The RELIC

The RELIC

Evelyn Anthony

HarperCollins*Publishers*

FIRST EDITION

Designed by Alma Orenstein

Library of Congress Cataloging-in-Publication Data

Anthony, Evelyn.
  The relic / by Evelyn Anthony.—1st ed.
    p. cm.
  ISBN 0-06-016101-9
  I. Title.
PR6069.T428R45 1991
823'.914—dc20   90-55961

91 92 93 94 95 WB/HC 10 9 8 7 6 5 4 3 2 1

*To BLANCHE KERMAN, my friend,
with love*

The RELIC

Prologue

COMMISSAR GREGOR LEPKIN was working at his desk. It was a handsome desk and it faced the big windows. His office was large and well equipped. He had status. He had been promoted. He was in favor. A beautiful little enamel clock with its matching calendar stood on the desk, flotsam rescued from the bloody tide of revolution. The rich translucence of the green enamel set off the delicate sparkle of diamonds. They gave Lepkin intense pleasure. He liked to wind the clock and change the date card on the calendar. He had done both that morning when he arrived. May 20, 1938. The Imperial cypher twinkled in the sunlight. The clock and the calendar had been looted from the Czarist Palace of Tsarske Seloe. Years ago he had bought the beautiful little objects from a drunken soldier for a few rubles.

He worked hard; he was a man who prided himself on his attention to detail. Best of all, he had a sixth sense for trouble. On his last three visits to his mother in the devastated Ukraine, he'd discovered that the State Security Services in Kharkov were rotten with corruption. Old Party men, grown fat and lazy, bloated like bluebottles on the corpses of Stalin's victims—five million of them—starved, imprisoned, hunted off their lands to die. The punitive forces had gone, their work completed.

The administration left behind had lined their pockets and neglected their duties. Lepkin had been compiling his report for months. It was not his province to question the methods Stalin used. He closed his eyes and hardened his heart in the name of the great cause he had followed since he was a student running from the czarist police. The Cheka, instrument of terror and repression, had been swept away. The Office of State Security had a new name, NKVD—a new hierarchy composed of dedicated men like himself, careerist officers, controlling an army of informers and armed enforcers. Even now the Revolution was threatened by foreign powers outside, and by traitors within.

Stalin was right. He had to be; the alternative was unthinkable. Lepkin wasn't brave like his old friend Alexei Rakovsky. He refused to question, to doubt. Without his beliefs, he was lost; without the Party and its leader there was nothing but chaos. He held fast to that, like a man on a cliff face who knows that to look down is to fall. The little clock had a sweet silvery chime. It was like music. Eleven o'clock.

He got up and went to the window overlooking Djerjhinsky Square. It was a bright spring day; sunshine struck gold off the cupolas of Saint Basil's Cathedral, a wonder of magnificence and imagination. It pleased his eye every time he looked across at the view. Czar Ivan had blinded the architect so he could never build another like it. Lepkin thought sometimes that this was Russia. The splendor and the cruelty that went hand in hand like lovers. He saw the car sweep into the courtyard below and he sighed.

Memories made him sad. Memories of the old, close comradeship that bound him and Alexei together. The faith, the fierce idealism. How he had admired Alexei, how he had looked up to him. The dangers they shared in those early days! Rakovsky was the elder by two years, and by temperament he was the leader. Lepkin was cautious, Rakovsky gloried in risks.

Lepkin was proud to be Alexei Rakovsky's friend and follower. Rakovsky had been caught delivering pamphlets and exiled to Gorki for two years. Lepkin was never arrested. He stayed on at university, quietly organizing.

Rakovsky joined the army when the war with Germany broke out. He was a Russian first and a Bolshevik second when the motherland was threatened.

Lepkin admired his patriotism, but remained in Moscow, coordinating workers' movements. When the czar's armies faced defeat in 1917, Rakovsky shot his officers and led his regiment back to fight for the revolution. He and Lepkin had stood together in the crowd that welcomed Lenin off the train when he returned from exile.

He watched the car draw up, the driver open the door for Rakovsky. Alexei had risen high in the Party. He had been a hero. He was secretary to the commissar of Internal Affairs— a high office complete with power and prestige. He had been chosen by Lenin. That, as Lepkin knew, was the reason for his downfall. All around them, men of the old Bolshevik tradition were toppling into the abyss.

He stepped forward as his door opened and he saw Rakovsky, his old friend. He held out his arms and embraced him.

"Gregor Ivanovitch," Rakovsky said. "It's so good to see you."

"Good to see you, Alexei," was Lepkin's answer. Rakovsky managed a smile; it was a poor thing that sat uneasily on his mouth. It never reached the eyes. Lepkin knew that look. He'd seen it many times in the eyes of other men.

"Sit down, my friend," he suggested. "A cigarette?" Rakovsky took one, lit it, and Lepkin noticed how his hand shook. He said, "Vodka?"

"Vodka," Rakovsky repeated. "Why not? Congratulations on the new office. It goes with the rank, I suppose."

"I've got more room," Lepkin said. "How are the family?

It's so long since I've seen them, but I've been so busy with the new job."

"You asked about the family," Rakovsky said. "That's why I've come."

"But why come here?" Lepkin frowned. He shook his head. Still rash, still taking risks.

"Because I didn't want to compromise you," Rakovsky answered. "I'm watched whatever I do, wherever I go. Your people are in my ministry, they're in my offices—everywhere. I've come to see you openly because no one can accuse you of plotting with an oppositionist."

He paused; the cigarette had burned down to its cardboard holder. "My name is on the new list, Gregor. You knew that, didn't you? That's why you've stayed away from us. Not that I blame you."

Lepkin said quietly, "That's not the reason, Alexei. But I do know about the list. I've seen your name."

"It's not just me, but my whole family." Rakovsky's voice trembled. "You know what happens—you know what they'll do to them? They came for Rosengoltz's wife and daughter in the middle of the night and they were never seen again."

He got up, a tall man grown thin, his clothes loose upon him.

"Stalin's a madman, Gregor. A devil. I should have seen it, I should have done something about it. Now it's too late. I did nothing. I stood there and applauded while he slaughtered millions in the name of Lenin. And now it's my turn."

He dropped back into his chair. There was a cold sheen of sweat on his face.

Lepkin said, "We're old friends, but you shouldn't say things like that. Not even to me."

"Why not? I'm already a dead man. But listen, listen, I've got something to show you. Something to offer you."

"No," Lepkin raised his hand to stop him. "No bribes,

Alexei. Don't offer me a bribe."

Rakovsky came close; he leaned across the desk. He had one hand buried deep in his coat. "This isn't a bribe," he said slowly. "I know money wouldn't buy you. But this hasn't a price. It could save your life one day."

"Then why can't it save yours?" Lepkin asked him.

"Because Stalin is Stalin," he said. "If I gave it to him he'd still kill me and send my family to the gulag. And it would help to keep his foot on our necks for as long as he lived. I'm giving you this, Gregor. In return, I want you to save Natalia and the boys."

He brought out a parcel. It was roughly tied with frayed cord. He took some time untying the knots because his hands were shaking. The paper peeled back, splitting with age, and a yellowing cloth with embroidered edges fell away at his touch.

Lepkin couldn't keep himself from staring. He swore an old-fashioned blasphemous oath. "Holy Christ! It's the relic!"

He reached out a trembling hand, and Rakovsky said, "Take it. Hold it."

Lepkin lifted it in his hands. The cross gleamed gold, the great red stones in the body flashed like huge drops of blood in the light. Lepkin shook his head. "Holy Christ," he said again. "I don't believe it. Saint Vladimir's cross. Alexei, where did you get it?"

Rakovsky said slowly, "The patriarch at Kiev gave it to my mother in 1919. The Red armies were winning; he knew they'd take the cross. My mother was only a poor woman, but she was devout."

"I remember your mother," Lepkin muttered. An illiterate *matiushka*, with Tartar blood. A figure who served her menfolk and kept in the background. She had been entrusted with the relic that could give victory to the Whites in the Civil War. Lenin had said publicly that he would grind the hated cross under the heel of his boot.

"My father was ordered to take it from the cathedral," Alexei went on. Serge Rakovsky was a fanatical Bolshevik, who had suffered the knout and exile to Siberia. Lepkin remembered him only too well. A terrifying man, brutalized by suffering and hate.

"You know what they did to the patriarch?" Rakovsky said. "They got nothing out of him. They shot the rest of the priests under the cathedral wall. My father was raging; he said to me, 'If the Whites have got it, they'll hold Russia from the Urals to the Black Sea.' And all the time it was in a box under his bed, wrapped in my mother's petticoat. He would have killed her with his own hands if he'd known what she did."

Lepkin laid the cross down on the desk. "How did you find it?" He felt shaken; he still couldn't stop staring at the cross. The red stones were full of shifting light. It drew him like a magnet. He thought suddenly, *This thing is in my blood. I'm afraid of it.*

He heard Alexei say, "She called me when she was dying. She hated my father, but she loved me. She gave me the cross, and she made me swear on her soul's salvation that I wouldn't give it up. I swore, Gregor. I swore to please her and let her die in peace. She said to me, 'There's goodness in you, my son. One day your soul will be saved because of this.' But there's no chance of that."

He poured himself another vodka and drank it down. He said, "It fascinates you, doesn't it? I was the same. I kept looking at it. In the end it troubled me, so I wrapped it up and hid it under the floor in my house. I haven't looked at it for many years, till I knew my name was on the death list. I want you to have it, Gregor. Stalin may not last forever. Then it could be your salvation. And Russia's."

Slowly, Lepkin made a parcel; the paper split, the string was raveled up. His hands were unsteady now. He put it in a drawer, closed the drawer, and turned the key.

He said, "I can save Natalia and the boys."

"And you will?" Rakovsky asked.

"I will. I promise you. I'll get them out of Moscow, to my mother. They'll be safe there."

Rakovsky nodded. He looked old and drawn. He took a deep breath that came out as a deeper sigh. "I'm glad. I know they'll be safe with you. I can try to be calm now. Do you know how long I've got? Is there a date fixed?"

"I wouldn't know," Lepkin said. "But it won't be long. There are two politburo members and eight army commanders on that list."

"They'll all be murdered," Alexei said. "They'll be drugged and tormented till they get up and accuse themselves and ask for death. That's what I fear most, Gregor. I'm afraid of what they'll do to make a broken puppet out of me."

Lepkin came close. He laid an arm around his shoulder. He looked into his old friend's face and said, "Don't be afraid, Alexei. I'm not going to let that happen."

As they embraced, he slipped his revolver out of its holster and shot Rakovsky dead.

The train to Kharkov was at Moscow station by the time Rakovska and her children were hurried through the barrier. But there was no sign of Rakovsky as she leaned out of the window, searching for him on the platform. When the train started moving, she turned back to her husband's driver. He was called Ivan. That's all she knew about him. A big, raw peasant with few words to say for himself.

"My husband," she shouted at him, "you said he'd be on the train."

He said, "Comrade Commissar Lepkin will come to you in Kharkov."

Lepkin. The old family friend who was a high officer in the NKVD. It was Lepkin who had put them on the train.

She saw the countryside rush by through a veil of unshed tears. The journey from Moscow to Kharkov would take two days and nights. Viktor, the younger twin, was nestled into her side. He fell asleep. Stefan, always boisterous and active, clambered over the seats. Ivan was showing him how to make paper men out of an old newspaper, folding and tearing with surprising delicacy.

"What's happened to my husband?" she asked in a low voice when both her sons were sleeping.

"I don't know," he said. "Please, it will be better if you sleep."

She drew the twins closer to her for comfort and gave way to the rhythm of the train. She knew she would never see Alexei again.

The body of Alexei Rakovsky had been removed from Lepkin's office, the blood stains scrubbed off the floor. His staff had rushed in when they heard the shot. He had dismissed them with calm authority; Rakovsky had been shot resisting arrest. They had heard that explanation before. He had time to send Rakovsky's driver on his secret journey. Time to hide the cross. Before the summons came.

He made his way up in the old-fashioned elevator to the little room at the top of the building with its sweeping views over Moscow. He paused by the door and knocked. His hand trembled.

Nikolai Yetzov was a small man; his hair receded and his skin was sallow. He looked unhealthy. He sat like a bird of prey in his aerie on the top floor. Next to Stalin, he was the most feared man in Russia. He called out, "Come in," and watched as Lepkin walked toward him. He stared at him. He didn't speak. He looked down at his papers as if there was no one there. He made a note or two, paused, added to what he'd written. The bile of terror rose in Lepkin's throat. He didn't dare cough to clear it. At last Yetzov said, still looking at his papers, "I am waiting for your report on the incident this morning, Comrade." Now he raised his head and stared at Lepkin. He had dark, cruel eyes and he delighted in other men's fear.

"Why did you shoot the traitor Rakovsky?"

Lepkin was word perfect. He had rehearsed his story again and again. He said, "Because he tried to bribe me, Comrade. I told him I didn't deal with traitors. Then he abused Comrade Stalin. He called him a murderer, a traitor to Lenin."

"Ah," the dry voice said, "Did he?—What else?"

Lepkin hesitated. The eyes bored holes into him. He had to be convincing because his life was forfeit if Yetzov didn't believe him. Perhaps even if he did. "He said he'd be revenged on me because I wouldn't help him. He said he'd name me when he was arrested. 'I'll take you to the cellars with me, Lepkin—I'll denounce you!'"

"And then what did you do, Comrade?"

"I drew my revolver to arrest him," Lepkin answered. "He resisted; so I shot him."

There was a long silence. Yetzov played with a pen, twiddling it between his fingers. There was anger in his eyes. He loved to inflict pain and humiliation on his victims. He had been looking forward to bringing Alexei Rakovsky to his knees. Lepkin had cheated him of that pleasure. At last he smiled; it terrified Lepkin to see that smile.

"You did what any loyal Party member would do," he said slowly. "You punished him for abusing Comrade Stalin, and you saved your own skin by shutting his mouth. Very sensible. We live in dangerous times."

"Yes," Lepkin agreed. "We do."

"You have an appointment in Kharkov," Yetzov's tone changed. It became harsh. "You'll have an opportunity to prove how loyal you really are, Lepkin. I want that area cleaned of filth, you understand? I want every oppositionist, every troublemaker, every enemy of the Party and the State hounded down and brought to me for justice. You mustn't fail, Lepkin. If even one escapes me, you will answer for it. You do understand, don't you?"

Lepkin answered boldly. "I understand, Comrade Yetzov. I won't fail."

"You'd better not," the voice sank to a whisper. "You can go now." Lepkin went out and closed the door very carefully, so as not to make a noise. He had robbed Yetzov of his victim. He was under a suspended sentence, and he knew it. He went back down to his office. He poured himself a glass of vodka. His hand shook, as his friend's had done that same day. He locked his desk drawer and called in his secretary.

She looked concerned and said, "Is there anything else you want, Comrade Commissar?" She thought he looked white and shocked. This surprised her. There had been many sudden deaths in the Lubyanea.

"Nothing," he said. "Thank you. I'm going home now. I have a lot of work to do tomorrow."

"Of course." She held the door open for him.

He thought suddenly, *I need a reliable staff. I can take her with me to Kharkov and my clerk Ivanov . . .*

He had a one-room apartment on Ouspenska Prospekt. He lived there alone. When he needed a woman, he went to a brothel reserved for senior officers in the State Security. The women were medically checked every month. He shut and locked the tiny cupboard that served him as a kitchen. The bathroom was communal.

Under the naked bulb in the ceiling he unwrapped the parcel. He whispered the old incantation at the coronation of the czars. "Who holds Saint Vladimir's cross has Holy Russia in his hand." A thousand years of mystic symbolism over the people of Russia. The concept was like a madman's dream. But without madmen and dreams there would be no Russia. He lit the stove and burned the cloth. He made a neat package of newspaper and new string.

He felt cold and sick to his stomach. He sat by the stove and tried to get warm and drank pepper vodka. It burned his tongue and lit a fire in his chilled body. He drank to his friend, Alexei, and talked to him aloud as he became very drunk.

"I saved you from the cellars. I saved you from the drugs and the stinking hole in the ground where they freeze men to death. A bullet is clean. You used to say that to me when we talked about the war, remember? I'll take care of Natalia and the boys. I'll keep my promise, don't worry. I loved you, Alexei."

Tears trickled down his cheeks. He struggled up from his chair. It overturned. The bottle rolled across the floor. It was empty. He fell on his bed and slept till the morning. His transfer to Kharkov was granted. By that evening he was on the train. The package was strapped to his body under his shirt.

Lepkin's mother took them in. The apartment was in a converted house; an old babushka came hurrying from the tiny kitchen with cries of excitement at having the children to look after.

Seeing the exhaustion on the woman's face, Marie Lepkin said, "You leave the little ones to us. We'll feed them and put them to bed. You lie down and sleep." Knowing the story, she was filled with pity.

Natalia lay under the quilt on the bed, staring at the ceiling. Tears filled up and overflowed onto the pillow. "Alexei, what are they doing to you?" At last she slept.

She was asleep and didn't hear the outcry from the kitchen. Stefan had kicked the babushka; he wanted to go to his mother. Viktor burst into weary tears. The babushka rubbed her shin and grumbled. Children were devils these days. They had no discipline, no respect. But then the devils were in charge. When the czar ruled them, Russia was a godly place.

Natalia was waiting for Lepkin when he arrived.

"Tell me the truth," she said, "he's been arrested, hasn't he?"

They were alone. His mother had taken the boys to play in the kitchen. Lepkin was shocked by how thin and white she looked. He didn't lie.

He said, "He's dead, Natalia. I'm sorry."

She turned away from him, her hands covering her face. After a while she asked him, "How? How did he die? Did he suffer?"

"No," Lepkin said gently. "He was shot. He felt nothing. It was over in a few seconds. I couldn't save him; he came to ask me to look after you and the twins. I could only promise him that."

She sat down, carefully smoothing her skirt. She was in control now, but as colorless as a dead woman. "I'm glad," she said at last. "He said to me in the last weeks, 'I'm not scared of dying. It's what they'll do to make me confess.' And you know how brave he was. Tell me how it happened."

"No," Lepkin refused. "You've suffered enough. The details don't matter."

She looked up at him. She had pale gray eyes the color of water under a clear summer sky. "You shot him, didn't you?"

He said simply, "Yes. It was all I could do for him."

She stood up. He waited for her condemnation, for tears and reproaches.

"Thank you, Gregor. I can bear it now."

"What's going to become of them?" Lepkin's mother asked. "They can't stay here, there isn't room for all of us. I'm so sorry for them, Gregor. The poor girl's been so brave. I'm not being hard-hearted, but the little boys need somewhere to play—the babushka finds them too much to manage. Especially Stefan."

"I know," Lepkin said. "You've been so good to them. So patient, Little Mother. Don't worry, I've found a place where they can live. It's in the country. They'll be safe there. I'll leave Ivan with them. You'll visit them, won't you? See they're all right? I'm going to be working so hard and I've got to be careful myself."

"Don't worry," his mother said. "I'll keep my eye on them. You've risked enough to help them. I do know they're grateful. Natalia calls you their savior."

He drove the family out to their new home. He helped Natalia out of the car and lifted the twins onto the ground.

"It's the best I could find," he said. "It's isolated, but you'll have Ivan to look after you, and it's safe."

It was an old farmhouse close to a wood. It had stood empty since Stalin decreed that every smallholder in the Ukraine was to be driven off the land. The peasant with a few acres was labeled a kulak, a rich enemy of the proletariat. The farms were collectivized. The cattle and crops were confiscated and the rebellious Ukrainians left to starve. Millions had died of hunger and disease in the breadbasket of Russia. The corpses lay in the gutters of the towns and by the roadsides where the people had wandered in their desperate search for food. Those who escaped that fate were herded into the terrible labor camps and worked to death. Stalin's Five-Year Plan for centralizing Russian agriculture was imposed on the Ukraine with merciless severity. The owners of the farmhouse were among the five million who perished.

Lepkin and Natalia walked up the path choked with weeds and into the house. It was a single-story wooden building. It needed paint inside and out; the window shutters were broken, hanging drunkenly on rusty hinges. The patch of garden was a wilderness of brambles.

Lepkin watched her anxiously. She had been living in luxury as the wife of a high Party official in a three-room apartment close to the Kremlin. He expected her spirits to sink as she looked round at the stained walls and the bare earth floors. Instead, he saw a rare smile as she turned to him and called the boys to come to her.

"We can make a home here," she said. "I was born in the country, Gregor. We'll be happy here."

He lifted the boys one after the other. "You be good," he admonished. "Take care of your mother and do what she tells you. Else I'll beat you with a big stick when I come back."

They giggled at the threat. He set them down and immediately they ran off shouting with excitement, to explore outside.

"You've been so good to us," Natalia said. "Alexei loved you like a brother. He was right. How can we ever thank you?"

He led her back into the house. "You can take care of this," he said. There was a black tin box on the table. He said, "It's locked, Natalia. One day we'll open it together. But not now. I know I can trust you to keep it safe for me. Nobody is to touch it. Hide it—hide it so no one can find it!"

She took it from him. It wasn't very heavy. Money perhaps. Ruble notes. Documents. She wasn't curious. Curiosity was a luxury for the idle. She was a woman of her word. "I'll hide it," she said.

"And forget about it?" he asked her.

She opened a drawer full of clothes and buried the box underneath them. "I've already forgotten," she said. "When will you come back again?"

"I don't know. I have a lot of work to do. Maybe it won't be too long. My mother will come to see you."

She watched him leave from the doorway. The car drove off into the path through the pine woods. She heard her sons calling to each other round the back of the house. She went back inside and looked around her. They had shelter, a man to chop wood for the stove, enough to eat.

That night, with her sons curled up beside her, Natalia slept long and peacefully.

It was two months before Lepkin came again. He found Natalia sewing. The sunshine streamed in from the window and her hair shone like a golden halo. His step made the floorboard creak and she looked up. The sewing fell to the ground and she hurried to meet him. There was a high blush in her cheeks.

He embraced her like a brother, kissed her forehead like a brother, and knew that he was in love for the first time in his life.

Natalia had changed from the city girl he'd known. The sun and the clean air had brightened her skin and burnished her fair hair. A little weight had rounded out her thin body. The shutters were strong and the rooms had been washed down and painted; the stove was blacked and shining clean. There was a bright rug on the floor. Ivan had found it, Natalia said. He slept on the floor by the door at night in case of intruders.

Natalia cooked for them that night. Gregor had bought vodka and wine and she made a vegetable stew with black bread and goat's cheese. Ivan had found a place where goats were kept.

They sat long at the table and the wine was finished. At last Gregor was silent. They'd talked of the old days, of Alexei and their memories of evenings spent together talking, getting a little drunk.

"In the last few years Alexei only laughed when he was with you," she said.

And Gregor said, "You haven't forgotten him, Natalia?"

"I'll never forget him," she answered.

He poured some vodka and swallowed it. "I wish you'd think of me sometimes," he said.

"I do. I've missed you."

"That's because you're lonely. I want more than that. I want you to think about me as much as I think about you. You're beautiful, Natalia."

She smiled at him. "And you're drunk," she said.

"Only a little. I love you, you know I love you?" He got up unsteadily. "I shouldn't say that. Don't worry. I'll sleep outside your door. Like Ivan."

She hurried to support him, her voice gentle. "You'll sleep in my bed."

He let her guide him to the bedroom. She put a finger to her lips.

"Don't wake the children." She undressed him and helped him into the bed. She covered him with the quilt. Then she stripped off her blouse and skirt, peeled off her stockings, and stood naked.

He groaned at the sight of the full breasts and the shadow between her thighs. "Natalia . . . I want you . . . I'm so drunk."

She turned down the lamp and slipped in beside him. He smelled the sweetness of her breath. "You won't be in the morning."

Lepkin and Natalia were married in the new Wedding Palace in the center of Kharkov.

On their journey home Natalia leaned against Lepkin, warm and submissive to his hands and his mouth in the darkness. "I wish I were a virgin," she whispered to him. "I want to do everything to please you."

When they had become lovers Lepkin knew that all she felt was gratitude. But now she loved him with a fierce intensity. For a still, quiet woman she was capable of a passion and abandonment that astonished him. And before they fell asleep he asked her the question he had never dared ask before.

"Alexei . . . Was it like this with him?"

She raised her head and looked at him.

"No," she said. "It was different. I loved him, but I would die for you." She bent and very slowly kissed him on the lips.

When he woke in the morning, she was already up, preparing food to start the day. He lay and listened to her singing. He felt he must be the happiest man in all of Russia.

They had been married for three months when he called her to him, sending the children out to play in the garden. Lepkin took her by the hand. He kissed her. "You remember the box I gave you—the day I brought you here?"

She liked to tease him, to flirt. "You told me to forget," she reminded him.

"I also told you we'd open it together one day," he countered. "Husbands and wives shouldn't have secrets. Get it, my darling."

She came with it in her hands. "You're so solemn," she said. "Is anything wrong? Why do you want the box? I don't care what's inside."

He didn't answer. He took the key from round his neck and opened it. She saw something wrapped in paper. He laid it on the bed and pulled the covering off. Natalia couldn't help herself. She gasped and stepped back.

"It's a cross! What are you doing with a thing like that?" She hated religion; she especially hated the old Orthodox faith.

He had forgotten that. His wife was a true child of her fanatically atheist parents.

"It belonged to Alexei," he said quietly. "He gave it to me."

"Why would Alexei want it? He had no time for all that superstition. It looks old—is it valuable? Where could you sell it? The stones might be worth something." She looked at it with distaste. She made no move to touch it.

"It is old," Lepkin said. "Over a thousand years. And

nobody could sell it because it doesn't have a price. It's Saint Vladimir's cross, Natalia. The holiest relic in all Russia."

Now she actually recoiled. "It can't be. It was destroyed."

"That's what the Party said when Alexei's father couldn't find it. The patriarch in Kiev gave it to your mother-in-law. He was roasted over an open fire to make him tell where it was hidden. But he died first."

She shuddered. "Don't. I didn't know. I knew they shot the priests."

"If we'd found this in 1919 half the White armies would have surrendered. Lenin knew what it meant and so did Stalin. To the people it means the God-given right to rule Russia. No czar was ever crowned without it in his hand. Even without God, it has a thousand years of power and mystical belief enshrined in it. It's buried deep in the Russian subconscious."

She said fiercely, "Not in mine. It's just ignorant superstition—only a peasant like my mother-in-law would believe in such a thing."

"Russia is made up of ignorant peasants," he reminded her. "We've shut the churches and driven out the priests, but there are icons hidden all over Russia. And if some leader was to rise up and show this—there are millions who would follow him. That's why Alexei kept it hidden. He hoped to bargain his life in exchange if he fell out of favor. But there are no bargains made with Stalin. He knew that at the end."

"Why do you keep it?" she asked. "It didn't save Alexei."

"Alexei said, 'Stalin won't last forever. It could be your salvation.' After what's happened he could be right," he said to her. "Everything is different now. The fascist Germans are our allies! Our ideals have been pissed on by Stalin."

She shushed him in fear, but he shrugged cynically. "I have a new boss. I work for Beria. Beria is a monster. I don't care. I do whatever is necessary to stay alive, because you and the children are the only things that matter to me."

She came and put her arms around him. "We live on borrowed time," she whispered. "We have each other, Gregor. I love you so much I couldn't live without you. If we were separated I'd die . . ."

They hadn't heard the door open. The child, Viktor, was standing there, watching them. "Mama," his voice quivered. "Why are you going to die?" His dark eyes were brimming with tears.

Natalia gathered him in her arms. "I'm not," she insisted. "I was just telling Gregor how much I loved him. It's the way grown-ups talk, you silly boy!"

"You're not sick, are you?" he asked.

He was the sensitive one, the child troubled by imagination. Gregor picked him up and swung him onto his shoulder. "Your Mama's not sick," he announced. "We were having a little love talk, that's all. And next time, you knock on the door, eh?"

"I did," Viktor protested. "You didn't hear. Stefan hit me and Ivan smacked him on the head. Stefan's very angry. But it wasn't a hard smack."

"Well," Gregor set him down. "One day you won't have Ivan to stand up for you. Then you'll have to hit Stefan yourself, won't you?" He saw Natalia watching them. He patted Viktor kindly. "You'll be as big as him one day."

Viktor wasn't listening. He pointed to the bed. "What's that red thing? That shining red thing?"

Natalia hurried and picked up the cross. Her children had never seen that symbol. It was forbidden. They knew nothing of Christianity or any other religion.

"It's nothing," she said hastily. "Just an ornament."

"Can I see?" he asked.

"No!" She sounded angry. "Go on, go out and find Ivan and play. And don't let me hear you and Stefan fighting or I'll beat both of you!"

When he had run out she turned to Lepkin. "Put that away," she said. "Lock it up quickly. Did you see him staring at it? Supposing he talks about it at school?"

"He won't," Gregor assured her. "It meant nothing to him. He won't remember." He wrapped the cross in its tattered paper and locked it in the tin box. "Natalia," he said. "We won't talk about it again. We won't think about it. But if ever anything goes wrong, you know what it means and where it is."

"I know," she said quietly. "I just wish it wasn't in this house."

Easter had been abolished. Instead Russia celebrated the anniversary of the October Revolution. There were parades and speeches in Kharkov and the factories were closed so that the workers could march through the streets. Everybody celebrated and got drunk. Red flags flew from every public building. Bands played, the radio blared rousing revolutionary songs. It was a day off work. There were huge posters of Lenin and Stalin, head and shoulder side by side. The face of the tyrant watched the people of Kharkov, a slight smile on the lips, an air of avuncular wisdom in the painted eyes.

The next morning, some of the wall posters had been daubed with red paint. It looked like blood streaming over the genial image. The culprit wasn't found, so a token arrest was made of a suspect factory worker. He was given a thorough beating in the police station and sentenced to three months hard labor.

Lepkin gave his wife the clock and calendar as a present. They were all gathered together: Lepkin and Natalia, his mother, the babushka, the children, and Ivan. There were tears in his eyes as he looked at them all. Natalia was pregnant and her beauty glowed. Lepkin was quite drunk and very happy. He laid his treasure before her. The diamonds glittered like frost; the green enamel was sheer as watered silk.

"Listen," he said and wound the clock forward. It struck the hour. Viktor stared at it, fascinated by the sweet sounds and delicate colors.

Natalia said, "They must be valuable. I don't deserve them."

"You like them, don't you?" Lepkin insisted.

"They're very pretty," she said. "But where can we put them?"

Though just a child, Viktor knew she didn't like the lovely things his stepfather had given her. He wondered why.

Lepkin embraced her; they all applauded. He wanted to take her to bed; he squeezed her breast and whispered to her.

She whispered back, reminding him they weren't alone. "I'll put them away," she said. "They might get damaged." She put the desk set carefully in a drawer. She was embarrassed by the gift. They were pretty toys for some spoiled aristocrat to play with. They had no relevance to her.

It was a bitterly cold winter. A time when they hibernated, as the winds and the snow turned the landscape into a frozen wilderness.

Viktor loved the quiet evenings gathered round the stove with his mother and Lepkin. Stefan preferred to help Ivan with woodwork; he was not a child who liked reading or solitude. Viktor was content; he drew in his book. It was full of pictures. He drew the rabbits he wouldn't see till the spring came and the yellow-eyed cat that had joined them as a kitten, curled up by his mother's feet. He drew the snow and the trees festooned with icicles. He drew the clock and the calendar. His mother had put them on a shelf. She had soon found an excuse to lock them away again. She didn't like them, but she hated the cross with the red, glowing stones that he'd seen on her bed that day. He knew it was a cross because he'd seen the babushka wearing one round her neck. His mother had told him not to say anything or he'd get her into trouble. He knew she hated it because he'd heard her say so to Lepkin.

"I hate having it in the house . . . especially since Viktor saw it."

He couldn't understand what she was afraid of. Ivan had told him once, people only hate other people because they're afraid of them. It must be the same with things. He went on drawing in his book. Ivan pulling a sled through the snow, Lepkin asleep in the chair, his mouth slightly open.

And he drew the cross with the red stones. He didn't show his book to anyone because he felt his mother would be angry if she saw that drawing.

The baby was born as the weather turned warm. It was a little girl, and they called her Valeria. Ivan had made a wooden cot, and she lay and gurgled happily as the spring turned into early summer. Life was peaceful in their isolated world. But to Lepkin that world was turning upside down. Their Nazi allies were massing troops along the Polish frontier and Russian armies were on the march.

Thousands of people were forcibly evacuated by Soviet forces in the first weeks of the German invasion. The Ukrainians were not to be trusted. Too many were fighting side by side with the advancing Germans. It was the time for revenge.

Captured political commissars or members of the NKVD were shot without trial. Soviet troops were throwing themselves upon the enemy. Soviet planes, slow and underarmed, were ramming the Heinkels and Stukas that commanded the skies. But the German armored divisions raced ahead, the Luftwaffe bombed and strafed at will. Kharkov itself was being evacuated and was devastated by daylight air raids. Lepkin couldn't persuade Natalia to leave without him. He had already sent his mother on ahead to Moscow. But Natalia wouldn't move. She wouldn't leave so long as he remained at his post in the beleaguered city.

Then in August Lepkin came back home unexpectedly. He called Ivan to bring the boys and went to find Natalia. She was holding the baby when she saw him. She looked at his face and cried out, "No! No!"

He took her in his arms. The child was startled and began to cry. Ivan waited, an arm round each of the boys. She wept and protested, but Lepkin stayed calm. And firm.

"I'm joining an active service unit," he said. "And Ivan will take you and the children to Moscow on the train. Places are reserved for you and you leave tomorrow. As soon as I've gone. The reports coming in are very bad. They're getting closer and closer. I only wish you'd have left sooner."

He held her closely and then turned, reaching out to his stepsons. They ran into his arms.

Stefan cried out fiercely, "We'll shoot them. Ivan and me'll kill them."

Lepkin said gently, "You'll look after your mother and the little one. You and Viktor will be good boys and take care of them till I get back. You promise?"

They promised. Viktor blinked back tears. Ivan took them outside. He knew what happened to the political officers if they were captured. His colonel wouldn't surrender. He'd die fighting. He sat the boys down and told them tales of the wonders they would see in Moscow. When he was a lad, he'd waited in line all night and a whole day to see Lenin lying in his tomb in Red Square. He looked just as if he was sleeping peacefully.

Natalia and Lepkin made love that night. They held each other and talked bravely of the future.

"I think I'm pregnant again," she admitted. "I've missed twice; I didn't want to tell you because I was frightened you'd make me leave."

He laid his hand tenderly upon her stomach. "It'll be a boy

this time," he said. "You'll be safe. Ivan will get you to Moscow. We'll beat these swine back into Germany, don't worry!"

She said, "If you're caught, they'll murder you, Gregor."

"They're murdering our people anyway," he said. "And you know I have to fight. I'm Russian. I'm not fighting for Stalin, I'm fighting for Russia. Once we've cleared the city, we shall blow up the buildings and the railheads and leave nothing for them. Nothing."

"Try not to get killed," she whispered to him. "Try to come back to us."

He kissed her. "I'll do my best," he said. He got up and dressed in the dawn light. "Don't forget to take the box with you," he said.

"The box?" She sat up, bare breasted with her hair hanging down over her shoulders.

"The tin box," he said. "That cross must never fall into German hands. And my present to you, Natalia. My clock and the calendar. Wrap them up carefully. Above all, keep that box close to you. Hide it somewhere safe when you get to Moscow. Remember!"

"I'll remember," she said. "It's unlucky. I wish we could just smash it to pieces and bury it!"

Lepkin held the battered box in his hands. He had a strange look and it frightened her. "I think we'd be cursed," he said.

The terrible separation was coming closer, minute by minute, as he finished dressing. Once more she held him, kissing him and weeping. Then he was gone; the car started up and she couldn't bring herself to go to the door or watch him from the window. Ivan was driving him into the city. Then he'd return for her and the children. He was armed with a rifle and ammunition. She sat at the table in the kitchen and bowed her head. Then she heard the little girl begin to stir and whimper in her cot. She got up and went to her. She soothed her and held her close.

THE RELIC

It was still early, but the sun was up. The boys were making bundles of their clothes for the journey. It kept them occupied. The baby was sitting on the floor in a pool of warm sunshine, playing with a wooden doll Ivan had made for her.

Natalia went into her room to dress. She brushed her long hair. She loved the house and garden and the cat with the yellow eyes. The children were begging her to take the cat to Moscow. She couldn't bear to tell them that it wasn't possible. Cats wouldn't be allowed on a train. It would be all right, left behind. It would catch birds. It would live.

As if summoned by her thoughts, it strolled into the room and came to rub against her legs. She bent down and stroked the rough fur.

"Silly thing," she said. "Why are we all so fond of you?"

And then she heard the noise. It was loud. It throbbed and roared like an animal. Her chair fell over. The cat fled. She ran from her room to the kitchen and saw them through the window. A motorcycle with a sidecar, painted gray with the black-and-white German cross on the side. Soldiers, with bucket helmets and gray uniforms. They were stopped a few yards away. She didn't scream. She couldn't. Fear made her dumb. Her sons had come into the kitchen. She heard one of them— Stefan? Viktor?—say, "What's that, *Mamushka?* What's that noise?"

Then she seized them, hissing at them to be silent. "Don't make a sound. In there, quick," she said, pushing them toward a cupboard. She thrust the baby in with them. "Don't let her cry, stay there. Don't *move.*"

She slammed the cupboard shut. As she stepped back, the first of the German soldiers walked in through the open door.

1

"I LOVE THIS VIEW," her father said. "It's the best on the Island." He held out his hand to Lucy. "Come and sit by me. It's so peaceful up here."

"The garden is looking lovely," she said.

He was a keen gardener, and the mild climate made Jersey a plantsman's paradise.

The sea stretched below them at the bottom of a cliff mantled in spring foliage and flowers, girdled by a thin line of yellow sand. Yuri Warren had bought the site twenty-five years ago and built the house. It was a minor heart attack at first, but the signs were ominous. He had a wife and two-year-old daughter. He had enough money to retire if he sold the business. Within five years his wife had died of cancer and he and Lucy were alone. He had lived far longer than anyone expected and he was grateful. The pace of life was easy, the gentle climate suited him. He had brought up his daughter, tended his beloved garden, and devoted himself to his life's work.

He had made it her cause as much as his. He had shared everything with her. From an early age he taught her to speak Russian. She looked like a child of his native Ukraine, with her Slavic bone structure and fair hair. He had bequeathed her everything but the piercing blue eyes. They were her Irish mother's legacy.

Lucy glanced anxiously at him. "I've been so worried about you," she said. "But you are feeling better, aren't you?"

He thought, *I've got to be brave. I've got to tell her. I've got to tell her everything. My time has run out. Hers has come.* He reached for her hand and held it.

"No, Lucy," he said gently. "I'm afraid not. Listen to me, darling, and be calm. I have only a few weeks left. Maybe a few days. It could happen any time." He heard her sob. "Don't do that," he said. "You mustn't. I've had a very good life and much happiness. It's coming to an end, that's all."

She stemmed her tears for his sake. With an effort she said, "How long have you known?"

"Since the last test. I've been putting everything in order. I don't want you worried with lawyers. It's all clear-cut now. There's only one thing left."

"What is it?" she asked him.

"To tell you the secret I've been guarding since before you were born. And to show it to you. Help me into the house."

It wasn't the safe where he kept his papers and Eileen's jewelry. It was a trap door under his desk. When she moved the desk and took up the rug, it was almost impossible to see the join in the parquet floor.

"Put your foot on the fourth square to the left, Lucy."

She did so and the flap rose up on a hidden spring. She knelt down to look inside. It was a cavity hollowed out and lined with lead.

"There's a box," he said. "Bring it to me."

It was plain wood with a ring handle and a simple catch. "What is it?" she asked him.

"A great treasure," Yuri answered. "But before I show it to you, I want to tell you how it came to me. Put the box there, on my desk. When I've finished, we'll open it together."

He waited for a moment. The past was dangerous for him. It made his failing heart beat faster. Keep calm, his doctor had insisted. Don't excite yourself. He had smiled and shrugged off the advice. For what purpose—to eke out a few more days. "Some of it you know already," he told Lucy. "How I was taken for forced labor in Germany. How my parents were shot. How Major Hope got me to England after the war. You know all that. But I never told you about Boris.

"Boris was in the camp at Spittal. There were ten thousand Ukrainians from the division that fought with the German army. The war was over and they were waiting to surrender to the British. There were women and children mixed up with them, kids like me who'd been caught up in the retreat and taken along. It was very hot. I remember men swimming in the dirty river and the women washing clothes along the bank.

"I was hungry and lousy and lost. I'd been kicked and beaten till I was scared of my own shadow. Then Boris found me. I can see him now." He paused for breath. "He was a big fellow, built like a bull. Ugly, with a shaven head. He had a loud voice and a laugh you could hear in the next camp. I don't know what he saw in me, although he said afterward I looked like his little brother who'd died. But he adopted me, Lucy. He scrubbed me clean and fed me, and kept me by him. 'Don't you worry, kid,' he'd say. 'You'll be all right. You stick with me and we'll get out of this shit.' He was coarse and people were frightened of him. I saw him hit a man with one blow and he fell as if he'd been poleaxed. Nobody bullied me with Boris around. I followed him like a little dog. I slept curled up by his feet at night.

"He talked to me, telling me about what he'd done in the war. He'd been in the SS extermination squads, killing Jews, he said. He was proud of it. 'I fought the bastard Bolsheviks,' he said. 'They threw my family off their land and my mother and my little brother starved to death. I fought them and the filthy Jews that were the cause of all the trouble.' He had no shame about it. I loved him, Lucy. Can you understand how

I could feel like that for such a man?"

He didn't wait for her to answer. "The German general and his officers had deserted the division. The place was full of rumors. The Reds were killing any Russian who'd worn a German uniform. Even the poor devils conscripted into labor battalions to dig earthworks. If they didn't, they were literally starved until they died in the prison camps. But there was no mercy from the Red Army.

"The Ukrainians were waiting, not knowing what would happen to them. Boris had changed his uniform for an ordinary infantry soldier's. He said anyone wearing the SS uniform was handed over to the Reds immediately. I was terrified he'd be taken away. I used to cry and he always promised me, 'I'm not going anywhere without you, kid. Now stop your sniveling.' And he'd give me a great bear hug that squeezed the breath out of me."

He was far away as he talked, reliving the trauma of those chaotic days. He could feel the heat of the sun on the trampled dusty earth and the smell of the camp in his nostrils. "The British came and took our surrender. I remember the officers had a big dinner after the terms were agreed upon. Our commander, General Shandruk, was dressed up like a real swell. Many of them were old czarist officers, some of them had been living in exile since 1919.

"The British were friendly to us. They gave food and sweets to the children and there was quite a bit of fraternizing and getting drunk.

"Boris didn't mix. I could feel he was uneasy, in spite of the way he talked. He kept in the background. We didn't know where we would be sent and one day it looked good, the next people were panicking because they heard we were going to be put on trains for Lenz. The Red Army was at Lenz. They were taking people back and shooting them in thousands. One night hundreds of Ukrainians and their families just slipped away and the British let them go. Then there was an announcement. The Ukrainians were going to be moved to a camp at Bellaria, outside Rimini. Beyond the reach of the Soviets. I'll never forget the cheering. People were dancing with joy, hugging each other, weeping with relief. Boris got very drunk that night. He was still drunk when a British officer and four men came in to arrest him the next morning. There was a separate list of SS criminals who were being entrained at Saint Veit and handed over to the Reds. Boris's name was on it."

Lucy saw his lip tremble and a tear rolled down her father's cheek.

"They took him by force. He fought and struggled and I was screaming at them to let him go, while the officer held me. I wanted to go with him. I wanted to die with him. He was all I had in the world."

"Daddy," she said in a whisper. "Don't. Don't. You mustn't upset yourself."

He didn't hear her. He said, "I begged the officer to let me say good-bye to him. I was crying and pleading in Russian; he called someone to translate. He spoke a bit of German. He said to me, 'All right. You can say good-bye. Come with me.'

"They were loading men onto a truck. The soldiers had Sten guns trained on them. I saw Boris and the officer gave me a push and said, 'Go on. But be quick.'

"Boris was handcuffed. There was a big bruise on his face. He couldn't embrace me, so I just clung to him round the middle. 'Look after yourself, kid,' he managed to say. I can hear him now. His voice was thick as if he wanted to cry. 'I've got a present for you. It's buried under my cot. It'll make you rich, Yuri. Hide it. Don't let anyone see it, or they'll take it off you. Promise me?'

"I couldn't take it in properly. He seemed to realize that because he said it all again. 'Under my cot. It's a treasure. Get it! Hide it!'

"They were separating us, pulling me away. They dragged him to the truck and he shouted back to me. 'Think of me, kid. And do what I told you!' They were all loaded onto the truck and driven away.

"I went to Boris's tent. It was empty. There was his camp bed where I'd slept on the floor to be near him. And I dug underneath and found what he'd given me. Now you can open the box, Lucy."

She held it in both hands. The red stones and the delicate gold flashed in the bright Jersey sunshine. In the garden outside she heard the buzz of a lawnmower.

"The holiest relic in Russia," he said. "It's been revered by Ukrainians for a thousand years. It's in our blood. We've been so close, Lucy. I've shared my dreams with you because one day I wanted to share this with you too. I had it planned, and then I had this last attack. Russia is in turmoil. It's the time for us to strike. I won't live to do it, so you must take my place."

"How can I?" she whispered.

"I want you to go to Volkov in Geneva. Tell him about the relic. Bring him and our people together. Kiss the cross, Lucy, and swear that you'll do it!"

She hesitated. His color was bad and his breathing uneven.

"You're the future," he said. "The young have shown us all the way. The students in China who died for freedom, the Germans, the Romanians, our Polish brothers. The day Volkov returns to Russia with the relic, the Ukrainians will rise and declare independence. And Communism will collapse. It'll die from the heart, from Moscow. All the murdered millions will sleep easy in their graves."

"I'll do what you would have done," she said. "I swear it." For a moment she touched the big central stone of the cross with her lips.

"Thank you, my darling." Her father's voice had sunk. "Get me some water . . . my pills . . ."

She laid the cross back on its satin cushion in the box. Made in her father's factory, like the flooring that concealed the safe. She pressed the hidden mechanism and the cover closed over it. She realized that she was trembling.

Her father had swallowed his tablet; his color was less gray. "I'm tired," he said. "But now I'll die a happy man. I'd like to rest now."

She helped him to the downstairs room that had been turned into a bedroom once he couldn't walk upstairs anymore.

As he lay down he raised his hand and stroked her face.

"I'm so glad I never had a son. There's an old saying, 'A daughter gladdens her father's heart.' How true it's been for me."

Ten days later he died.

It was a private funeral. There was a requiem mass in the local Catholic church for his many friends in Jersey, but only a dozen came to the graveside. Like Lucy, the women were in mourning. It was their custom, and they cherished the old ways. One by one they came and kissed her, murmuring their sympathy. Then they came back to the house for the traditional funeral breakfast. Lucy didn't weep; she had no tears left. Part of herself had been buried that morning. Side by side with the mother she hardly remembered. He often told her how much he had loved Eileen and how beautiful she was.

His old friend, Mischa, made a solemn speech. He called Yuri by his original name, Warienski, and spoke of his patriotism and his lifelong devotion to Ukrainian freedom from the Communist yoke. He reminded them of his generosity in time and money, his involvement with the human rights activists inside the Soviet Union. His letters and articles denouncing the arrest of the bravest of the young intellectual dissidents, Professor Volkov. Mischa had tears in his eyes and Yuri's Russian friends cried openly. Vodka was passed and drunk in Yuri's memory. And then Lucy called him aside. He was the closest to her father and the president of their English association. She brought him into her father's study and closed the door.

He said quietly, "Yuri wrote to me before he died. He said you would take his place."

"I'm going to try," Lucy said. "I promised him."

He said, "He asked a lot of you, even when you were a child. Perhaps this is too much. If you change your mind, nobody would blame you, Lucy. One of us could approach Volkov."

She shook her head. "You're known," she said. "You never made a secret of your activities. You'd be watched. Nobody will connect an English woman called Warren on a holiday in Geneva with anything subversive. I'm the one to see Volkov. My father insisted on that. And he was very wise. I shall go, Mischa."

"Say nothing about the relic," her father had warned. "All our organizations have been penetrated by the KGB ever since we helped to expose the Yalta Agreement. . . . They learned we were more than a few exiles shaking puny fists at them from a safe distance. . . . Only Volkov can be trusted. No one else must know."

Mischa said gravely, "He was wise. Even so, it may not be so easy for you. Volkov has been silent for five years. He hasn't written a word or given an interview. There have been rumors that he was very ill. And his wife is an infamous woman. She worked in the Lenin Institute."

"I know," Lucy said. "But my father believed in him. He said he was a patriot who wouldn't spit on his own country as an exile."

"Yuri was an idealist," Mischa said gently. "He wouldn't believe that Volkov might have changed."

He came close and laid a hand on her shoulder. He had known her since she was a child. He had watched her grow into a beautiful young woman. She should have married by now, produced grandchildren for her father. But he had dedicated her on the shrine of his own fanatical beliefs. And he was sending her out to fulfill his mission from the grave.

He tried once more. "You know how much I loved Yuri," he said. "But I do urge you to consider very carefully. This could bring you into danger, Lucy. Take time to think about it."

She shook her head. "I haven't got time. I'm booked to fly to Geneva tomorrow. Don't worry about me. I'll be careful. Wish me luck."

He bent and kissed her on the forehead. "I do," he said. "God go with you, Lucy. But promise me one thing. If Volkov is not the man you think he is, abandon it and come home."

"I promise," she said. "But I know that's one promise I won't have to keep. I feel my father's near us. Do you feel it?"

"Yes," he said. "He's here. Open the windows in the house. It's what we do in the old country. It lets the spirit leave in peace."

When they had all gone, Lucy walked out into the garden. She sat on the empty seat and stared out at the sea below. Sailboats glided into view, swaying and dipping like swallows in the breeze. It was so peaceful and secure. Sailing had been her father's hobby. As a child he had taken her out on a simple sailboat, taught her the rudiments of handling a small craft, navigating the little inlets and outcrops of rock around the coast. She was an apt pupil; she loved the sea and had no fear of it.

The little boat had been replaced by a motor cruiser. Soon it was Lucy who sailed to Saint Malo and Yuri who crewed happily for her. They spent their holidays at sea; he had taught her to navigate and she took them down to the South of France the year before his last illness.

She thought of that time, watching the sea and the boats below. They had been so happy together, so deeply companionable. She'd had boyfriends, but no one had engaged her heart. That belonged to Yuri and to the man whose faded photograph was still pinned on her bedroom wall. The face haunted her; she kept it as others kept an icon, to remind them of their faith and to give them strength. Imprisoned, persecuted, defiant to the last, Dimitri Volkov was the dream that hadn't faded like his photograph. Mischa was wrong to doubt. Volkov hadn't changed.

She thought of the ancient cross, in its dark hiding place. A thousand years ago it had been given by the tyrant Vladimir when he converted to the Christian faith. Ever since men had woven legends around it and invoked its mystical powers. Dark superstitions had invested the cross with a God-given power to bless or to curse. No czar dared take the oath at his coronation without holding it in his right hand. Hands tainted by murder and sacrilege had reached out to seize and destroy it. But the shrine was empty. The priest who had been its guardian had died in torment rather than betray where it was hidden.

A life span later, the old tyranny was crumbling. A people who had never known freedom were demanding it. All it needed was a man of vision and heroic courage to bring the cross back in triumph to Russia and rally the millions of Ukrainians against the power of Moscow. Volkov was that man.

It was a smooth flight the next morning. The weather was glorious; Geneva was a lovely city, built round the immense, spectacular lake. Lucy landed at the airport and took a taxi to the Hotel Arbalete, a modest family hotel in the Rue Tour Maitresse.

She checked in; the room was pleasant and not too expensive. She explained to the proprietress that she was on a working holiday and would need to rent an apartment.

The first estate agent suggested several properties, but none were suitable. Too smart and high priced, or too geared to short-term family lets. There was one, the girl suggested, that might suit her at Petit Saconnex, but it was for a six-month tenure. Lucy didn't demur. The setting had to be right. Unobtrusive but congenial. The time didn't matter.

Volkov couldn't be won without careful preparation. He had to accept this strange emissary, to trust her. And she needed a place where they could meet without attracting attention.

She arranged to view the apartment the next day and went on a brief tour of the city. That evening she sought out the proprietress. Unlike many Swiss, Madame liked to gossip. She accepted Lucy's explanation that she was a journalist on a popular English women's magazine.

A journalist with a special assignment. Her curiosity was aroused. Was Lucy after a film star? There were plenty living in the region. A pop singer, perhaps? No, Lucy said, hesitating before she let Madame into her secret. Professor Volkov, the famous Soviet dissident who had been exiled from Russia— her magazine wanted an interview with him that would exploit the women's angle. Nothing political, Lucy shrugged that aside. Just domestic details. How he'd adjusted . . . what were his hobbies? That kind of thing.

Madame nodded her agreement. Just the sort of thing she would like to read about someone so well known. "But, he never gives interviews. Never been seen on TV," she said. "I remember there was an uproar in the press when he came here first . . . must be several years ago. But he wouldn't see anyone or talk to anyone. His wife said he was too ill. I don't think anyone bothers him now. When people settle here they soon become private citizens, never mind who they are. It's our way. His wife's a doctor; she works in a very exclusive clinic up in Cologny. Only very rich people can afford to go there."

"I've got to try and talk to him," Lucy confessed. "It would make all the difference in the world to my job if I could write something about him."

"You could try his wife," Madame suggested. "But she's never encouraged the press."

"I wouldn't want to bother her," Lucy answered. "If I could just bump into him. He must go out. They're not in the telephone directory; I looked."

Madame was sympathetic. She was such a pretty girl and so friendly. It would be a pity if she went back with nothing.

"I can ask around if you like," she offered. "Hoteliers all know each other; I've got relatives in the business. Everyone goes to bistros and bars at some time. A lot of Swiss have regular places where they eat every day. Let me see if I can find out anything for you. After all, he's a well-known figure."

Next day Lucy hired a car and drove to Petit Saconnex and viewed the apartment. It was in a pleasant block on the Chemin de la Tourelle. She rented it, but she didn't move in. And the next morning, when Lucy came down to take breakfast, Madame hurried over looking pleased with herself.

"I've got some good news for you," she said. "I've asked around and friends of mine say he's a regular at the Bistro St. Honoré! It's a pleasant little place by the lake on the Place de Truinant. Apparently they say he goes there every morning for his coffee."

"Oh," Lucy exclaimed. "Oh, how kind of you, Madame! I can't tell you how grateful I am! At least if I go along I can see him."

"Smile nicely, my dear, and I expect he'll talk to you," the older woman said. *What man wouldn't?* she thought privately.

Lucy didn't finish her breakfast. She took a bus to Quai Gustave-Ador and walked along. The Bistro St. Honoré was small, as Madame had said. Clean and bright like all Swiss bars and restaurants, with a fine view over the smooth water and tables where the customers could sit out, sipping their coffee and watching the passersby.

She took a table set back a little and ordered coffee. The waiter lingered over the order. She was a foreigner and very pretty. He had picked up foreign girls by offering to show them the sights after work.

"You on holiday, *M'selle?*" he asked.

She gave the same answer. "Working holiday. I'm doing some articles for an English paper. It's my first visit to Switzerland. It's very beautiful."

"Thank you," he said. "You staying long?"

"I'm not sure," Lucy answered. "Tell me," she said, "is that Professor Volkov?" She nodded toward an old man reading a newspaper. He was old enough to be Volkov's father.

"Oh, no. That's Monsieur Fritche. He's one of our regulars, like the Professor. *He* hasn't been in since last Thursday. Maybe he's sick or something. He's here most days."

"I've read so much about him," Lucy prompted. "What's he like?"

The young man shrugged. "He's quiet, doesn't talk to anyone. Just sits around. Wanders off after a couple of hours." He hesitated, but she had a beguiling smile. He really hoped she might meet him one evening after work. He lowered his voice and said, "He's drunk most of the time. He starts on the cognac as soon as he gets here. Never causes trouble though."

"How awful," she said. There was a sick feeling in her stomach. Drunk! It couldn't be. The waiter said he hadn't been into the café since Thursday. Sick or something. Starts on the cognac as soon as he gets here.

"Talk of the devil," the man said. "Here he is!"

She recognized him from the faded photographs. The tall, slight figure. The face with the distinctive Slavic cheek bones and broad brow. He looked ill. There were bags puffed under his eyes; his dark hair straggled over his collar. He walked with his shoulders stooped under an invisible weight.

"He's pissed," the waiter whispered. "Same as usual. I better take his order. He still brings in the gawkers now and again."

Lucy sat very still. She watched him take his place at a table under an umbrella. She saw the careful movements as he shifted the chair and lowered himself into it. As if he were in pain.

Oh, God, she said silently, *What am I going to do?* She was close enough to hear him speak. She started at the sound of the voice. It was deep and heavily accented. It reminded her of Yuri. She flinched at the memory.

"Some coffee—and a cognac. Lovely morning."

And the sneering waiter, writing down the order, looked briefly across at her and winked.

She took a deep breath to calm herself. Her father's life-long dream, the hopes of so many helpless people, the saving power of the relic that men had died in torment to protect . . . all to be abandoned, sacrificed in vain because a great man was drowning himself in drink . . .

She ignored the waiter. She pushed back her chair and walked up to his table. She stood in front of him and he looked up.

"Professor Volkov?"

"No," he shook his head. "I'm sorry, you're mistaken."

"No, I'm not," Lucy said. "I know who you are. Can I sit down?"

He frowned for a moment. She thought suddenly, *He isn't drunk. That oaf was wrong. He's* been *drunk, but he isn't now.*

"If you're a journalist, you're wasting your time. I don't give interviews. Please go away. I don't mean to be rude, but go away."

She pulled out a chair and sat opposite to him.

She leaned toward him. "I'm not a journalist," she said in Russian. "Please can I talk to you? Just for a few minutes?"

Immediately the shutters came down. Suspicion, fear, then blankness. "I've nothing to say to you," he said. "If you don't leave me alone, I'll call the management."

Lucy shook her head. She spoke gently. "Professor, you needn't be afraid of me. I just want to talk to someone I've admired all my life. That's all. Please believe me."

The waiter came, bringing the coffee and a large cognac. Lucy looked up at him. "Coffee for me too," she said. Behind Volkov's back he pulled a face and winked again.

She said to Volkov, "Thank you for not getting him to throw me out."

"Who are you? What do you want?" He reached for the cognac; his hand was shaking. He said defensively, "I'm not frightened of you. I need this because I've got a hangover."

"I know," she said. "Why not take some coffee? It's better for you."

"How do you know?" he demanded. "You don't know anything about me!"

She answered quietly, "I know everything about you, Professor. I've read every word you've written. I know your great speeches by heart. I've had your photograph on my wall since I was twenty. The waiter told me you were drunk when you arrived. My name is Lucy Warren. Will you at least listen to me?"

"Why should I?" he asked. "I don't know you. I don't want to talk to you. I don't talk to anyone from home."

"I'm English," she explained. "I've never been to Russia. My father was Ukrainian; he taught me to speak Russian. His name was Warienski."

"It means nothing to me," Volkov said. "I never knew anyone with that name." He fumbled in his pocket and brought out a packet of Disque Bleu. He put one in his mouth and searched for matches. On the second attempt he lit it.

"There's no reason why you should know him," Lucy

answered. "He wasn't famous, like you. He was an exile who loved his country and thought you were the bravest man in the world. He worshipped you, Professor, and he brought me up to feel the same. He's dead now, but I promised I'd come and see you just before he died. That's why I'm here."

"Well," he looked down, fiddling with the coffee cup. "Well, you've kept your promise. You've seen the great Volkov at close quarters. A bit pissed from the last three days. Got the shakes. So you can go now and leave me alone."

"I've come all the way from England," she said, "just to meet you. Here, let me give you some sugar."

"I don't take it," Volkov muttered.

"You should. It gives you energy. Try one spoon."

"You must be English," he said. "English women are so bossy."

"If you really hate coffee with sugar, have mine instead."

"No, no. It doesn't matter. Now will you go away?"

"No," Lucy said. "I won't. You said to the waiter it's a lovely morning. Can't we just sit together and enjoy it? I won't talk if you'd rather not."

He'd been trying not to look at her. He didn't want to see her; she realized that. With his eyes lowered, he felt safe. Now he gave in and met her eye-to-eye. His head ached and his nerves were a screaming mob clamoring for alcohol instead of blood. But she was still pretty, with piercing blue eyes like the lake water when the sun shone.

Why would they send her? Why would they try and trap him after all this time? He was broken, disarmed. They'd nothing to worry about from the wreck he'd become.

"Are you genuine?"

The question caught her by surprise. "Genuine? What do you mean, Professor?"

"Are you real? They use pretty girls to trick people into

saying things. And then they punish them. Are you sure you're not one of those?"

"I'm not," Lucy said firmly. "I'm Lucy Warren. I was born in England and you said yourself, I'm bossy. You really can trust me, Professor."

For a moment she saw him smile. It was brief, but it lit the sad, dark eyes.

"I was locked up for a year," he said. "You learn not to trust anyone after that. I've been very rude to you. Most people would have gone away."

"I'm not most people."

"I can believe that," he said. His cigarette had burned out in the ashtray. He lit another, blew out the smoke, and stared at her. The coffee and the cognac were soothing; he felt better. He thought, *She has the most beautiful eyes. She keeps staring at me. I wish she wouldn't.*

Lucy let the silence continue. Under the table her hands were gripping tight with tension. So far so good. He hadn't got up and walked away. For a brief moment she had made him smile. He had drunk the sugared coffee. One ill-judged word, one mistake and flimsy contact would be broken. "I was locked up for a year . . . You learn not to trust anyone . . ."

He'd thought she was a KGB plant. How foolish not to have reckoned on that . . . she had a lot to learn about people who had suffered as he had done. You didn't grasp the reality from books and articles. The reality was in his haunted eyes and trembling hands. In the deadening refuge of drunkenness.

The waiter was back again. She avoided his inquiring glance.

"Anything else, Sir, Mademoiselle?"

"Have you had breakfast, Professor?"

Volkov shook his head. "No. I don't eat much."

"Would you mind if I had something. I'm very hungry."

"I don't mind. Of course."

She ordered croissants and more coffee. She didn't want them. Her throat was tight and her stomach knotted. Anything to keep him there, even food that she doubted she could swallow. She said gently, "Why don't you eat anything in the morning? Isn't there anyone to get it for you?"

He shrugged. He finished the cognac.

"My wife leaves early. I'm asleep. It doesn't matter. I haven't felt hungry for a long time. When I was in prison I tried to eat the straw out of the mattress. They stopped my bread ration for five days." He put down the empty glass and looked at her.

"You don't want to hear about things like that. You're pretty and young. Here's your breakfast."

Lucy couldn't help it. Her eyes filled with tears. One slipped onto her cheek and she tried to brush it away. But Volkov saw it. He leaned a little toward her.

"You mustn't do that," he said. "Don't cry. Nobody cries for me anymore."

"I was crying for them too," she said slowly. "For all the people like you, Professor Volkov. The ones who died and the ones who are still locked up. There are thousands and thousands of them."

"Millions," he corrected. "I shouldn't talk to you like this."

"Are you forbidden to talk?" she asked him. "Did they make you promise?"

"I wouldn't promise," he answered. "My wife promised for me. I wouldn't cooperate. Now." He raised his hand for the waiter.

Lucy said desperately, "Don't have any more to drink, please!"

"That's what she says," Volkov nodded. " 'Don't drink, Dimitri. Stop feeling sorry for yourself.' Please don't sound like my wife."

"I don't mean to," Lucy said. "I'm sorry. It's just selfish, that's all. Talking to you means so much to me."

He let his hand fall. He had been a handsome man once; the face was drawn and hollow-cheeked, the fine eyes sunken and bloodshot. He looked so desolate that Lucy almost gave up.

"I'm being a nuisance to you," she said. "I shouldn't do it."

He said slowly, "Why should it mean anything to you to sit and talk to a drunk who's opted out? Tell me, Lucy Warren."

She said quietly, "Because you're not a drunk and you haven't opted out. I'd no right to say that about drinking. Please forgive me. They've tried to crush you in exile because they couldn't do it at home and the whole world was watching. People like my father were praying for you, working for your release. You gave so many people someone to look up to. I know that's how I felt. So long as Volkov stood against the system, there was hope. That's what you mean to me. My father said you were so young and brilliant and you couldn't be bribed or threatened into keeping quiet. At the worst time, when they were sending dissidents to mental hospitals, driving them mad with drugs, you drew the world's attention to what was being done. If you want a drink, Professor Volkov, I'll go to the bar and get you one!"

"You're very strange," he said. "I knew girls like you at home. They were strange too. Full of strong feelings. Brave. Oh, much braver than some of the men. They were more cruel to women than they were to us. They hate courage. They hate heroism. It's just as well you're English. If I'm not going to get drunk, I'm going for a walk. We'll pay the bill and I'll say good-bye."

"I'll pay the bill," Lucy said. "And if you don't mind, I'll walk with you."

* * *

They walked slowly and in silence for most of the time. Once Volkov paused at the lakeside. Sea gulls were swimming close to shore, looking for tidbits. He felt in his pocket absentmindedly.

"I forgot," he said. "I get some stale bread from the café. I like to feed them."

"We'll get some tomorrow," Lucy suggested. "I'll remember. At home we have a lot of sea gulls; they come screaming in over the garden. They get so tame they'll come down and take food out of your fingers."

"You live by the sea?" He said it politely.

"I live on an island," she said. "Jersey, it's very beautiful."

"I've never heard of it. You said you lived in England."

"It's one of the Channel Islands; they're English. The Germans occupied them during the War. I was born in England. We only moved there because my father had a heart attack and had to retire. It was very cheap and he had made some money. You pay hardly any tax."

"Oh, that must be useful."

He was still being polite. Drifting away from her. Lucy caught his arm. She felt him start nervously.

"There's a seat over there. Could we sit down for a while?"

"If you like."

They sat and he lit another cigarette. He offered her the packet.

"Do you smoke?"

"No, I never really liked it."

"My wife chain smokes. She only likes Russian cigarettes. They get sent over specially."

"You don't smoke them?" Lucy asked.

"I hate the smell. I told her once and she said, surely I'd got over all that."

"Why do you hate it?"

His attention was focused again. *He can't relate to anything outside his own experience*, Lucy thought. *I mustn't talk about myself or he'll drift away.*

"My interrogator used to smoke them. He'd say, 'You'd like one, wouldn't you, Volkov? You'd like a cigarette and a hot meal and some coffee...and shoes? Your feet are cold, aren't they?'"

He was looking out over the placid water.

"Your wife should give them up," Lucy said quietly. "It's unkind when she knows it upsets you."

"She loves me," he said. He turned his head and looked at Lucy. "If it wasn't for her, I wouldn't be here now. They took my shoes away when I was arrested. I got frostbite."

"I don't know what to say," she murmured. "I've read what happens to prisoners, but hearing you say it makes it so much worse."

"There's a man coming," Volkov said. "I hope he doesn't sit down here. What's the time? I forgot to put on my watch this morning."

"Nearly twelve," she said. "I think he is going to sit here. Do you want to go? I'm not tired anymore."

The man's shadow fell on them, directed by the bright sunlight. Lucy glanced up at him. He was elderly, gray haired, well dressed. He looked ill. He didn't speak. He sat at the far end of the seat and stared out over the lake.

"Ready?" Lucy whispered.

"Yes," Volkov muttered.

They got up and as they did so, the man glanced at them without interest. In turn, their shadow fell on him.

Adolph Bruckner had been walking. There was an hour to kill before his appointment. He believed in taking exercise, but his head was starting to ache and he was tired. He saw the seat in the distance with a man and woman sitting on it. He would have preferred to sit down alone, but there might not be another seat for some distance. His head was aching. It wasn't the skull-splitting pain that immobilized him for days on end. Just the faint warning of the agony that was to come.

He had told his secretary that he was going on a short holiday. His wife knew the truth. She was so worried about him. Adolph was touched by her concern. She loved him in spite of the age difference. He had promised to let her know what happened after the first consultation.

He came up to the seat and sat down, as far from the couple as possible. The last thing he wanted was a casual conversation with strangers. His doctor was a woman. He didn't like the idea of that; he had old-fashioned ideas about the female role. But she was said to be the best. His friend, Peter Muller, had recommended her. He trusted Muller's judgment in this, as he did his knowledge of antiques and works of art. He glanced up briefly as the couple got up. The girl was blonde and very pretty. He liked beautiful women and beautiful things. Collecting was his passion. He watched them walk away together.

He stared out over the lake; he couldn't appreciate the splendor of the view. His mood was bitter because he was afraid. Afraid of the headache, afraid of submitting to a science he had derided as the refuge of fools and weaklings. Psychiatry.

He had tried everything else. Brain scans showed nothing. No tumors, no abnormality. Business pressure was blamed and he went on a long cruise with his wife and his adopted children. It was useless. He lay in his cabin and groaned aloud with the intolerable pain. There was no rhythm in the attacks. They came without warning and as suddenly they stopped, leaving him shocked and exhausted. He had taken his head between his hands, crushing the temples as if he could drive out the excruciating agony. At times he had thought of suicide.

He had been forced to this as a last resort. Switzerland. He muttered the word to himself. Cuckoo clocks and numbered bank accounts. Watches and ski resorts. And clinics. Clinics as discreet as the banks.

A group of children passed by, laughing and shouting. He winced at the noise. He loved children, but he couldn't father any. His first marriage had broken up because he was sterile and his wife wouldn't adopt. Eloise had been different. He had worn his second wife like a jewel. Thirty years younger, elegant, intelligent, a medal Adolph Bruckner had awarded himself for his phenomenal success. His wealth and his power couldn't help him now. Here he was, the famous West German industrialist with his millions and his influence from the Bundesbank to the Bundestag, sitting on a seat, alone and vulnerable, while the headache tuned up for a terrible concert of relentless pain.

Clinics and cuckoo clocks. The words chased each other round his brain like some idiot jingle. He looked at his watch. He sighed. He had left his car and chauffeur while he walked. They were waiting for him on the road.

It was a short drive up the hillside. The clinic was built on a promontory, with spectacular views across the lake to the distant Jura Mountains in their bridal wreath of clouds. He went up the steps and into the reception.

It was a handsome modern building, with lots of glass. Cool colors, plenty of air. Pastel flower arrangements and smiling faces coming to greet him. Empty eyes and painted smiles. *To soothe the mad*, he thought savagely. *Am I, Adolph Bruckner, mad? What is it, inside my head, that all the skill of technical science cannot find?*

A nurse guided him to a silent elevator that stopped at the third floor without seeming to move. She came with him and he read the nameplate on the door. Doctor Irina Volkov. The nurse knocked, and then opened the door for him. Her smile was painted too. He stepped inside.

He had formed a mental picture of the famous Russian

doctor. He was expecting a big, butch woman, with spectacles and shorn hair. The woman who came to meet him was slight, fair haired, and in her thirties. She wore a well-cut blue dress and a gold necklace. She smiled at him and held out her hand, as if it was a social encounter.

"Monsieur Bruckner. Good morning. Do come and sit down, please. Make yourself comfortable."

A big leather armchair faced her across her desk.

"Do you smoke?"

He shook his head. "Thank you, no."

"Very sensible," she said and smiled. "But I'm afraid I do. If you don't mind."

"I don't mind."

She wasn't a health freak; that helped. He had no time for the anti-alcohol and -tobacco lobby. People should make their own decisions on what was bad for them. He had interests in the tobacco companies.

"I've been looking through your notes," she said. "You're a very healthy man. No illnesses apart from a remedial operation for a war wound."

"I was shot in the leg on the Russian front," he said. "Army surgeons cocked it up. I walked with a limp till it was put right."

She nodded. She wore her blonde hair in a short swinging bob. The color of corn swaying in a light breeze.

Fields and fields of corn as they rumbled through, cutting across them, scything down the crops.

"But you have this one problem," he heard her say. "Headaches. Acute attacks lasting for days sometimes. Clinical investigations show no malignancy or physical cause. Migraine has been eliminated. Psychological stress is the diagnosis, but the attacks occur as frequently when you're on holiday or during leisure activities. You play golf, I see."

"And I ski," he added. "I keep myself fit."

"Well," the doctor said; she drew on her cigarette. "I'll start by asking you some routine questions. Do you have any secret anxieties that you can't discuss with anyone? Any business problems? Personal relationships? Money?"

He said no, to each one.

"Sex?" she inquired and smiled at him, as if it was a foolish question.

"I'm seventy-one," he said. "I'm still able to perform, if that's what you mean."

"I'm sure you are."

He knew he was being aggressive; she didn't seem to mind. "No aberrations, no perversions you're ashamed of? Don't think you can shock me. I've heard everything. I've great sympathy with problems of that kind."

"I'm not a sadist, masochist, pedophile, or anything else," he said. "And I don't want to fuck men, or dress up in women's clothes."

"Would you like a cup of coffee?"

It was a gentle put-down, and he knew it. She had a slight accent, not very thick, but with the lilt he recognized from all those years ago. He said, "Doctor, I didn't come here to drink coffee. What can you do for me?"

"It's what you can do for yourself," she said. "Your headaches are self-induced, *M'sieu* Bruckner. You are punishing yourself. *I* don't know why, but *you* do."

He glared at her. "That's nonsense. I'm not listening to a lot of psychiatric crap."

"Then get up and walk out of here," she suggested. "I guarantee you'll have the worst headache of your life."

He didn't move. He rubbed one hand against his forehead. There was sweat on his palm.

"What am I to do?" he said at last.

"You can trust me," she said quietly. "Try to think of me as a friend. Let me help you in the way I think best. I'd like to give you an injection, something to help you relax and make it easy to talk.''

He jerked suspiciously. "Sodium pentathol? I'm not having the Truth Drug!"

"No, you're not," she assured him. "You've been reading too many spy novels, *M'sieu*. That's a lot of nonsense. I'll give you something called Buscopan which simply relaxes the muscles and stops you feeling tense. It will hold that headache at bay for a little while. Now, why don't we start. Would you prefer to lie down?"

He grimaced. "No couch for me, thank you."

"If you're comfortable, you're just as well sitting up. Take off your jacket and roll up your right sleeve, please."

She straightened up. He hadn't even felt the needle go in. "You won't feel drowsy," she assured him. "Just loose, not uptight. So," she went behind her desk and lit another cigarette. He remembered the smell. Strong, scented Balkan tobacco. "Tell me about yourself. From the beginning."

It was the third time Volkov had said good-bye. They'd been walking aimlessly, stopping to sit and watch the lake and the passersby, mostly in silence. There was a bar up a side street. Lucy saw him glance toward it and then stop.

"I must go home now," he said.

"I must go back to my hotel," Lucy said. "It's lonely when you don't know anybody. There's a café over there. I wouldn't mind a glass of wine and a sandwich. Then I'll say good-bye. I promise."

He didn't argue with her. They left the quayside and crossed over; Lucy asked if she could take his arm.

"I'm not used to the traffic yet," she explained. She knew he didn't want the contact, but he was not going to refuse. He was a naturally gentle man, she realized that. A kind man. The courage, the self-respect had been stripped from him, but the kindness remained. He guided her across the stream of traffic.

"This is a nice little place," Lucy remarked. "Do you come here often?"

"If I walk this way. I have a routine, you see. I have a drink at the St. Honoré, then I walk to the end here and sit down for a bit in the Jardin Anglais. Or I stop off at this bar. There are bars and cafés everywhere. The Swiss eat and drink a lot."

They sat down; the bar was already full of people eating a snack lunch, drinking beer and coffee. The waitresses were busy. Volkov fidgeted.

Lucy said, "What do you do when it rains?"

"I go to the *bibliotèque* in the Place aux Vives and buy a book. Or I go to the cinema." He was looking round, trying to attract attention.

Lucy waved at a passing waitress. "The menu please and a glass of cognac. Bring the cognac right away, my friend's not feeling very well."

"You asked me not to drink," he said suddenly. "Why did you do that?"

"Because I know you need one," she said quietly. "Tell me, what sort of books do you like?"

"Books on religion. I'm very interested in religion. I'm reading about Buddhism at the moment. Ah, thank you." He took the brandy and sipped it.

Lucy waited. "Do you believe in Buddhism?"

"No. I don't believe in anything. I live in a vacuum. Rather, I exist. I might try Shintoism. It would be nice to be converted to something. There was a Protestant pastor in prison with me. He was a good man. He said I'd find it easier if I was a Christian. I wonder what's happened to him . . . If he ended in a labor camp he's probably dead. He wasn't very strong."

"But you survived," she pointed out. "That's what's important."

He watched her, finishing the brandy, the sense of not being, not caring, spreading through him. She had such a delicate face, such an innocent intensity.

"You're a nice person, Lucy Warren. But you're wasting your time with me. I don't know what you want, but I've nothing to give anyone. So, for the last time, go away and leave me in peace. Please."

"All right," Lucy stood up. "All right, I'll go. But I'll be back tomorrow and the day after and the day after that. You're not going to get rid of me, Professor."

Then she was gone. He saw her walk away down the street. It was peaceful now she had gone. Nobody to ask questions, to fix him with that intent blue stare as if there was anyone worth looking at. And suddenly he was lonely. The day ahead of him seemed very long. He knew the remedy for that. He called the waitress.

Lucy went to the rented apartment. She felt tired and drained. Despair was creeping up on her. The hero didn't exist; the fiery orator, the fearless protester against injustice and oppression had become a lost soul. Introverted, withdrawn, alcohol dependent. And so vulnerable that he made her heart ache with pity. And pity began changing to anger.

She kicked off her shoes and paced up and down.

"I'm damned if I'm going to let them win!"

They were brave words; she said them more for herself than for Volkov. The system had broken him and contemptuously cast him out. He posed no threat, especially in the new age of *glasnost*. He was no Andrei Sakharov to enter politics and rally opposition. He was dying visibly without the martyr's crown. It was hopeless. It was cruel to harry him. As he said, he had nothing to give anyone.

She sat down and closed her eyes. All for nothing. Her father's dream of a crusade, her hopes, the trust of Mischa and the friends who had lobbied and marched in protest all over the world when Volkov was arrested. A year in prison. That was all they needed to break his spirit.

She opened her eyes and sat up slowly. A year wasn't very long. Others had survived much worse and come out strengthened. Was Volkov flawed? Was he so weak under duress? He hadn't seemed so when the world was watching. Ringing statements of defiance had been smuggled out of his cell in the Lubianka prison and published to the rage of the Soviet authorities.

She remembered her question, "Are you forbidden to talk? Did they make you promise?" And the swift answer, unusually decisive. "I wouldn't promise . . . My wife promised for me . . . I wouldn't cooperate." He had disintegrated afterward, in exile.

His wife! He had spoken of her in an ambivalent way. She smoked cigarettes that he associated with torture and dismissed his protest. She nagged him for drinking, when even Lucy knew it was the wrong way to approach the problem. She was a famous Soviet psychiatrist, involved with the medical establishment that declared dissidents insane and locked them away in asylums.

Her father, Yuri, had warned her about the wife. Surely she was the best person to help her husband? Unless she hadn't helped him. "She loves me." He'd said that too. Coldly and without emotion. "If it wasn't for her, I wouldn't be here now."

Lucy got up and opened the window. She took deep breaths of the clear Swiss air and thought, *I'll be back tomorrow and the day after and the day after that. For as long as it takes until I reach him. If his wife is part of what's happened to him, then she's not going to win either.*

She slammed the window shut so hard the glass rattled.

Adolph Bruckner was relaxed. The chair was comfortable, He had no sense of drowsiness or lack of control. It was natural to talk about himself; the doctor was so unobtrusive. She just asked an occasional question to focus his mind.

He'd had an unremarkable childhood, devoid of traumas. His parents were affectionate, his home life stable. He was the only son; he got on well with a younger sister. Yes, he'd joined the Hitler Youth. It was compulsory, after all. And not a bad training either, he insisted. Discipline, physical exercise, pride in achievements. The present generation of young Germans could benefit from such a system. He wasn't a Nazi, no, he rejected that. He was a patriotic German.

"The army," Irina Volkov prompted. "Tell me about the army. What was it like being a soldier?" She was sitting just out of his view, a disembodied mentor. She could see his reflection in a cleverly placed mirror in the wall.

He tensed. His jaw clenched. He shifted in the chair. He didn't want to talk about the army.

"There's nothing to tell," he snapped back. "War is filthy. I survived with a bullet in my leg and that got me out of it and home."

"You were lucky," she remarked. "Millions of Germans never got back at all."

"Ten million," Bruckner said. "Ten million dead. Don't talk to me about war."

She had lit another cigarette. Her eyes narrowed against the smoke. "Twenty million Russians," she amended. "If you went through that campaign, no wonder you get headaches."

"It's got nothing to do with that! I was invalided out by the end of nineteen-forty-two." He was visibly disturbed; sweat was trickling down his face in the air-conditioned room.

Irina stood up. "I think that's enough for today, Monsieur Bruckner. You've made a good start."

He was up, pulling on his jacket, running his tie into place under his collar. He was anxious to get away.

"I don't see any point in going on with this. All I've done is waste time talking about myself."

She said quietly, "Do you have a headache?"

He paused. "No."

"You were starting one when you came here, weren't you?"

"Perhaps. Yes, it was throbbing slightly." The fear came back, swamping him.

"Well, it's not hurting now, is it?" she said firmly.

"No. No, it isn't." He was buttoning his jacket. He wiped his damp face with a handkerchief. "I may not have another attack for weeks!"

"I wouldn't like to bet on that." Her voice was very cool. "I'd like you to come back tomorrow. Unless you want to wait till you get another headache."

He raised his voice. He was used to shouting at employees and servants when they frustrated him in any way.

"What good can all this talking do me? I'm busy. I've a business to run, I haven't time to waste on a lot of claptrap."

She was quite unmoved. She shrugged slightly. "It's up to you. I can't do anything for you except help you to help yourself. If you want to come back, there's a ten o'clock appointment reserved for you. Believe me, *M'sieu*, I have a waiting list of patients. I'm only seeing you because I know it's urgent."

He went to the door. He turned the handle. Irina Volkov didn't move. He opened the door; then he turned back and said, "All right. Ten o'clock tomorrow then."

She left her desk and came to him. She smiled and nodded in a friendly way. "I'm glad," she said. "You've made the right decision." She gave him her hand to shake and gently closed the door on him.

Then she bent down to the recorder hidden under his chair and pressed the button to rewind the tape.

There were four more appointments in the afternoon. It was already dusk when she closed up her office. Just before she left she checked with her secretary. Yes, Monsieur Bruckner had confirmed the ten o'clock session.

Irina drove home, taking her time. She wasn't in a hurry to get to the apartment. She knew what she would find there. It was a lovely evening; Geneva was beautiful in the springtime. On an impulse, she stopped outside the Hotel d'Angleterre. She felt like relaxing with a drink before going home. And it was a good place to make her telephone call.

She knew she was attractive. Men glanced at her appreciatively. She gave no encouragement. She ordered a glass of Moselle, smoked a cigarette, and watched people come and go without much interest. She was thinking about her patient, Adolph Bruckner. She knew the type. A number of others like him had come to the clinic over the years: arrogant, greedy products of the capitalist society she hated. Their women were no better. Their children were typically spoiled and neurotic.

She loved her work; the mysterious mechanism of the human psyche fascinated her. She was euphoric when she dismissed a patient, cured and ready to resume a normal life; depressed when she failed and the solution eluded her. It was like winning or losing a chess game at championship level— she played chess as a hobby. She had been trained to regard human beings in her care no more personally than amoeba under a microscope. Without that professional attitude, she couldn't have worked at the Lenin Institute.

Bruckner was different. Bruckner wasn't there to be cured of his agonizing affliction. Peter Muller had sent him, as he'd sent others over the past five years. Muller hadn't made one mistake in his selection so far. Bruckner was going mad with guilt. He was driving himself to the point of suicide.

A ruthless opportunist who had fought his way to riches and power in postwar Germany must have something dreadful gnawing at his subconscious to torture himself like that.

Irina stubbed out her cigarette and asked for the bill. And

for a telephone. She dialed a number in Munich, closing the cubicle door. The phone rang for some time, and she exclaimed impatiently. Where was he? He was expecting a call. At last he answered. She heard Peter Muller's voice.

"It's me," she said. "I've been ringing for ages. Are you having a party? There's a lot of noise. . . . All right, so long as you can hear. Our friend came today. You're right, I'm sure we're on to something. I didn't rush him. He's coming again tomorrow . . . Yes, of course, I'll keep him in. Can you come up at the weekend? . . . What an awful row. You must have hundreds of people!"

It irritated her trying to talk against a background of cocktail party noise. It was unprofessional of Muller. She didn't like him from the beginning. He was too smug, too sure of himself. Now she had reason to hate him. But he was good.

"Oh, have you? That's nice for you. Make it Friday. I'll know a lot more by then."

He was celebrating, he said. A very big sale to some American collectors. She rang off and checked her watch. It was late. Time to go home.

Volkov was sober when the front door opened. He'd slept off the afternoon drinks, showered, and made himself coffee. He didn't switch on the lights. He sat in the deepening gloom and thought of the girl who had come into his empty life that morning, and refused to go away. "I'll be back tomorrow," she had promised and he knew she meant it. When he was released he'd been plagued by waking nightmares; often reality and fantasy became indistinguishable. Irina's care had got him through the worst period. Her care and her medical skill. She'd healed his damaged lungs, insisting that he rest and avoid all mental and physical stress. No interviews with the clamoring Western media, no press conferences till he was stronger. He was so weak he didn't resist. His will seemed to ebb away; the fighting courage that had sustained him even when they forced him on the Aeroflot plane in handcuffs to fly him out of Russia had deserted him.

He was in Irina's hands. Something in him had broken. Not in the cruel misery of cold and deprivation in his cell, but in the comfort of the Swiss environment. For many months he'd lived only to hear the door open and her step in the hall. He had depended upon her like a child. Irina loved him. Irina had fought for his release and finally persuaded the authorities to let him go. It was a long time since he had discovered the terms negotiated for that act of mercy. That was when he started to drink. He felt the helpless rage well up in him. And the despair.

She switched on the lights.

"Dimitri, what are you doing sitting in the dark?" She came toward him; he wasn't drunk and gratefully she bent and kissed him on the cheek.

She loves me, he said to himself. *She takes me in her arms in bed and I can't touch her . . .*

"What have you been doing today?" It wounded her when he flinched away. She bit at her lip, as if one pain would drive out another.

"I went for a walk. I had a few drinks." He heard her sigh. "I came home again." He didn't say, "I met this strange girl who told me how brave and wonderful I was and wouldn't go away. And she'll be there tomorrow." He said, "I won't ask what you were doing."

"I'm going to change. You might pour me a drink instead of being nasty, darling. It doesn't do any good."

She went into the bedroom and stripped off the smart dress. *He has to hurt me,* she told herself. *He has to punish me. I must try not to mind. If only, if only that swine Muller had kept his mouth shut.*

He hadn't moved when she came back. She poured herself a glass of wine. "I'll make some dinner in a few minutes," she said. "Unless you'd like to go out?"

"I've been out," he said. "And I'm not hungry."

Irina looked at him. "I wish you'd try," she said suddenly. "We could still be happy. We could have a good life here together." She leaned close to him; he saw a film of tears in her eyes. "It's all over, darling. It's all in the past. You could stop drinking and start on your book. Don't you realize how things have changed at home? We could even go back one day."

"There's nothing to stop you from going," he remarked. "You've given them enough victims by now, haven't you? Not to mention me. Why don't you go?"

"And leave you here alone to drink yourself to death?"

He shrugged.

She said desperately, "I still love you, that's the reason. We go over and over it and nothing changes. You can't forgive me and you won't try. All you want is to destroy yourself and blame me."

She got up, fighting back tears. At the door of her room she turned back and faced him. "You were dying of TB," she said. "You wouldn't compromise, so I had to! You might think of it like that!" She slammed the door.

He might have been able to forgive her. He still loved her in those days. He might have been moved by her distress. He might have accepted her explanation. If it hadn't been for Peter Muller.

"Peter, darling, the Baxters are going. Come and say goodbye to them. Who was on the telephone at this hour?"

Peter Muller followed his wife back to the party. The Baxters were rich American clients; they specialized in early German Gothic carvings and enamels. He had sold them a highly important ivory triptych for an incredible sum of money. His wife, like all clever American women, had made a friend out of Mary Baxter and organized the party in their honor. She was a great help in the business. They had been married for fifteen years and were happy together.

"Who was it?" she whispered, the smile already in place on her lips as they emerged from his study.

"Only a runner," he said. "Thinks there's something to be looked at in Geneva. I chewed him up for calling so late. Ah, Joe, Mary—do you really have to go so soon?"

He had a wonderful warm manner. A typical Bavarian, cultivated, charming. Not at all like a German. Mary Baxter felt he was a friend. And that wonderful, wonderful triptych! She couldn't wait to see it in their house in San Francisco. Thirteenth century, and the crispness of the carving! Joe loved it too. Joe loved their collection. It had made them famous, introduced them to interesting people in the art world. There'd been a whole profile on them in the *American Connoisseur*.

They were escorted to the door, handed into their car. Peter Muller kissed Mary's hand.

"Enjoy your treasure, Mary," he said. "There's only one other like it and that's in the Getty Museum."

"I wish we'd known you then," Mary Baxter said. "We'd have bought both!"

The party didn't break up for some hours. The Baxters were flying to London early next morning en route to the States. The Mullers' friends settled down to enjoy themselves and talk about their clients and their businesses. He saw the slim, elegantly dressed woman getting a drink from one of the waiters and came toward her. She was thin and dark and had been a photographic model in her youth.

"Eloise, my dear," he said. "Aren't you being looked after? You're always surrounded with admirers!"

"Not so many at my age," she smiled at him. He made a gesture, dismissing the idea as absurd.

"My dear, a mature woman is more attractive than any girl. Have you heard from Adolph?"

"I spoke to him before I came this evening," Eloise Bruckner said.

"And how was he?" he asked. "It's been so worrying for all of you."

"He said he'd had one consultation. He was grumpy. You know what he's like. But no headache, thank God. I'm so grateful to you for persuading him to go and see this doctor. He'd never have listened to me!"

"I couldn't see an old friend suffer like that," Peter Muller said. "I've known people who went to this woman; they swore by her. It can't do any harm. Please God, it may help him."

"I hope so," she said. "Thank you, Peter. You've been wonderful."

She didn't include his wife, Susan. The omission amused him. The two women didn't like each other. They were good at disguising it for the sake of their husbands.

It was past two o'clock when the last guest left. Susan Muller looked round at the room. It was littered with empty glasses, plates of half-eaten canapés, full ashtrays. The staff were being slow about clearing up.

"Well," she said. "Let's hope it was worth all the expense. I've made a note of the spongers who come here and never buy a goddamned thing! Next time, they won't get an invitation."

"From what we made out of that Baxter sale we could give a party every night for the next ten years," Peter reminded her. She was always irritable after a party. She resented the expense. "Come on, it was very successful. Let's go to bed."

Before she went to sleep, she turned on her back and said, "Peter? Is there something in Geneva?"

"There may be," he said. "I might fly up on Friday and take a look."

"What is it? Why don't I come too?"

"Because it's silver and most likely a fake. I'll only go for the day."

"I don't know why you bother," his wife said. "There's no real market for silver at the moment." She was far more dedicated to business than he was. Unfortunately she had no natural feel or sympathy for beautiful things. She only saw the price tag.

He heard Susan's deep breathing. He lay beside her till he was sure she was asleep, then he got up and slipped out of the bedroom. He made some hot milk in the kitchen and sat down to drink it. The debris of the party was cleared away. The kitchen was its clean, clinical self.

He had known Adolph Bruckner for nearly ten years. Bruckner was a big prize for any antique dealer. He had a large fortune and he had taste and knowledge acquired over years of collecting. He was an expert on early Russian art. Muller was as shrewd in his business as he was in his other profession. He set out to charm Adolph Bruckner's wife. Eloise Bruckner was a beautiful woman and he found he liked her very much. He didn't flirt; she wouldn't have welcomed that. He was astute enough to realize she loved her husband. He wooed her in a different way, by praising Bruckner's knowledge. She began inviting him to parties. He thought back to that first party in the sumptuous Munich house. The big drawing room was set out like a museum, with rare Italian masters expertly lit and displayed and what caught his attention instantly, a large cabinet filled with Russian works of art. Fabergé boxes, photograph frames, copies of Japanese netsuke in various hard stones with tiny jeweled eyes. And in pride of place, glittering with frosty diamonds and translucent green enamel, a desk set from the Russian Imperial collection: a clock and an exquisite calendar. He noticed that the original Russian date card had not been changed. The set was priceless.

He cultivated Bruckner carefully. He wasn't a man to be rushed into friendship. He didn't try to sell him anything. He flattered him by asking his advice and soon Bruckner was con-

sulting him. First one expensive rarity was found and pur-
chased, then others followed. Bruckner and his wife became
close friends of the Mullers. Muller made a lot of money out
of that friendship. And one day, by chance, he caught Adolph
Bruckner in a lie. They had discussed his collection of Fabergé
at length. He had been allowed to handle the treasured clock,
listen to the delightful silver chimes, adjust the calendar. And
he had accepted Bruckner's story without question—that he
had discovered the desk set in Paris after the war. He had named
a famous French dealer, long since dead.

It was a lucky coincidence, a one in a million chance that
brought Muller on a buying trip to Sotheby's in New York in
pursuit of a Fabergé Easter egg made for a rich Russian mer-
chant in 1912. He was acting for Adolph Bruckner, who wanted
this exquisite rarity for his collection. The estimate was over a
million dollars. Muller had his authority to go above the top
estimate to buy it. He failed. The buyer was a New York dealer
with a French name. The same name, he remembered, as the
dealer in Paris who had sold Bruckner his desk set. He had
approached the man after the sale and introduced himself on
behalf of his client. If the egg had not been bought on com-
mission, might he be interested in an immediate profit from
the underbidder?

And Muller added the story of his client's purchase from
the French namesake. No namesake, the American said, but
his grandfather! The desk set rang no bells with him, he added.
And he knew every important item of stock his grandfather
had bought and sold. The old man kept a meticulous record
stretching over forty years. He'd check, but he would surely
have remembered something so unique. Muller got a call from
him that evening at the Sherry Netherland Hotel.

There was no desk set listed. He'd been through the led-
gers. The name Bruckner was not on his grandfather's list of
clients either and he was equally meticulous about them. And

he regretted that the egg was not for resale. His tone suggested that he regarded Muller and his offer as highly suspect. That was when, as Muller put it, he changed hats.

Adolph Bruckner had lied about the Fabergé set, which meant he had come by it dishonestly. And dishonesty was another commodity that excited Muller's interest. Theft, sexual delinquency, scandal—Muller traded in all of them. He had been working for Moscow Center since 1957, using his contacts in the art world to supply them with agents. And for the last five years he had routed several highly important potential victims via the Geneva clinic—and Doctor Irina Volkov.

Muller alerted Moscow. Bruckner would be a very useful tool. He finished his milk, grimacing because he had sat there letting it get tepid. Eloise had told him about Bruckner's headaches. No physical cause had been diagnosed. He wouldn't accept that it was psychological. She was in despair. Muller promised to talk to him.

He waited till he knew that Bruckner was recovering from a terrible attack. Then he recommended the Russian psychiatrist in glowing terms to Bruckner. Between them, he and Eloise persuaded him to consult her. It was possible that his lies about the Fabergé treasure were part of something far more serious. Once in Doctor Irina Volkov's hands, he'd make a good confession. Thinking that, Muller grinned. He had been brought up a Catholic and it was the old injunction to children on the weekly visit to the priest. Make a good confession, Peter. Bruckner would confess, but there'd be no comforting absolution at the end of it.

He rinsed out the cup and went back to bed. Susan was lying on her back, snoring lightly. She had no idea of his other life. No idea of the bank account in Liechtenstein that was topped up so generously every time he pleased his Soviet masters. His controller over the last eight years was at the present moment leading a trade delegation in Berlin.

The Russian was an enigma to Peter Muller. Over the years he had surfaced in the West under a number of aliases and jobs. When Muller first came under his control, he was a military adviser to the East German army. He wore a moustache and cultivated a hard-nosed image—dour and stiff necked. A year later he appeared as a naval commander attached to the Soviet Embassy in Paris. This time he appeared with no moustache and a very different personality, that of a fun-loving, pro-Western Russian, with an eye for the ladies and the good life.

He had told Muller once that the French Intelligence, SEDECE, had tried to recruit him. He was much amused by the incident. He had, in fact, recruited one of *their* senior officers who'd been caught in bed with one of Rakovsky's young naval lieutenants.

He left Paris to reemerge as a respected official in the Soviet Trade Ministry. And this time he used his own name and assumed his real identity. The cloak and dagger days were over. He still ran a few selected agents like Muller, but in the new age of Gorbachev and *glasnost*, intelligence work was more specialized. A lot of the action men, as the assassins were called, and the sleepers waiting to be activated, would have to be retired.

As Muller would be one day, he realized. That made the nest egg in Liechtenstein so important. When Muller talked of retirement to his wife, he wasn't thinking of their pleasant Munich apartment and a holiday house on the Baltic coast. He had the golden shores and sunny skies of the Caribbean in his mind's eye.

He'd make the trip to Geneva on Friday. By that time Irina Volkov would have opened Bruckner's skull to see if there were worms inside. He drifted off to sleep.

He was late. Lucy looked at her watch again. It was nearly midday. The smirking waiter had given up trying to talk to her. She remembered the other routine he'd mentioned. "Sometimes I sit in the Jardin Anglais for a bit." Perhaps she should try to find him. She had slept badly and woken with a sense of apprehension. He wouldn't show up. Then just as she was giving up, he came into view.

He walked slowly, *A traveler without a destination*, she thought. If there was a ravine at the end of the road instead of a café, he'd step over the edge without looking down. She got up to meet him.

"I thought you weren't coming," she said. "Where do you want to sit?"

"Anywhere. I didn't mean to come. I thought you'd have given up," Volkov said.

"No, you didn't," Lucy told him. "I never give up. And you wanted to see me again. What would you like? Coffee?"

"If you like. It's hotter today."

"Then let's go in the shade," she suggested. "I've been thinking so much about you."

"I wish you wouldn't," he said. "I'm not worth the trouble."

"Do you always feel so sorry for yourself?"

It was a quietly spoken question and it took him by surprise.

"That's not very nice. I enjoyed talking to you yesterday. Why are you being unkind?"

"I didn't mean to be," Lucy answered. "It's just that I'm not sorry for you. Not now. I thought about the awful time you had in prison and I cried. You saw me. But there's nothing wrong with you now, Professor. Nothing really wrong, or you wouldn't have come back here."

"It's my favorite café," he said. "It wasn't all that bad in prison. It was much worse for some of the others."

"Then why have you given up now when you didn't then?"

"My wife, Irina, says I won't try," he remarked.

"Well, she's right about that," Lucy answered.

He looked up at her quickly. "No, she isn't," he said. "She doesn't mean what you mean. She wants me to forget and forgive and go back to Russia with her one day. The good dog on a leash who's learned to love *glasnost*. I'll see them all in hell first. I think I'd like a cognac."

Lucy said nothing. Forgive and forget? It wasn't hopeless. There was a spark alive under the ashes and she'd just seen it.

"I'll have one with you," she said.

He smiled at her. "You don't have to do that, Lucy Warren. I'm not in need of company. I can drink alone."

Lucy opened her bag. "I brought these," she said. "Copies of the speech you made about the Helsinki Agreement and the article published just before you were arrested. I was reading them last night. Have you looked at them lately?"

"No."

"Then why don't you? They're inspired. I know them by heart."

He took the photocopies from her. He didn't want to read what he'd said and written when he was in Russia. A phrase caught his eye. He remembered it.

"Liberty is the life of the human soul. The system that denies that to its people must be resisted even at the cost of that life." He put the page down.

"Why are you doing this? Why are you trying to revive a corpse?"

She said quietly, "Because you owe a lot of people. Like my father, who spent his time and his money campaigning for you. And all his friends. And *your* friends, Professor."

She reeled off half a dozen names. Members of the human rights movement. Imprisoned, dead, driven insane.

"You got out," she declared. "But they didn't. What

would they say if they could see you now, if they were able to speak for themselves?"

He hadn't touched the cognac. He looked at her; there was a tinge of color in his face.

"You hit hard, Lucy Warren. I don't have to listen to you."

"No," she agreed. "No, you don't. You can turn your back on me, just like you've done with them. But you won't. You need me. If you're dead, Volkov, then I'm going to bring you back to life."

"Where are we going?" he asked her.

She had hold of his arm. She'd been walking quickly, forcing the pace. Now she hailed a taxi cab.

"To my apartment. It's not far now. I've just moved in. I want to show it to you."

"That's not the reason."

"It'll have to do till we get there. We can't spend our time in cafés when I've got a perfectly good place where we can go."

When they got out at the entrance to the block he paused. "Why am I doing this?"

"I told you," Lucy said. "You need me. We need each other. Please, come up with me."

He followed her through the front door, into the apartment. It was a large sunny room, pleasing to the eye. He looked down at her.

"You're very beautiful," he said.

She came and put her arms around his neck and gently touched his lips. After a moment she parted them.

He said, "I'd better warn you. I'm impotent."

"You won't be with me."

The blinds in the room were drawn; a single light shone on the ceiling above the bed. Adolph Bruckner lay on his back and

looked at it. He couldn't see Irina, he couldn't see his surroundings. He only saw the little circle of light over his head; it held
him concentrated.

He felt weightless; there was no pain, no sensation in his
body. He had been talking, answering questions that unlocked
doors he had kept closed for fifty years.

Irina's voice was cool and distant.

"You were sent ahead to scout the land," she reminded
him. "What happened?" The tape recorder by the bed was
taking it all down.

"We went too far. Boris wasn't looking for partisans. He
was looking for someplace to loot. I was scared. I thought we'd
run into a Red Army patrol. He only laughed at me. He was
like a bull. He didn't give a damn about anything."

She had heard a lot about Boris, the big Ukrainian who'd
volunteered to fight with the Germans when they entered his
village. A powerful brute who couldn't wait to put on a uniform
and rob his own people.

"We went through a wood," the monotonous voice continued. "We saw this house. Boris said, 'We'll get some pickings
in here! Come on, let's take a look.' We had our submachine
guns out; Boris could move like a cat. He didn't bother being
quiet. He'd seen through the window. We just shoved the door
open and went in. There was a woman. She had long blonde
hair hanging down. She stared at us."

As he talked he became a spectator. He saw it all happening
again, as if it were a play. The blonde woman, terror contorting
her face, backing away from him and Boris.

"She turned and ran into a room, slamming the door. Boris
laughed." The laugh was ringing inside Bruckner's head.

" 'Oh, no you don't. I'll get you, you bitch!' " exclaimed
Boris. And Boris hurled himself at the door and burst it open.
Bruckner saw himself following; Boris had the woman by the
hair. He was bending her backward onto the bed, one hand

ripping her skirt off. He felt the sexual excitement rise in him all over again as he watched Boris expose her naked thighs and the round belly. She had been silent until then. The scream echoed in his head as the man fell on top of her, his breeches dropped round his ankles. He was thrusting into her, grabbing at her breasts, shouting at Bruckner to shut her up . . . to sit on her head.

Sweat was running down him. He saw himself pinning the woman down, half smothering her while Boris heaved and grunted, ripping her blouse away.

From far away he heard the doctor's voice.

"You held her down while he raped her. How many times was she raped?"

"Boris did it twice. He turned her over and buggered her. He was like an animal. Then he said, 'Here you are, kid. Now you get stuck in.'

"She was still struggling, kicking out. He held her for me while I got on top. She managed to scream once. It was so loud . . . like a trapped animal.

"Next thing there was a boy in the room. He was punching at me, trying to pull me off by the leg. He was yelling. Boris picked up his gun and smashed him over the head. I heard the skull crack. It made me finish too quickly.

"She was bleeding. She was bleeding all over the bed. I looked down and saw the boy was dead. I said to Boris, 'Come on, let's get out of here.'

"'Get your pants up,' he said to me. 'That little bastard spoiled a good fuck for you.' He kicked the boy's body. Then he started pulling open drawers. Throwing stuff out, looking for money or jewelry.

"I ran out of the bedroom, I was watching out of the window. I was so scared someone might come and find us. The place was miles from our main force. I was scared of the partisans. I heard a shout from Boris and he came out holding a cross. Holding it up. It was big and flashing with red stones. I thought, 'My Christ! He's got something there.'

"'Well now, get a look at this,' Boris was laughing. He was excited. 'The Red bitch's been robbing a church! This might be worth a few rubles, eh? Gold and jewels, lad, gold and fucking jewels!'

"He told me to go back in and pick up some ornaments he'd found."

In the shadows Irina sipped water. Her hand shook. She said, "What did you steal, Adolph?"

On the monitor his pulse rate had steadied. He was past the worst trauma of the rape and the murder of the child.

"My desk set," he answered.

"Volkov," Lucy whispered. "Wake up."

He was lying across her, his head pillowed on her breast. She stroked the dark hair, trying to rouse him gently. He stirred and lifted himself, gazing at her. She reached up and kissed him on the lips.

"You were so strong," she said softly. "I want you to make love to me again."

He said in Russian, "You're a witch. A white witch."

It had been an extraordinary lovemaking. Compulsive, mindless, and without words. Words might have given him time to doubt . . . to remember the empty shell his body had become. She didn't let him speak; she kissed him till his mouth burned and suddenly his tongue thrust fiercely back against hers. They undressed each other, still in silence. Their bodies had taken control; their senses spun them in a daze of desire, bringing them to the bed.

There was no sophistication in their lovemaking. She opened herself and grasped him to her and he reached a swift and violent climax. He fell into an exhausted semisleep, while Lucy lay passive under his weight and held him in her arms.

He was spent, but he was a whole man. She had made him whole. No failure, no impotence with her. "If you're dead, Volkov, then I'm going to bring you back to life." *And that is what I've done*, she thought, holding him close.

"Wake up," she'd whispered and he was awake, looking down at her, touching her face, tracing her lips with his finger, saying, "You're a witch. What did you do to me?" And stopping her mouth with a long, slow kiss before she could answer.

It was not like the first time. It was leisurely and there were many words, even laughter, between them. They were intimates now, finding out about each other, exploring their bodies with sensitive touching.

"You're beautiful," Volkov told her. "You smell like flowers."

And he made love with subtlety and tenderness, stifling her sharp cry of pleasure with a gentle hand over her mouth.

Then they both slept in one another's arms. It was dark when they woke. They lay and watched the lights blink and flicker from the window and Lucy said, "Would you believe me if I told you something?"

"Not that I'm wonderful," he chided her. "It's you! You're the one with the white magic."

"I'm going to make you love me, Volkov. I'm going to make you want me and love yourself because I love you. That's a promise."

He smiled at her. "And you keep your promises, don't you, Lucy Warren? Beautiful Lucy Warren."

"I keep them," she said. "Are you hungry?"

"No. Are you?"

"Yes. Stay there and I'll make something for us."

"You're always hungry. You wanted breakfast the first time we met."

"I didn't. I only ordered it to keep you talking to me. Do you want a drink? I've got some wine."

He lay back against the pillows, watching her. She put on a dressing gown. She switched the light on and drew the curtains.

"I might get drunk," he said. "I'm always drunk by now."

She paused by the door. She said, "You'll never get drunk again. You're not alone anymore. We'll have a glass of wine together." She sat on the bed and they touched their glasses in a toast. "To my lover," Lucy said simply.

She made sandwiches and they ate them cross-legged on the bed, finishing the wine together.

"Why aren't you married, Lucy Warren?" he asked her.

"I never found anyone I loved," she said.

"But you've had lovers?"

"Yes. Only two. I met a student at the college where I was studying interior design in London. It lasted about a year. It wasn't serious, we were both very young. Then there was a man at home in Jersey. I decorated his house for him and we became involved. I didn't want to marry him so we broke up. It was nothing compared to you."

He said slowly, "I don't want to hurt you, Lucy. I don't want to disappoint you. I must go home before my wife gets back." He sat forward, not touching her.

"Tell me about your wife," Lucy said. "Talk to me about her. You said she loved you."

"She calls it love," he answered. "She's tried in bed with me for a long time. I can't bear to touch her. She says we could start again. Just the other night she said we could be happy. There were nights when I lay there and felt her breathing beside me and I thought of killing her."

After a moment Lucy said quietly, "Why? Why do you feel like that? What did she do to you?"

He lay back and she moved close to him. He let her take his hand, as if she knew he needed strength.

"When I came here first I had TB. I caught it in prison. I

was ill and couldn't concentrate, I couldn't see people or face interviews. I didn't know what was the matter with me. Then I had an accident. I hadn't left the flat for so long. I remember it was sunny outside. I wanted to go out, to walk on the street alone. The flat was like a prison. I didn't get far. I fell and knocked myself out. Someone called an ambulance and I woke up in the hospital. They found the pills I was taking twice a day. I believed they were for my lungs. My wife, Irina, prescribed them. They were drugs, Lucy. The strongest mind-numbing sedatives. The dose was at such a high level the doctor at the hospital said no wonder I fell down.

"They kept me in overnight. I wouldn't let them send for her. I wouldn't see her. By the time I went home I'd thought it out. My wife had been controlling me, just like they do with the poor devils in the special wards. Keeping me quiet, doping me so I didn't talk to journalists, give interviews . . . turning me into a sleepwalker who'd never cause Moscow any trouble. I threw the bottle of pills at her.

"She tried to lie. But the hospital had x-rayed my lungs and they were clear. She cried. She's not the sort of woman who cries, but she did. She begged me to forgive her, to understand that she'd had to promise to do it before they'd let me out of prison.

"She kept saying, 'You'd have been dead of TB if I hadn't agreed to what they wanted.' She said it the other night."

"You couldn't forgive her," Lucy said at last.

"I could have forgiven her for what she did to me," he said. "I'd escaped addiction; that was lucky. I wouldn't let her give me an aspirin for a headache, so I had a drink when I got the withdrawal symptoms. They weren't pleasant, but I managed. I could have let her persuade me, I suppose. She'd given up so much to follow me. I reminded myself about that. She had a brilliant career; she was dedicated. Her father was a powerful Party man with friends in the politburo. She'd worked so hard to get me released. I told myself all that over and over, and tried to come to terms with the way she'd betrayed me.

"Yes, in the end I'd have forgiven her. Till I found out why she was really in Geneva. That's when I wanted to kill her. But I'm the one who died."

He turned and looked at her. "I thought of killing myself many times. But I didn't. I gave up on life and went on living. Drinking. Making Irina suffer. I can still do it. But one day she'll turn. I don't know what will happen then."

"What is she doing?" Lucy asked him. "Can you tell me?"

His voice had the same dead tone she had first heard.

"She works for the KGB," he said. "She has special patients at the clinic. She tortures them with drugs; she breaks them into little pieces so they can be blackmailed into doing whatever Moscow wants. It was part of the deal she made when they let me go.

"I said I'd denounce her. She just looked at me and said, 'I got you out of prison. I'm doing it for you. Go on, have me arrested. I'll get twenty years under Swiss law.'

"I did nothing. I couldn't betray her, Lucy, and I couldn't speak out on the old issues unless I did. So I opted for the Russian alternative. I got drunk."

After a time he said, "You despise me, don't you? You wouldn't have compromised."

"I would have done the same as you did," Lucy said. "She saved your life; you couldn't have denounced her. You're not that kind of man. And you'd been so ill, Volkov. Don't forget that. You'd suffered so much and she'd undermined you with drugs. You needed love and care to get your strength back. Instead she set out to destroy you. She didn't have to do it. She didn't have to work for them once you were out of Russia. I hate her!"

She put her arms around him. He saw how pale she was. The blue eyes blazed.

"I hate her for what she's done to you. But she's not going to win! You're free of her, Volkov. Don't you realize that? You won't feel guilty and you won't drink. And very soon the world will hear your voice again. Don't go back tonight. Stay with me."

"I want to," he said slowly. "But it wouldn't be wise. "She mustn't know about you. She'd find some way to hurt you."

"Where do you live?" she asked him.

He told her. "You mustn't try to contact me," he said. "You must be careful."

"I'll wait for you outside, tomorrow," she said quietly. "If you don't come down I'll know there's something wrong. I'll come up and get you. I'm not afraid of your wife. We'll come back here and talk and spend time together. We'll make love. You want that, don't you?"

He held her tightly, kissed her hard and hungrily. "You've made me alive," he whispered. "She leaves for the clinic before nine. There's a flower shop on the corner. I'll be there at ten o'clock."

He let himself out of the apartment. Lucy watched him from the window. He turned, looked up, and waved. Then he disappeared from her view.

"I won't take any calls this afternoon. I'm having a long session with Monsieur Bruckner."

"Yes, Doctor," the nurse said.

At the door of Bruckner's room, Irina Volkov paused. He'd been given a light sedative after the morning; she'd watched him drift off to sleep. He'd laid his bloody ghost to rest. Or so he thought.

While she wrote up her notes and locked the first of the tapes in her desk, she thought of the woman, violated and degraded, and the child who had tried to save her. She opened the door and went in. He was still drowsy. She prepared another injection, pinched up a vein, and shot the drug into him. Then after checking her watch to let it take effect, she slapped him hard across the face.

"Wake up! Wake up!"

She had hit him so hard there was a red mark on his cheek. Her own hand stung. She lit a cigarette and took her seat. He was awake and muttering in confusion. She reached over and switched on the powerful light above his head.

"Look at the light! Look at it, or I'll have to slap you again. Good. Now, Boris had killed the woman. The boy was dead and you'd stolen the desk set. Tell me, Adolph. Tell me what you did then."

"Boris was gloating over the cross." The voice was low. "He kept rubbing the red stones and holding it up to the light. 'Gold and jewels,' he said over and over. 'It's worth a fortune. Boris, you're in luck, you clever fucker! You'll be rich when this war's over.'

"I was wrapping the clock and the calendar in a skirt I'd found in the bedroom. He'd thrown everything on the floor, emptied the drawers. I wanted to get out, take the stuff and get the hell away from the place. I remember I was so scared I was peeing myself, thinking what would happen if a Red Army patrol caught us coming out of that house. Then I heard a moaning noise.

"I shouted at Boris. He heard the moaning too, and he shoved the cross into his jacket. He picked up his gun. 'Watch outside,' he told me and he went back into the bedroom. I thought we'd killed her, but she was still alive. I stood by the window looking out again. The sun was shining in. Then I heard a noise. It was coming from a big cupboard by the door. I got ready to open fire and then I opened it."

Irina noticed that the monitor attached to his wrist showed a violent rise in his pulse rate.

"Tell me," she said. "What was in the cupboard?"

"Two kids. A boy, holding a baby. He had his hand over its mouth to stop its crying. He just stared up at me."

"Did you kill them too?"

"No. I heard shots in the bedroom. I knew Boris had finished off the woman. I made a sign to the boy to stay quiet and I shut the door. I didn't say anything about them to Boris. I knew what he'd do. I used to dream of that kid's face and the eyes, staring up at me. I had nightmares about it for a long time."

"Didn't you have nightmares about the woman and the boy being murdered? Didn't that worry you?"

"Not so much. I'd seen a lot of corpses by then. We always looked for women when we took a village. Everybody did it. She wasn't the first one I'd had. But the boy in the cupboard, holding the baby. I couldn't get it out of my mind. The way he looked at me."

"That must have been his mother then, and his brother," Irina remarked. "She tried to save them by hiding them in the cupboard. She didn't have time to save herself."

Bruckner's mouth trembled and tears spilled out and ran down his cheeks.

"It was the war! It was the same everywhere. I wasn't the only one. I could have shot them. Boris would have done it. I just couldn't. That boy staring up at me. I couldn't. Oh, Jesus, my head hurts." He began to sob.

Irina stood up. She looked down on him. Remember, remember your training. You are not involved. You are objective, unemotional. It means no more to you than a test tube experiment. You struck him because you had to wake him up. You had to demonstrate your power over him. You are a scientist, a rationalist. You are superior to feelings of hatred and rage.

She switched off the tape recorder, put the tape in her

pocket, shut down the harsh overhead light, and rang for the nurse. Bruckner was moaning, holding his head and tossing to and fro.

The nurse came in and Irina said, "We've had a very good session. Very productive. But he's experiencing some distress."

"Yes, I can see. What medication shall I give, Doctor?"

Irina paused on her way out. She said coolly, "None. He'll just have to suffer through it. It's part of his therapy. If necessary, restrain him. I'll be in early tomorrow morning."

She closed the door.

Volkov saw her car draw up and turn into the garage space reserved for residents in the apartment block. She was late; another special patient. He hurried in ahead of her. *I must be careful*, he kept saying to himself. *She's clever, she's trained to observe people. She mustn't notice any difference in me. And surely it shows—isn't a man who's found his sexual powers after five years of flaccid impotence visibly changed? Isn't it obvious when a dead man comes to life? Won't she see at a single glance that something has happened to me? Part of me wants to flaunt it. Part of me wants to taunt her. What did I do with myself today? She always asks that question, never expecting an answer, but the same sullen negative. Nothing. I walked, I had a few drinks. But not this time.*

What did I do? I spent the day with a woman. I made love to her. Yes, I made love several times. She said I was wonderful. I'm going to see her tomorrow.

How much I hate her, he realized, waiting for Irina to let herself in. *Perhaps it's because I loved her so much in the beginning. I wanted to change her, to open her heart and mind to the goodness and truth in human beings. I failed. I couldn't change her. The only thing that touched her soul was love for me. And that's why I've tried to kill it. That's why if it wasn't for Lucy Warren, I'd cut her heart out tonight. So long as she loves me, I'm not free of her. I'm tainted with her cruelty, her heartless commitment to the Soviet ideal.*

"Hello," Irina said. "Sorry I'm late, darling. How was your day?" She wasn't really listening. She was making herself a drink, frowning, absorbed in something far from her surroundings.

He shrugged. He didn't answer. She didn't notice.

"Oh!" she exclaimed impatiently. "I forgot. I said we'd have dinner with the Schmidts tonight. I'd better hurry up or we'll be late."

The Schmidts were her friends. He was a lawyer, his wife a research chemist. They tolerated Dimitri, ignored his drinking. They were sorry for Irina, with such a burden to carry.

She had a circle of acquaintances. They all treated him as if he were some kind of mental defective who had to be humored. Poor Volkov. Just a shell. Put him in a corner with a bottle and forget about him.

"I don't feel like going," he said. "You go. They won't mind."

Irina didn't mean to lose her temper. She didn't realize how the sessions with Bruckner had frayed her nerves. She wanted to relax, regain her professional composure. She liked the Schmidts. Dimitri didn't like anyone. He had no friends. He lived in a limbo of his own making.

She swung round on him.

"They're expecting you. Frieda's cooking dinner. What am I supposed to say at the last minute?"

"I'm drunk," he suggested.

Irina glared at him. She was trembling.

"You're not," she countered. "You're just being swinish. I've had a long day and I'm not going to play games with you. We're going out to dinner and that's the end of it. Get drunk if you like. They won't be surprised! Now I'm going to change."

He said. "I don't like them. He's a bore and she talks about animal experiments. She makes me sick. I'm not going, Irina.

I'm not going out with your friends anymore."

She paused then. She made a great effort not to lose control. He was challenging her in a way he never had before. Not with the petulance of the weak; not striking a feeble blow that she could ward off easily. She was used to his gestures of defiance, tokens of independence that meant nothing.

"What's the matter with you? Why are you suddenly saying all this?"

"Because I'm sick of being put on display. Here's Irina with that poor dummy of a husband. . . . Wasn't he something to do with the human rights movement in Russia? Never sober. Must have had a hard time in prison. Only it wasn't prison, Irina. It was you! What would the Schmidts say if I got up tonight in the middle of their horrible dinner and told them how you fed me mind-bending drugs? How you manipulated me till I couldn't think or speak straight? Apart from the other things you do. I wouldn't make me go if I were you."

And then he said, from the comfort of his armchair, "What kind of a hard day *did* you have? Found some poor devil to set up for those bastards at home?"

She snapped. Shaking with anger, she stood facing him and shouted, "I'll tell you. I'll tell you about the poor devil! I spent my day listening to how he helped to rape and murder a Russian woman and her child in the war. How he held her down while she was sodomized by another brute. A Ukrainian, one of the scum who joined the Germans. Ukrainian like you! He robbed her and he's got the loot out on display in his nice big mansion! He's going to pay for it. And I'm going to see that he does!"

She rushed into the bedroom and slammed the door. She stripped off her clothes, changed into a silk dress, put on earrings and a necklace. She took deep breaths, urging herself to be calm. She dialed the Schmidts' number and said she'd be a little late. And Dimitri wasn't too well, so she was afraid he might not make it.

She lit a cigarette and walked out to face him. He was reading. There was a glass full of cognac beside him.

"I'm going," she said. "I made up some excuse for you. I'm sorry I shouted at you. Forget what I said. It's nothing to do with you anyway. It's my problem. Try not to drink too much."

"Enjoy the evening," he said, putting the book down. "I hope she doesn't talk about blinding rabbits while you're eating. I think I'll take up Buddhism. It's such an interesting religion."

She turned her back on him and left the apartment.

Volkov waited. He went and watched from the window till he saw her car edge out from the garage, its headlights raking the road, then turn and speed away. He took the glass of brandy into the kitchen and poured it down the sink.

2

G OOD MORNING, Sister Duval." Irina had changed into her white coat. She never wore it with ordinary patients. It intimidated them. She liked to project herself more as a friend than a doctor.

"Good morning," the sister said. Her tone was hostile. "Here are the night staff's notes on Monsieur Bruckner. As you instructed, we gave no sedatives. He became seriously agitated. We had to call in male nurses to restrain him. I couldn't take the responsibility for what was happening. At six A.M. I called in Doctor Minden and he sedated the patient."

She was a very experienced psychiatric nurse and she knew Doctor Volkova's callousness verged on deliberate cruelty. The unfortunate man had suffered such violent panic attacks that he tried to throw himself out of the window. She saw the Russian flush angrily.

"Doctor Minden had no right to interfere with my treatment program," she snapped. "I shall take this up with him. You should have called me, Sister."

The sister said, "I'm sorry," in a chilly voice.

"I'll see my patient now," Irina said. "We're not to be disturbed."

He was unconscious; his face was gray and he'd bitten

through his lower lip. He was strapped down to his bed and as Irina stood watching him he stirred, the eyelids fluttering open for a second and then closing tight. There was nothing she could do till the sedative wore off. She had canceled all other appointments. The morning was free.

She'd slept very badly. She felt tired and low spirited. And frustrated because Bruckner was out of her reach for some hours.

Volkov had been asleep when she came home. The dinner with the Schmidts hadn't been a success. It was her fault; she had been tense and ill at ease. Volkov worried her. She sensed he was pretending to be asleep when she got into bed. How many times had she reached out to him, trying to rouse the passion they used to share only to be rejected? In the end she had subdued her body as she disciplined her emotions.

Sex had brought them together, bound them through the difficult and dangerous years when he was actively opposing the authorities. Sex and a strong maternal instinct made her love him. There was no child at her breast, but a vulnerable, misguided husband who was doomed unless she took control. They might still have come together in spite of what she had done. If it hadn't been for Muller.

She sat in her bright office and thought of Muller coming to the apartment that day. He often visited her in the early months, talking as if the passive figure in the background wasn't there. It hadn't mattered what he said. Dimitri Volkov was in a fog of mental apathy and confusion. Muller had said to her once, "How can you live with him like that? Why don't you just keep him in the clinic?" He had shrugged her angry retort aside. And then that fatal day when he came early. She hadn't time to get Volkov out of the room. He had been off drugs for three months. Muller in high spirits, boasting, announced, "I've got a client for you, Irina. A French diplomat. Likes little boys. Doesn't fancy anything over six years old. He's got a big job

in the French Foreign Ministry. The Center will love this one!"
And he'd laughed out loud, talking through her, ignoring her
frantic attempts to stop him.

It had been too late. He had seen the signals too late. He
had stared at Dimitri Volkov and grimaced. "What's the matter?
He wouldn't know if it was Christmas or Easter."

That was how Volkov had discovered the real implications
of his release. His wife had been put in place as a Soviet agent.
The Center was Moscow Center, the heart of Soviet Intelligence. They had financed the clinic and prepared the setup in
Geneva especially to make use of her talent. A unique talent,
honed and polished in the Lenin Institute. They had invented
brainwashing.

Muller had brazened it out. He'd tried to bluff and bully
his way out of his terrible mistake, but Volkov wouldn't be
intimidated. He was physically frail, but mentally clear. He had
got up and faced them both. He'd said to Muller, "You do it
for money. You'd have sold Christ for dollars," and turned his
back on the German.

"You fool," Irina remembered shouting in desperation at
him. "You big mouth! Get out! Get out of here!"

She sat on, the inevitable cigarette burned out in the ashtray.

She had tried to explain, to make excuses, but he wouldn't
listen. His contempt shriveled them on her tongue. She had
burst into tears. He was so soft-hearted, he hated anyone to
cry. But he recoiled in disgust when she came near him. He
had actually held up his hands as if to ward off something evil.

"If I'd known what you were, I'd have killed myself in
the Lubianka."

He'd locked himself in their room and drunk himself in-
sensible. He hadn't denounced her. Irina had waited, gambling
on the challenge she had thrown down to him. "Go to the

Swiss. Tell them. I'll get twenty years. I only did it to save you!"

For the next four years he had lived in his private hell and his silence had condemned her to live in it with him.

But last night he had been different. It wasn't brandy bravado that spoke. She knew that too well. She was reminded of the man she had seen fight the invincible power of the KGB and refuse to back away. For only a moment, hardly discernible, except to a trained eye, the old Dimitri Volkov had shown himself.

Her telephone rang. She was startled back into the present. It was the ward sister.

"Your patient, Monsieur Bruckner, is awake."

"Thank you," Irina said. "I'll come right away."

Bruckner was sitting up in a chair. He was gaunt and hollow eyed; his voice trembled. Irina sat behind him, a disembodied voice asking questions through the drugged haze in his mind.

"Why did you spare the two children, Adolph?"

"I didn't want Boris to kill them."

"That was a good thing you did. A kind thing. I'm proud of you for doing that. Did Boris like killing people?"

"He didn't care. If it suited him, he'd kill them."

"Were you together for long?"

"About a year. We were a team. We fought at Kiev together. Boris was decorated. He only laughed. 'They can stuff the Iron cross,' he said. 'The one I've got is going to make me rich!'"

"The cross he stole from the woman?"

"Yes. He was always talking about it. He was going to sell it to some Jew. That's why he joined the Einsatz Commando."

"The SS extermination squads?"

"They were wiping out the Jews in the rear. He thought

he'd find a rich one and sell him the cross for a good price.
And then shoot him. He thought it was a great joke."

"Did you join with him?" The quiet voice asked him.

"No. I was a soldier. They were murderers. The Ukrainians hated the Jews as much as we did. A lot of them joined
the SS. We got drunk together the night before Boris left. He
got the cross out and showed it to me. He kissed it. 'There's
my beauty,' he said. 'With what I'll get for it, I'll live like a
prince! All the girls I want, all the drink. You'll make a few
rubles out of that clock, old lad. But I'm going to be rich!' "

"When did you see him again?"

"I never saw him. I was wounded and sent back home. I
was put on light duties. My leg was very bad."

"So you never found out what happened to him?" She
went on probing.

"No. I didn't even think about him. I wanted to forget. I
never told anyone about what it was like. I kept the clock and
the calendar. I didn't want to sell them. They were beautiful.
I wanted to make money so I could have more things like
them."

"And you did," she encouraged him. "You worked hard
after the war. You made a lot of money and became a powerful
man, didn't you, Adolph? You're well respected. You have a
lovely wife and three nice children. And a fine art collection.
So long as nobody knows how it started."

She had inserted the point of a knife. He didn't seem to
notice.

"That's the irony," he muttered. "If it wasn't for the desk
set I wouldn't have got interested in Russian art. My God—
I'll never forget the day I saw it. I couldn't believe it. There it
was. Boris's cross! The medieval treasure lost during the Revolution."

She said sharply, "What was lost? What are you talking
about?"

"The holy cross of Saint Vladimir. Priceless. Thirteenth-century gold and jewels. It was the same. It was the cross Boris stole. And he'd taken it. Without knowing what he'd got. I could have wept thinking what I'd missed. I made inquiries. I tried to find it. I'd have paid anything."

"What did you find out?"

"Someone had taken it to a French jeweler after the war and tried to sell it. The jeweler said the jewels weren't rubies. They were spinels. He offered very little, so the man didn't sell."

"Was the man Boris?"

"No way of knowing. The jeweler was vague. He said the man was a foreigner. He wouldn't part with the cross. If that fool had known what it was, he'd have given him the money." Bruckner wiped the saliva from his mouth. "To think of it—what a treasure I missed! With such a history! I found out all about it. It's in all the reference books. The Bolsheviks never found it. It disappeared from the cathedral at Kiev. The White armies would have beaten the Reds if they'd got that cross."

Irina didn't move, she didn't interrupt. He was ranting now, venting his frustration.

"When I think of that marvelous treasure being hawked around for sale . . . I went back to that idiot, the jeweler who turned it down. I kept asking him questions. What did the man look like? Couldn't he try and describe him? He couldn't. I told him what Boris looked like. He didn't think it was the same man. I could have strangled him. He was my only link with the cross. I put detectives on it; they found nothing. I even advertised in the art magazines. I was careful, very careful." He looked sly. "I didn't want the Russians on my track if they knew what I was looking for—just think what it would mean if it turned up now? Just think—that'd put Gorbachev in trouble! There'd be a bloodbath." He cackled wildly. He was becoming very agitated.

Irina interrupted him. "You were mistaken," she said firmly. "It wasn't a treasure. The jeweler would have known. You've imagined it, Adolph. It's not what you think."

He croaked at her, trying to raise his voice. "I held it. I counted the stones. It's unique! There's not another cross like it in the world. Don't you know I'm an expert on that period? Just because of that cross. I've spent all these years thinking about it, wondering how it got into that house. Like the Fabergé." Sweat was running down his face. "If Boris had known they weren't rubies, he'd have taken that instead."

He leaned back exhausted. "He couldn't have sold it to a Jew. All the Jews were killed. Perhaps he was killed. Perhaps it was stolen from him. I'll never know. I'll never find it now."

"No," Irina said quietly. "You never will. But you couldn't have shown it to anyone, could you? You couldn't have risked people finding out you'd stolen it from a woman you'd raped during the Russian campaign. Fabergé pieces were on sale. You could lie about them. But not a holy Russian cross. The only one in the world. People would have found out you were a thief and a rapist who'd let a woman and child be butchered in cold blood. No wonder you got headaches, living with a crime like that for all these years. No wonder you were driving yourself mad. You wanted to kill yourself last night, didn't you?"

He had sunk again, his eyes were full of tears.

"Yes." It was a mumble.

"And you will kill yourself if I don't help you. You know you can trust me, don't you?"

"Yes."

"You're safe, so long as nobody else finds out. And you won't have headaches anymore because you saved the other child and the baby. That was a good thing to do, Adolph. Boris did the killing. But other people wouldn't care about that. They'd think you were as bad."

He was crying. "I was punished. I was sterile. I was punished."

"That's enough for today." Irina got up. "You'll have a sleep now. We'll talk again tomorrow. You'll feel better. Much better. Get up."

She wouldn't help him; he was weak and unsteady, but she wouldn't take his arm or guide him to the bed. She let him stumble and fall on his knees. For a moment he looked at her with lucidity.

"You hate me," he said.

Irina pressed the bell for the nurse. "I'm helping you," she said. "You hate yourself."

Muller arrived at Geneva Airport just after eleven in the morning. He wandered down the Rue du Rhone, admiring the window displays. It was a rich city, comfortable and self-confident. He stopped to inspect the latest Piaget watches and was tempted to buy one for Susan. She loved jewelry. She had done a lot toward making that sale to the Americans. She deserved a present.

They had two boys, both at college in America. He didn't want his sons to grow up in Germany. They were not going to be involved in what he did. Their lives lay with the Western world he had hated so bitterly in his own youth.

He didn't hate it now. He accepted it, enjoyed what it had to offer and lived his secret life because he loved it. He loved the game for its own sake. If it had ever been necessary he could just as happily have switched sides.

He decided to be generous and went into the shop. He bought a gold Piaget with a diamond-set face, had it gift wrapped, and went out to find a cab and go to meet Irina.

He was on the pavement, waiting, when he saw Volkov on the opposite side of the road. The same familiar figure, untidily dressed, with hair too long and a hangdog look about him. Then he saw the girl. She was beside him and she had taken his arm as they waited on the pavement across the road. Muller stared hard. She was young, in her late twenties, very blonde and pretty.

I'll be damned, he said to himself. *I wonder what Irina would think of that.* He turned away, not wanting Dimitri Volkov to see him. He was in luck because a cab drew up alongside him and a man got out. He jumped in and set off for his rendezvous with Volkov's wife.

Muller grimaced at the thought of her. He had grown out of fanaticism. He despised the single-mindedness of people like Irina Volkova. They were blinkered by their own convictions. Often they did their cause more harm than good. Even more important to Muller, they harmed others more flexible than themselves. He didn't like her. She was a type he found threatening.

But he had despised her husband from the beginning. A fiery orator, and self-styled leader of the persecuted and oppressed, consumed with a reckless urge to sacrifice himself for his ideals. Muller hadn't admired him for it, even when he was a thorn in the Soviet government's side. He thought Volkov was a fool. There was no place in Muller's scale of values for a loser. He had long since abandoned heroics. They were all losers: the Jewish refuseniks, the intellectual dissidents, the scattered Christians asking to be eaten by the KGB lions. All the men and women of conscience who had confronted the invincible system. The jails, the labor camps, and the asylums were full of them. They were building railways and digging roads in the frozen wastes of Siberia. They had changed nothing. Change had come in spite of them, that was the irony. Change was a mass movement; it owed nothing to the puny efforts of the individual. Gorbachev and the new era in Russia were the result of the great pendulum swing of economics. Inequity and deprivation had brought Marxism to birth. The same forces were calling for freedom and democracy. What people wanted was food in the shops and a slice of the materialist cake they saw being gobbled in the West.

Few things surprised Muller; he had lived through the trauma of Germany's defeat and the painful reconstruction of a shattered and divided people. He had come out of it successful, respected, and secretly wealthy. But the sight of Dimitri Volkov with a woman gave him pause. It was no chance acquaintance. They were isolated from the crowd, their arms linked, the woman gazing up into his face. Volkov had been written off for the last five years. He was drowning himself in booze and self-pity. He posed no threat to anyone. He was the last man in the world with the guts to deceive his wife. But even in that brief glimpse, Muller was certain that he *was* deceiving her.

She should be told, of course. He should mention it, alert her in their mutual interest. But he disliked her enough to postpone it. What harm if she were being fooled for a change. He had never forgiven her for reporting his indiscretion in front of her husband. Even though the husband had made no use of it. She had rounded on him without mercy. If his controller had taken her seriously, he might have been in real trouble. No, he decided. Let Volkov cheat on her. A little adultery now and then was harmless. As harmless as the man himself. And Muller could play that particular ace if and when Irina Volkov needed a slap in the face.

"Tell me about yourself, Lucy. I want to know about you."

She smiled at him. They were together, sitting in the sunshine on the balcony outside her apartment. They had made love that morning and it was better than the day before.

"I've told you all there is," she said. "The only interesting thing about me is finding you."

He had a strand of her hair in his fingers; he played with it, twisting it round until it curled.

"You have lovely hair," he said. "Tell me about your father then. How did he get to England? And your mother?"

He was happy—a feeling he had forgotten. The elation, the excitement, and the wonderful aftermath of making love to her had left him in a mood of carefree tenderness. The sun was shining and they were warm on the pretty little balcony with its boxes of flowers. He was in the mood for confidences. He wanted to extend their intimacy, to hear about her childhood, her family. He wanted to imagine her growing up.

"My father was in a camp at the end of the war," Lucy said. "He'd been taken back to Germany for slave labor. His parents were shot. The camp was run by the British and one of the officers had taken an interest in him." The same officer who had let him say good-bye to his friend Boris, but she didn't tell him that.

"He got my father to England after the war and gave him a job and helped him to get settled. My father became naturalized, but he was always a Ukrainian. My mother was Irish; she died when I was seven, but I remember her very well. She was so pretty. My father brought me up. Major Hope left him the business when he died; he'd lost his only son through drugs, I think, and he more or less adopted my father. They were very close."

He held her hand. "Poor Lucy," he said gently. "Now you're an orphan. I'll take care of you. You mustn't be alone in the world. And he taught you to speak Russian—your father taught you?"

"He taught me everything," she said. "He'd had so little education, but he loved books and he said learning was the key to living. And being free. That's why you meant so much to him, and to me too. He'd lost his freedom; I couldn't imagine what it must have been like, seeing your parents executed, being dragged off to work in a factory . . . he was beaten and half starved . . . But he never gave in. He was brave, like you, Dimitri.

"He wrote letters to politicians, to church leaders. He got up petitions and raised money when you were arrested. And he gave me a picture of you to put up in my room. Every Sunday we went to mass and prayed you'd be released. I wish he'd lived long enough to meet you."

"You make me sad," he said slowly. "I didn't deserve anyone's prayers. I don't deserve you. What are we going to do, Lucy? This can't go on forever."

"No," she said. "It can't. But we've got a little time left. We've got today and we're going to be happy together. The sun's gone in, and you look cold. Come inside and I'll warm you."

"I said I'd take care of you," he whispered as they embraced. "But you're the one who's looking after me."

"I want to," Lucy whispered. "You need love and care to strengthen you. And it's coming back, isn't it—your strength and your courage? I can feel it." She held him a little away from her. "I've got so much to tell you, Volkov, but it must wait until you're ready. Now come to bed with me. I want to make you so happy. So happy you won't remember anything but what we do together."

In the evening they went walking, hand in hand, as if it was the first love for each of them. And he said suddenly, "What have you got to tell me, Lucy?"

She said simply, "Why I came to find you."

"How long have I got to wait?"

"Not very long, I think," Lucy answered. "I never thought I'd love you, you know that? I imagined meeting you, talking to you, but nothing like this. I'd built up a picture of you, like the one my father cut out and gave me, but it's nothing like you, Dimitri. You don't fall in love with heroes. You trust me, don't you?"

"I have trusted you," he said. "I've told you about my wife. That's put my life in your hands, Lucy. And your life in mine. That's what frightens me."

"It mustn't," she said. She stopped and they faced each other. "Your wife won't find out about us," she said. "Or when she does, it won't matter because you and I will be out of her reach. I'm going to say good-bye, Dimitri, my love. It's getting late and you should go home. I don't worry about you going home anymore. I know you won't drink. I know she can't hurt you. I won't come to the flower shop tomorrow. I'll wait at the apartment."

He bent and kissed her. She gasped as he opened her lips. He held her tightly.

"I'll come to you tomorrow," he said.

Irina was early. They met in the cocktail bar of the Richmonde. It was an old Intelligence adage that if you want to hide something, put it on public view. If two subversives want to meet and pass unnoticed, then do it in the smartest, most exclusive hotel in Geneva. She waited irritably, smoking, checking her watch.

He came into the bar without any sign of being flustered. He walked up to the table, smiled, pulled out a chair and sat down.

"Irina," Muller said. "What can I get for you?"

"You're late," she said icily. "I have afternoon appointments."

"So have I," he retorted. "I'm going to waste my time visiting two dealers, both of whom will try to sell me items I don't want and one I know is a nineteenth-century fake. But I had to have an excuse to see you, so I'm not complaining. I shall have a Kir. The same for you?"

"I hate fruit juice in wine," she said. "A glass of Moselle will do. Now, can we be serious?"

"You're always serious," Muller remarked. "How is our friend Adolph? Have you discovered why he has his headaches?"

She was a very cool, self-composed woman, who seldom showed her feelings. Except when she lost her temper and shouted at him like a fishwife in front of her husband. He would never forget that. Now he saw anger in her eyes and a faint flush of color in her cheeks.

"Rape and murder," she said. "It's taken a long time for the guilt to surface."

Muller raised his brows and pursed his lips in a tiny whistle. "Adolph? My God! Tell me about it."

"He and a Ukrainian Nazi attacked and killed a woman during the Russian campaign. He stole the Fabergé desk set from her. That's why he lied about it. That's not the important point. The Ukrainian stole a cross. Does Saint Vladimir's cross mean anything to you?"

He set his glass down on the table. "It does indeed. What are you saying?"

"In a minute," she leaned toward him. "What do you know about it?"

"It was an early-thirteenth-century gold cross which vanished from Kiev during the Revolution. Most likely the Bolsheviks destroyed it. With all due respect, my dear Irina, they were a lot of barbarians in those early days." Then he frowned. "You're not suggesting there's a connection with it and this cross Adolph told you about. That would be impossible!"

She said quietly, "It was a humble farmhouse. They were country people. But they had a czarist treasure hidden there—that desk set. He told me about the cross. He ranted and raved because he found out years afterward what it was the other swine had taken. He's a world expert on Russian art, isn't he?"

Muller said, "He likes to think he is. I've told him so anyway. So?"

"He swore it was the genuine cross. He tried to find it after the war. He thinks the Ukrainian probably was killed and someone stole it from him and got it to Europe." She paused. He didn't interrupt her. "He used his resources to try and trace it and he came up with a French jeweler who'd been offered it about twenty-five years ago. He wouldn't pay good money because it was set with spinels instead of rubies, so the man took it back."

Muller said slowly, "It would be spinels. There weren't any rubies of large size at that period. And that was all? He got no further?"

"No," Irina said. "He knew its significance. He said he didn't want the Russians getting on to him, so he had to be very discreet. But he came to a dead stop with that jeweler."

"What exactly is its significance?" Muller asked. "I assume you mean political?"

"Political disaster, if the wrong people got hold of it," she retorted. "Bruckner knew how dangerous it was. He said it this afternoon. 'If it turned up now, that'd put Gorbachev in trouble. There'd be a bloodbath.'"

"And you want me to make inquiries?"

"I want you to tell our friends at home. This is too big a responsibility for us to take on our own. It must go to the top. At once."

"You don't think you're being alarmist," he suggested. "It's very unlikely that it survived the Civil War in 1919 and even less likely that it was looted during the war and brought out of Russia in one piece. Personally, I don't believe the story." He shrugged. "No doubt there was some cross or ornament they found, when they robbed that poor creature and Adolph had made a fantasy out of it. He's half mad anyway, from what you tell me. I'll pass it on, but I must add my own disclaimer. I don't want to look a fool."

Irina got up. "I have to see my evening patients," she said.

"As for looking a fool, I wouldn't play this down if I were you. I have an instinct that he's right."

Muller summoned the waiter for the bill. He got up, bent briefly over her hand. It was a charming display of good manners by a suave middle-aged man to an attractive woman.

"I have a great respect for female intuition," he said. "But I never suspected you relied on it. My contact is in Berlin at the moment," he added. "It wouldn't be wise to communicate with him in the usual way while he's there."

Irina looked at him. "You can fly there yourself. If you don't, I'll make contact." She turned and walked away.

Muller sat down again and ordered another Kir. He had time to spare before his appointments. She meant what she said. If he didn't go to Berlin, she'd preempt him. She believed in Adolph's fairy story. *But then she would,* he thought, sipping the delicate drink. Superstition was embedded in the Russian psyche. Not even the dehumanizing process of Soviet medical training could eradicate the myths and legends of a thousand years of Russian Christianity. A brand of religion peculiar to the country and its people, where saints and miracles were part of everyday life and idiots were revered as the children of God. Part of Irina Volkova would believe in a cross that might cause people to rise up and start a counterrevolution. Being Russian she knew it was possible. . . . After seventy years of atheism, religion was reemerging in the Soviet Union. When official attitudes relaxed, the Easter services had been packed with worshippers. And not just the babushkas, mumbling their prayers, but with young men and women. Perhaps Irina was right to be alarmed.

He finished the glass of Kir and decided he had better see his controller in person. He traveled all over Europe on buying trips. He wouldn't be suspected. He paid and left for his first call at a dealer's house in the Place du Bourg-de-Four. He planned to catch the ten o'clock flight back to Munich. And then go on to Berlin the next day.

Irina had cooked dinner; she noticed that Volkov refused wine.

"What's the matter," she asked him. "Aren't you feeling well?"

He said, "I've decided to give up drink."

On an impulse she reached over and touched his hand. "I'm so glad, darling. I'll help you. It won't be easy."

He pulled his hand away. "No thank you," he said. "I'm never taking medicine from you again. I'll manage."

She said, "Why? After all this time, when I begged and begged you to cut down, why suddenly say you're going to stop?"

"Because I'm taking your advice," he answered. "I'm pulling myself together. That's what you keep telling me to do, isn't it?"

"Yes, yes of course it is. But why do you have to be so hostile to me?"

"How's your patient?"

She saw the contempt in his eyes. She bit her lip; he knew the mannerism well. It signified that he had hurt her.

"He's recovering," she said. "I don't want to talk about it. There's a play on television. I want to watch it."

They didn't sit together. He avoided contact with her even more these days, she noticed. She tried to concentrate on the screen, but she kept looking at him. Watching him. He made her uneasy.

"What have you got there?" she asked. He was eating something out of a box.

"Chocolate," Volkov answered.

"You would need sweet things," Irina said. "It'll help if you feel a craving."

He stared at the screen. She knew he hadn't been paying any attention to the play.

"I don't feel a craving," he said. "And I don't want advice from you. I thought you wanted to watch this nonsense?"

She got up. She switched the set off. "I'm going to bed," she said. "I've been miserable with you for five years, Dimitri. I don't know why I don't throw you out onto the street!"

"Because you love me," he said coolly. "You said so not long ago. 'I love you, Dimitri. I betrayed your trust and I betray sick, helpless people who come to me for help, because I love you.' That's why, isn't it, Irina? Love for me?"

"Don't count on it," she said slowly. "I'm only human. There's a limit to what I can suffer."

"Unlike your victims."

He didn't turn round when he heard the door bang. He switched the set back on, changing the channel to a news program. It was so long since he had taken an interest in anything. Years of self-induced coma. An abdication from life and from reality. Sexless, motiveless, enmeshed in guilt for the crimes of someone else. He knew she would cry when she was alone. He had seen her weep when he turned away, chilled into impotence at her touch. He had made her suffer and further imprisoned himself by doing so.

Courage was what he needed. The courage to leave her and beg public forgiveness for his desertion of his cause and his friends. He thought of Lucy and it warmed him, in body and mind. "Love," his terrible wife called her obsession with him. But love was what he felt for the stranger who'd thrust herself upon him. Not just the love for her body, for the softness and the scent of her, but for the person inside. The spirit that believed in him and would dare anything in its innocence. She had rekindled the sexuality he'd lost. But she had made him come alive in heart and mind. That was what love meant. She would want him to watch the news review, to involve himself.

He sat forward and concentrated on the interview being screened.

THE RELIC

*　　　*　　　*

A first-floor office had been made available to Muller's controller in the new Soviet Embassy in Berlin. From the windows
he had a clear view of the Brandenburg Gate. So much had
changed in the city. The Wall was long gone, the divided city
was united like the country. Germany was one.

Viktor Rakovsky had made a sketch of the scene; he would
finish it later. His speciality was watercoloring. He had exhib-
ited in Moscow under a pseudonym and been well pleased with
the critical reaction. The painting of Saint Basil's Cathedral was
highly praised. He preferred not to think that everyone knew
the artist had painted his best-known work from the window
overlooking Djerjhinsky Square.

He had chosen his stepfather Lepkin's old office when he
made his permanent headquarters in Moscow. He had a photograph of him enlarged and framed in silver gilt on his desk.
There was another photograph, the same size and framed iden-
tically. It showed the famous partisan leader, Ivan Zobev, wearing the medals bestowed on him by Stalin. The two men that
Viktor loved. There was no picture of his mother or his murdered brother, Stefan. His childish drawings of them were in
his bedroom, the only visible memento of their lives.

Rakovsky was thinking of them as he sat there in the borrowed office. It was late afternoon and the sky was turning red
outside. He remembered the vivid sunsets of his boyhood and
the way the sun would hang like a crimson ball above the edge
of the trees surrounding their house and then plunge out of
sight as if it had been dropped in a moment of carelessness by
God. He had been frightened until Ivan explained to him that
the sun went to bed like everyone else and would be up and
shining for them in the morning. Ivan was a fanciful fellow,
and he loved to tell the boys stories. Who would have thought
he could turn into a hero—leading his partisans against the
Germans.

Ivan had become a legend, a symbol of all the other Ivans who died on the battlefields and fought village by village and street by street to drive the invader out of Russia. He had stood for them all, when he was made a Hero of the Soviet Union by Stalin himself.

Rakovsky thought of him too. He was old and dying, but he lived in Rakovsky's handsome dacha and his days were comfortable. Rakovsky called him Little Father and Ivan called him Son.

There was a report on the desk in front of Rakovsky. His agent, Peter Muller, had prepared it and left it in one of the embassy "letter boxes" for collection. It was in the sleeve of a classical album that Rakovsky's junior secretary had picked up from one of Berlin's best-known music shops on the Tiergarten.

The words leapt at Rakovsky off the page. The words of a man confessing under duress from drugs and a long-festering guilt. Rakovsky could see it all. The house in the woods. His mother screaming as she was raped; his brother bursting from their hiding place to run in and try to save her. Sweat broke out over his body. He couldn't go on reading. He had a bottle of Scotch whiskey in his office; he poured a half tumblerful and drank it down. Now he saw the missing details in his nightmare. His brother lying on the floor with his skull crushed. His mother stretched out mute and bleeding on the bed. The sound of shots as her ravager murdered her. And then the moment when the cupboard door opened and he looked up in terror at the German soldier staring down at him. He was still stifling his baby sister's cries. Then the door closed.

He heard the roar of the motorcycle being started up and then fading until it was silent. A long silence followed. He hadn't dared to move. He was trembling with shock. He was in the dark. At last he let the baby cry. He was afraid she might suffocate. He didn't open the cupboard door till he heard Ivan's voice calling when he came in. Then Ivan's terrible cry of anguish from the bedroom.

Ivan had gathered Viktor and the baby Valeria in his arms; tears were streaming down his face.

He heard his own voice saying over and over, "Germans. Germans did it." Ivan had held him back from the bedroom by force. They had dug the grave together. He remembered how deep it was and how hard it was to break the earth. He hadn't seen their bodies. Ivan had wrapped them together in the curtains his mother had made for the sitting room, and laid them in the bottom of the grave. Even so, Viktor had seen the red stain spreading among the bright colors.

They didn't get the train to Moscow. The terminal at Kharkov had been bombed. There were no trains and the roads were under constant air attack.

The days afterward were blurred in his memory. Viktor was in shock. He screamed if Ivan left him alone, even for a few minutes. They journeyed into the countryside, sleeping under the trees, eating what Ivan could trap or shoot. When the partisans found them, they gave Valeria to one of the women to look after, but he stayed with Ivan. The camp in the forest was their home. It moved as the Germans advanced. They lived like nomads, ambushing, killing the enemy, moving on.

Some were captured. Viktor had seen their bodies swinging from a gallows in a little hamlet after the Red Army had retaken it. He had been given a rifle and Ivan taught him how to shoot. He'd said, "You're a man now. You're old enough to kill Germans."

They never took prisoners. They hanged them from trees. The first time Viktor saw it, he vomited. Then he remembered his mother and Stefan and made himself go back and look up at the bodies till he didn't mind anymore. Ivan had understood. Ivan was beside him when he shot his first German. He was ten years old.

"Now you'll sleep better," he had told him. "Your mother is smiling on you from heaven."

He drank more whiskey. He had lived through the war with the partisans. He had learned to accept death. His little sister had sickened and died before her second birthday. There were no drugs in the camp. A lot of the children died. He had seen horrors committed by the enemy, and horrors that were the doing of his comrades-in-arms.

Lepkin had been captured during the Battle for Smolensk. He had been denounced as NKVD by one of his own men and executed.

He was twelve when the war ended and by that time he had forgotten how to cry. Now he sat and stared out at the Brandenburg Gate, lit by the bloody glow of a German sunset, and saw it through a mist of tears.

After fifty years he could come face-to-face with the soldier who had spared his life. And raped and robbed his mother. Lepkin's gift to her was on display in his Munich mansion. He'd sketched the green enamel and the twinkling diamonds in the tattered book he'd taken with him from the charnel house that was his home. Ivan had given it to him, with the wooden doll he'd made for Valeria. They'd buried the doll with her in the forest.

And he'd drawn and colored the cross that he'd seen on his mother's bed. The cross she spoke of with hatred, as if she feared it. Her ravisher and murderer had stolen it.

Muller had ended his report. "If the cross Bruckner describes could possibly be the genuine relic from Kiev Cathedral, it could present a serious threat to Soviet stability in the Ukraine."

Rape and murder, wartime looting—a dark stain on the past of a very important German industrialist. Such incidents were not unique. It was the cross that had prompted Muller's journey to Berlin, and the rarely used "urgent" signal he'd sent to the Embassy.

And he was right. The threat was incalculable. Rakovsky forced himself to be calm, to consider the wider implications. The great Soviet Empire was only just holding together; if a group of Ukrainian nationalists were to raise Saint Vladimir's cross as a rallying point, one of the most important states within the State would erupt into rebellion against Moscow.

Muller was not only a very good agent, but an old partner. He had asked for an urgent meeting with Rakovsky to discuss the report and get instructions.

They hadn't seen each other for a long time. Both had been comparatively junior when their association started. Rakovsky was embarking on his career as a diplomatic spy, moving under different names and jobs from one Western embassy to the next. He had personally recruited the antique dealer. Over the years they had worked well and closely together until the political situation in Russia underwent the first dramatic changes. It was time for Rakovsky to leave the field and work in Moscow. Another reason was his beloved Ivan. Terminal cancer was diagnosed. But Rakovsky kept one or two special agents under his control. He wouldn't relinquish Peter Muller to anyone else.

The light was fading; lamps were aglow in the streets and the shop windows were lit invitingly, tempting the late shoppers.

There was a reception at the Italian Embassy; Rakovsky was expected as a special guest. A dinner and the theater were to follow, arranged by his own ambassador to entertain the trade delegation he was leading.

Trade interested him now, as other intelligence spheres had done in harder days. Industrial espionage was high on the list of Soviet priorities. They were starved of the technical skills of Western manufacturing industries. The best brains and resources had gone into military research and development until Gorbachev came to power.

Rakovsky drank another whiskey. He would go to the Italians. He would attend the dinner and the theater. He would smile and talk engagingly and hide his feelings. And then when he was alone, he would get drunk enough to sleep without dreaming of his mother screaming.

Muller was a little early for the rendezvous. Rakovsky was visiting a Russian arts and crafts shop selling embroidery, pottery, and lacquer work. Muller arrived ahead of him by twenty minutes and waited in the private room at the back. He thought the goods on display were crude and tasteless; but sometimes it was possible to find a little gem among the mass-produced dross. One small lacquer box had caught his eye. It was the work of an original craftsman. He asked to buy it. His wife liked little trinkets for her dressing table.

He was surprised at how much Rakovsky had aged when he came in. They hadn't seen each other for so long. They shook hands and then embraced like old friends. He *had* aged, Muller decided, noticing the puffy skin under his eyes. He looked as if he had hardly slept.

They drank tea together and Muller went over the report with him. Rakovsky was quiet, which was unlike him. He let Muller talk while he listened. He was not only older, but subdued.

Muller said suddenly, "You don't seem well, Viktor. Is anything wrong?"

"It's been a heavy schedule," Rakovsky said. "Too many parties every evening. Peter, I've decided to go to Geneva. I'm going to see this man, Bruckner, and check his story for myself. I'll make the travel arrangements. What you must do is tell Irina to keep him in the clinic till I can come. And not to lean on him too heavily. I know her methods. They don't leave much at the end. I want to talk to him myself."

Muller hid his surprise. Rakovsky had never visited the clinic. He knew Irina very well from her Moscow days. He had been instrumental in getting Volkov released so she could take up her appointment in Geneva. But he had left the running of the operation to Muller.

"Of course. I'll tell her."

"And Volkov? Still drinking?"

Muller shrugged. "Still drinking. She leads a hell of a life with him. And he's cheating, which is interesting."

Rakovsky glanced up at him. "You mean with a woman? How do you know?"

"I saw them together, by chance. Young, very pretty. They looked like lovers to me. Irina doesn't know. I saw no reason to tell her. She might do something stupid. She's still obsessed with him."

"It was her one weakness," Rakovsky remarked. "Everyone warned her—her father, all his friends, but she would marry him. Her own career was at risk, even her loyalty came under suspicion because of his activities. I remember her coming to see me and begging me to help when he was arrested. She was crying. She was an attractive woman, but I never thought she had a human feeling in her. To me she was just a brain, a scientific machine in a bedworthy body. She'd have agreed to anything to save his life and get him out. And this is how he's showing gratitude. Well!" He paused, then he offered Muller another glass of tea. Muller declined. He didn't like Russian tea.

"Perhaps we'd better find out about the woman. Just routine, Peter, but we don't want that drunken fool getting into mischief. And we don't want Irina upset. She's much too valuable." He finished his tea and stood up. He shook hands with Muller.

"You were right to bring this to me direct," he said. "I'm going home at the end of the week and I'll make arrangements to go to Geneva as soon as possible. And I'll authorize another payment for you. Look after yourself, my friend."

"And you, Viktor. I'll go out the back way."

"My love," Lucy said, "he wants to speak to you." Volkov hesitated.

"Go on," she urged. "He's waiting."

He took the receiver from her. She had dialed the number in London.

"Mischa is my father's oldest friend," she said. "He worked so hard for you, getting signatures, writing to the newspapers. It'll be the proudest moment in his life to talk to you."

She had described Mischa to him, and his wife and his children. How they worked for the dissidents, raised money, edited a Ukrainian-language broadsheet. Now he was going to talk to the man himself.

Lucy watched him; she came and stroked his hair with tenderness to give encouragement.

"I love you," she whispered, and then left him to speak.

He had changed so much in the time they'd spent together. He was still hesitant, still uncertain. But stronger, prouder. His life force was returning. And he was sober. His hands shook and he was suffering, but he didn't drink. And she nursed him with love and matched his moods. Mother, mistress, friend. Lucy had filled whatever role he needed, when he needed it. Her little apartment had become their home, where she cooked for him and they shared all the daylight hours together. He went back to prison at night. They were his words and as soon as he said them, she knew she had won him to freedom. Mischa was the next step. Mischa knew what to say. Lucy had primed him carefully.

Volkov mustn't be rushed. He'd been terribly debilitated, ill used in prison and worse used after his release. She didn't mention alcohol. Mischa wouldn't understand that route to oblivion. Only she knew how bravely Volkov was fighting against the habit and what it cost him to throw away that crutch and seek to stand alone. But not alone; that was the source of his resolve. She loved him and she endured with him.

She went out of the room while he spoke on the telephone. There was a fine line to walk between protecting him and urging him to self-reliance. If she crossed it, he regressed.

When she came back he had finished speaking. There was a little color in his face and a brightness in his eye. He got up and held out both hands to her.

"I'd forgotten how good it felt to talk to someone like that," he said. "We felt the same about so many things. He must be a fine man, Lucy. He made me feel very humbled. And grateful to you, my darling. So grateful for everything."

He drew her close and kissed her gently. They sat with their arms round each other. He wanted physical contact with her at all times.

"You were talking for a long time," she said.

"He reminded me of things I'd half forgotten. The way we used to fight at home; our little victories. I never realized how the world was watching us. That was the worst thing they did to you in prison. They said it every day. 'Nobody even knows you're here. Nobody cares whether you're alive or dead. You're just a number. You'll be a number till the day you die.' It used to frighten me. I kept saying my own name so I wouldn't forget it. Your friend told me they held vigils outside the Soviet embassies all over the world when I was arrested and when Sakharov went on hunger strike. Lucy, how could I have abandoned people like that?" He wiped tears from his eyes.

She said quickly, "You didn't. You mustn't say that. All that is in the past; you're not to think about it. You've come back to lead them. Mischa knows it. They're all waiting for you, my love. And very soon you'll be strong and well enough to do it."

He looked at her solemnly. "How can I lead them, Lucy? History's overtaken me. I've been left behind. If I'd been braver, if I'd exposed my wife and let her go to hell, I might have been respected. I might have had the right to take a place among the free people in the world. I could have helped my country."

"You can help it," she said. She stood up and looked down at him. "When my father was at the camp at Spittal, another Ukrainian looked after him. He'd joined the SS. He'd done some dreadful things, but my father was only a boy and this man took care of him. He was sent back to be shot by the Red Army." She paused for a moment. "Do you want me to go on? Are you strong enough?"

He said, "I'm strong, Lucy. Tell me. I've been waiting for you to tell me."

"Before he was taken away, this man gave my father something he'd stolen during the war. He thought it was valuable and my father could sell it. He knew he was going to die. But my father kept it. Then when my mother was so ill, he did try and sell it to get money for treatment for her. He told me that. He said, 'The hand of God saved me, Lucy.' The jeweler didn't know what it was my father showed him. He saw an old paste cross and he wouldn't offer any money for it." She slipped to the floor and knelt beside him. "My father came back with the cross; his friend, Major Hope, paid for my mother's treatment. Before he died, he showed it to me. He'd kept it hidden for fifty years. He'd tried to sell the holy relic, Saint Vladimir's cross. And that's why I came to Geneva. To find you and give it to you."

She couldn't help herself; she burst into tears. He raised her up and held her. Saint Vladimir's cross!

He said very gently, "No, my darling. That was destroyed. Everyone knows the Reds destroyed it."

"It's at home," she said. "In my house. It's the relic. I can prove it to you."

He left her early. He took one of the water buses that ferried across the lake. He needed to be alone. She understood and accepted it. When he left her she was very pale and quiet.

"I'll come back," he promised. "Just give me a little time to take it in."

She'd shown him the book where it was illustrated. And he had the article written a few years ago about the missing czarist treasures. It featured another illustration, large and faithfully depicted: the delicate gold filigree, the massive red gems— which the writer described as spinels, since rubies of that size were unknown at the time.

"Paste," the jeweler had said, refusing to buy the cross. Missing from the cathedral at Kiev since 1919. It was a learned article; it went into details about the workmanship, the size and influence of Byzantine art on the beautiful object specially commissioned by Vladimir to mark his conversion from paganism. And the writer hadn't spared the legends, because it explained the Bolshevik obsession with the relic. If the White armies could claim it, the Civil War might go in their favor. The Reds spread the rumors of its destruction, but there was no evidence to support this. There was evidence that despite torture and execution, the clergy at the cathedral had managed to conceal it. *No evidence of its destruction.*

Volkov had the article in his pocket. The pages, scissored out of a famous art magazine. They were creased and folded, a little frayed at the edges. He looked at the cross. Besides the color reproduction, there was an old scale drawing, and an enlarged section of a painting of the last czar's coronation, with the relic in his right hand.

Lucy had said simply to him, "It's the real cross. This is the photograph my father took. Compare them. The scale is right, the gold work is identical. No one ever copied that cross; it would have been blasphemous."

He put the pages back in his pocket. There was a restaurant on board the ferry. All he had to do was get up and walk a few steps and he could escape it all.

He could be what his jailers had told him he was. A number. No identity, no name, just a set of numerals. Numbers didn't have responsibilities. They weren't presented with ancient symbols of faith with powers to topple a tyranny. They weren't challenged to do anything. They hardly existed. Prisoner 36672. That's who he was. Five digits. One brandy would make him into a number. His hands trembled. Sweat broke out all over his body, chilling him. One brandy. Then two and afterward he'd lose count. He wouldn't remember his number even. He got up and went to the restaurant. He put money down.

The waitress said, "What can I get you?" She had very pale blue eyes. Not the same limpid color as Lucy's eyes, but pale and blue.

He said, "A glass of mineral water, please. I'm thirsty."

He had been gone for a long time. The little clock in the sitting room struck an hour. It could have been the span of her whole life. She paced up and down; she went backward and forward to the windows, stepping onto the little balcony where they sat together in the afternoon sun, peering down the street.

There was no sign of him. Other men walked along, passed underneath. But not Volkov. Volkov had gone away to think. Or to escape! To step backward into the limbo of the last five years.

She almost cried out in desperation and self-blame. She'd acted too soon, burdened him before he was ready. She went into the bedroom, gave way to a burst of weeping. She had done more than destroy the hopes of Mischa and the chance of the unhappy millions in the Ukraine to win their freedom. She had destroyed the man she loved. If he drank, she would never get him back again.

It was only two hours; she heard the clock strike again. She washed her face and went wearily back to look out for him, but she was losing hope. She was leaning by the window, watching the first clouds creeping up from the horizon to challenge the sun, when the door opened. She heard her name.

"Lucy?"

She turned and saw him. He walked toward her. He was steady, sober. She ran into his arms.

"I took the water bus," he said. "That's why I was so long. Were you worried? Did you think I wouldn't come back?"

Lucy held tight to him, "No," she lied. "I knew you would."

He didn't contradict her. In her place, he would have doubted too. Then she managed to smile up at him.

"That's not true," she said. "But thank God you did."

Later he said, "I'm not going home tonight."

"You must, what will your wife think? Darling, you mustn't be reckless. You said she was dangerous."

"Dangerous to you," he corrected. "But she doesn't know about you. I've stayed out before. I went to sleep at an all-night cinema once. I don't want to leave you tonight. We've got so much to think about. I'm going to make love to you and I'm going to go to sleep in your arms. Will you let me stay?"

Lucy drew him down to her. "Kiss me," she said.

Irina hung up in exasperation. She had been trying the apartment since seven o'clock. She had an emergency patient to attend to. A rich Italian suffering severe postnatal depression had been brought in by ambulance, having tried to kill her six-week-old son and then taken an overdose. The family were following on in a state of high Latin hysteria.

Irina didn't know when, or if, she would get home that night. There was no answer to her calls. He was either out and hadn't switched on the answering machine or he was tormenting her by ignoring the telephone. He sometimes did that.

She wondered whether he'd started drinking again. She hadn't taken him seriously when he said he was giving it up, even though he'd never said it before. Miracle cures for alcoholism didn't happen. He'd slip. It was inevitable. And he'd been more unkind than usual in this odd period of sobriety. That was a common symptom, but she didn't welcome it. Mute, drunken dislike was easier than the cold hatred of the last few weeks.

She put her unhappiness aside. She had a seriously ill patient to contend with and she'd just had a telephone message to say that Bruckner's wife wanted to come up and visit him. She'd deal with that in the morning. Muller's instructions were clear. Keep him quiet, but don't disorient him. Viktor Rakovsky wanted to talk to him. A most significant departure for someone so senior to involve himself personally. She had been right about the importance of Bruckner's story. Right to overrule Muller's judgment. No doubt he had claimed the credit for himself. She would let Rakovsky know the truth. *I hate Muller,* she thought. *He ruined my happiness. If it wasn't for him, I'd have talked Dimitri round. We'd be living together like in the old days.*

Her internal phone rang. The patient was recovering consciousness. Her mother was being treated for shock by one of the junior physicians and the husband was creating hell. Could she *please* come down and deal with the situation. Irina hurried out. She forgot to call the apartment again, and decided by two in the morning that she might as well stay at the clinic for what was left of the night.

"We've got to think it through," Volkov told Lucy. "I've got to plan every move I make from now on."

THE RELIC

He had woken early. He was restless and excited. She watched him in wonder.

"I nearly drank yesterday on that boat," he told her. "I went to the restaurant and put the money down for a large brandy. Then I thought of you, my darling. It was easy then. I can't believe how easy it was. That's over; I know I'll never drink again. You said you'd bring me back to life, remember? And you have. You have!"

"You've got to get away from here," she insisted. "We can go to England. Mischa will organize meetings. He has contacts inside the Ukraine. We can't plan anything till you're safe and out of their reach."

Volkov said, "I disappear and then I reappear very publicly. I do all the things I didn't do the first time. I give interviews. I hold a press conference. I've thought it out already. I draw so much attention to myself that they won't dare touch me."

"We shouldn't waste time," Lucy said. "We should get away from Switzerland."

He was bold and confident, almost euphoric. Suddenly she was afraid. Afraid for him and for herself. And the fear was growing as he made his plans. She came up and put her arms round him.

"We could leave here tomorrow. Why don't we? Why don't we just go to the airport and get on a plane?"

He shook his head. "We can't travel together," he said. "We must plan very carefully. First I have to find my passport." He frowned. "It may be out of date. It may have been renewed. I wouldn't remember. Irina took care of everything. I was just a piece of luggage to be labeled and sent wherever they wanted. You speak to Mischa. Ask him if he could help with papers. Say I'm sure it won't be necessary, but just as a precaution. There were people at home who forged passports and exit visas. They were shot if they were caught. My darling, I'm going now. Meet me at seven at the St. Honoré. We'll hide ourselves in a corner and celebrate."

He hugged her. He was like an exuberant boy. She remembered her father saying, "There's nothing on earth that flies higher than a Slav when he's happy, or sinks lower when he's sad."

"I feel like Lazarus," he said. "Out of the tomb and into the sunshine. How much I love you, Lucy! Seven o'clock—at our café."

Then he was gone and she watched him striding away down the street—a traveler without a destination. That came back to her; the figure shuffling from one bar to another, one aimless walk from place to place. Now this was the Dimitri Volkov the world had watched in admiration. The focus of so many people's hopes and dreams.

But the fear stayed with her, its cold hand on her heart.

The big Illyushin jet made a smooth landing at Sheremetyevo Airport. Viktor watched the descent over the city he loved. He was glad to be home. He had always felt the same elation at the end of his long tours abroad. When he came back to Russia he shed his aliases. He was himself.

The official Zil, with his driver, was there to meet him. There were no airport formalities for him and the rest of his delegation.

It was a warm evening and the air was sweet. He opened the window after they reached the country. He had a handsome dacha in the woods on the banks of the Moskva River. He loved Moscow, but he didn't like living there. His dacha was home to him. The forest and the lapping water of the great river were a balm to the spirit.

His housekeeper came to greet him. He kept his mistress in an apartment in Moscow. He never brought women to the dacha. He made his way to the upper floor. He opened the door of a big airy room with views down to the great river itself. The old man sitting in his chair by the window turned round and smiled at him. Ivan! Cancer had eaten into him, but he was still alive. A wraith with bright eyes in his gaunt face. He was too feeble to leave his room now, but Viktor had the window specially made so he could sit and watch the river.

Viktor embraced him. The body was a skeleton wrapped in a winding sheet of clothes. But the eyes were bright and the smile was glad.

"How have you been, Little Father?"

"Well, Son, well. And you?"

Viktor offered him a drink. A very small drink, since he had only half a stomach. In the old days Ivan could swallow a bottle of vodka and keep his legs.

"I want to show you this," Viktor said.

He put an exercise book on the old man's lap. The cover was faded from bright red to pink. It was creased and frayed. He turned the pages to the childish drawing of rabbits sitting under the trees among the spring daffodils, his sketch of Ivan on the sled, of Lepkin dozing in his chair by the stove, of the cat with yellow eyes crouched in the long grass in pursuit of a bird.

The old man nodded. "Your drawings," he said. "You could have been an artist."

"A bad one," Viktor answered. "Anyway the times weren't right for painting pictures, Little Father."

The sketch was from memory, but he had an eye for detail. He had drawn the cross he'd seen so briefly and colored the stones red and the setting yellow. Ivan looked at it and didn't speak.

"I can't remember why I drew that," Viktor prompted.

"It belonged to your father," the old man said at last.

"To Lepkin?"

"No, your real father. The Minister Rakovsky. I think he gave it to Lepkin as a bribe."

"How do you know?" Viktor asked gently.

"I saw him look at it in the car when we were driving to the Lubianka. It was tied up in a parcel. I saw him in the driving mirror. I thought, He's got something valuable there. He's in trouble; he's going to buy someone with that cross. It was full of red jewels. He didn't know I could see him. I saw a lot of things, but I never let on. It was safer to look stupid."

"You're a fox, Little Father," Viktor said.

The light was fading. Clouds were creeping up over the edges of the trees and the river's surface was turning black. His father had given the cross to Lepkin. A bribe, Ivan had said. Viktor watched the darkness spreading. Lepkin had saved Rakovsky's family. He'd married the widow and been a father to Rakovsky's children. Rakovsky had bought their lives with that cross.

He took the drawing book and said, "I have work to do. I'll come up later and say good night. Is there anything you want, Little Father?"

"Some tea," the old man murmured. "And that stuff that stops the pain."

"I'll send the nurse," Viktor promised.

The crude little colored sketch drawn by a child was a picture of the cross given by the first Christian ruler of Russia to celebrate his conversion. His own grandfather, the Bolshevik Serge Rakovsky, had led the search for it. He had murdered the priests. He must have found the cross, hidden it and given it to Viktor's father Alexei. It had left Russia. Bruckner had established that. He had the money and the resources. A dealer had been offered it by a man who was hoping for money—the Ukrainian Boris, red-handed from rape and murder, boasting of how rich he was going to be. Bruckner thought he had been killed. But someone had tried to sell the cross. Only to find it worthless and disappear with it.

Viktor had dinner alone. He went up to see Ivan and found him asleep.

"He was uncomfortable, Comrade Rakovsky," the nurse explained. "I increased the dose as you instructed. He drank some tea and then he slept." No pain, no sorrow, no cloud to blur the sunset . . .

That was his decree for the man he loved best in the world.

"Watch him tonight," he instructed. "Call me if he wakes or asks for me."

The next morning he was assured by the nurse that Ivan had slept peacefully and eaten a little breakfast. He was in good spirits. There was no immediate danger.

Viktor went into his Kremlin office. The necessary papers were provided for him, the traveling arranged, and by noon he was on an Aeroflot plane to Geneva.

He was met at the airport. He traveled on a Polish passport. His occupation was given as manufacturer of industrial components. He went unnoticed through Swiss immigration. Poles were traveling freely these days, seeking business, Western commercial and technical expertise. He spoke perfect Polish, as well as excellent German and fluent English.

He had learned his languages at the highly sophisticated KGB special school in Leningrad. He had been recruited on the strength of his life with the partisans. He was the kind of material Stalin's Intelligence Services needed in the Cold War.

The taxi took him through the city and up into the countryside beyond the lake, where the Amtel Clinic commanded its famous views. He was shown up to Irina's office immediately.

He hadn't seen her for five years. She had changed. She was slimmer, more sophisticated. He noticed the artful makeup, the elegant hairstyle. A very good-looking woman with a bedworthy body.

He was fond of women; he enjoyed their company and he liked making love. He wondered whether she had taken a lover during the last five years. Then he remembered that it was Volkov who was being unfaithful.

They shook hands. They were on first-name terms. He and her father were friends.

"It's good to see you, Irina. You're looking very well. Swiss air suits you."

"Thank you. You look well too, Viktor. Please sit down. Can I get you a drink? It's not too early?"

He smiled. "It's never too early. But I won't have anything. How is your husband?"

She shrugged slightly. "The same. He's never recovered from Muller's visit."

She still held that grudge, he noted. *Muller, beware*, he thought.

He said, "That was a long time ago. Muller wasn't to know he'd come off your medication. And I haven't come all this way to listen to the same complaint, Irina. You've made it officially and it's been noted. I want to see Adolph Bruckner. How is he?"

"I've kept his sedation to a minimum. And I haven't advanced his reeducation since I got your message. His family are agitating to get him home. I'm glad you've come; it was getting difficult to stall them."

"So far," he said, "he's responded well?"

"Well enough. The trouble is, he hates himself. There's a strong suicidal tendency. That's why I've decided to let his wife and children come and see him. He needs motivation. I can advance the program; that's no problem. He's already highly suggestible."

Rakovsky listened to the cool voice describing the intensive hypnosis and subliminal suggestion that would distort Bruckner's mentality. Visual images flashed on and off at fractions of a second to imprint themselves on the subconscious mind. Images of guilt, of fear, of himself suffering the excruciating self-inflicted headaches that only the doctor could hold in check. Obedience and trust. The treatment hammered them into the defenseless mind. Trust in the doctor. Obedience to the doctor.

"I'm glad you've come," Irina said again. "I insisted that Muller contact you at once. He thought it was a fantasy. I had such difficulty persuading him to take Bruckner's story seriously. I had to practically draft the report myself."

Oh, yes, Rakovsky noted, *Muller had better beware.* He said, "I'd like to see him now."

"Of course. He's had some medication. He'll be pliable."

They went down in the elevator. Irina spoke to the nurse on duty in the corridor.

"I have a visitor for Monsieur Bruckner."

He stood back while she approached the bed. Fifty years had passed. The man lying there was in his seventies. He was white haired, with dull eyes and a slack mouth; saliva dribbled from one corner.

"Wake him up!" Rakovsky commanded.

Irina bent over and shook him. She shook him hard. "Adolph! Adolph, pay attention!"

He focused on her, he mumbled something. Viktor came to the edge of the bed.

"He can see you," she whispered. "He's not that doped."

"It won't matter," was the answer. "I'm going to question him. Tell him he's got to answer me. Go on, tell him!"

Irina glanced quickly at him. There was a terrible rage in him; she could feel it like an electric charge in the room. She raised her voice to the tone of command that meant, obey me or you will suffer for it.

"My friend is going to ask some questions. You'll answer them, Adolph. You tell him everything he wants to know. You understand me?"

"I understand." The voice was tremulous.

Viktor Rakovsky came very close to him. He loomed over the prostrate man in the bed. "Tell me about the cross that was stolen," he said. "Describe it to me."

"It was gold. Very old workmanship. With big red stones. I thought they were rubies. It was so beautiful."

"How many stones?"

"Seven. Boris counted them. Three in the traverse and four in the body. He kept saying he'd be rich."

Rakovsky's hands were clenched into fists. Irina thought he was near to striking the old man. She had begun to feel uneasy. This was no ordinary interrogation.

"How big was the cross?"

"As big as my palm. He let me hold it once. It felt so light. It covered the palm of my hand."

The description fitted exactly: filigree gold work, seven red spinels, the right measurement. He leaned closer, nearer to Bruckner. Bruckner was watching him with wide, frightened eyes.

"What happened to the man you call Boris? Tell me!"

"I don't know. He was SS. I heard they'd all been killed. The Reds never took SS prisoners."

"No," Viktor said. "They didn't. You raped the woman in the house, didn't you?"

Irina protested, "Please, you mustn't talk about that. You don't know what harm it could do now."

She came and caught Rakovsky's arm. He thrust her away. He seized Bruckner by the jacket of his pajamas. He heaved him upright.

"You raped her, didn't you? You held her down for the other one. Didn't you?"

"Yes." It was a quavering cry. "Yes."

"You raped my mother and you're going to die for it. You

understand me? You hear me? You're going to die for what you did to her."

Behind him, Irina gasped. He didn't hear her.

"You should have shot me. I was the boy hiding in the cupboard, gagging my little sister so she wouldn't cry out. You made a mistake. You didn't kill me. Now you're going to be punished. You're going to die!"

Bruckner screamed. It was a thin sound of rising terror.

Viktor turned to Irina. She was filling a syringe. She paused for a moment, staring at him.

"Is it true? *You were there?*"

"It's true," Rakovsky said. "What are you giving him?"

Bruckner was moaning, tossing to and fro.

"I'm going to knock him out," she said. "I don't want that busybody nurse coming in if she hears him."

Viktor stepped away from the bed. He laid a hand upon her arm. It gripped so tightly it hurt.

"I meant what I said. Give him a lethal injection. That is an order. I'll wait in your office."

He didn't look back. He walked out of the room and closed the door. He went up in the lift and sat down in Irina's pleasant office. He wiped sweat from his forehead. He would sleep as peacefully now as his mother and brother in their unmarked grave in the woods. The time passed. He was calm. He waited. At last the door opened and Irina came in. She was very pale. He stood up.

"Is he dead?"

"Yes. Why did you make me do that? I've never personally killed a patient."

He dismissed the protest. "Don't be a hypocrite. You kill their minds. It's not much different."

She sat down. She gripped her hands together.

"I feel shocked," she said. "I've killed in cold blood. You must excuse me."

"You'll get over it," Viktor said. "You did your duty, Irina. I gave the order. You obeyed it. That's all. How did you explain it?"

"Cardiac failure. I overdosed him and then rang for emergency resuscitation. I knew it couldn't work. They went on and on trying. I can't believe it, Viktor. Your mother and your brother."

"She hid us," Rakovsky said slowly. "She didn't have time to get away from them. I heard her screaming. That Fabergé desk set was an Easter present to her. I want it back. I'll talk to Muller about that. And the cross is genuine. It's the relic. That was another reason he had to die. He knew about it."

"I'll have to call his wife," she said. "I have to make a full report. There'll be an inquest."

"But they won't find anything?"

"Nothing. Not a trace. He had a heart attack. I gave him digitalis. His heart couldn't stand the shock."

He could see she was regaining her composure.

He said, "You were serving your country. Times are dangerous for us all. One life is nothing compared to the survival of our system. He'd lived fifty years too long. Remember that. I'm staying at the Hotel d'Angleterre. Get through to Muller and tell him to contact me there. I'll be in Geneva for only two days. There's a lot of work to be done. If the cross still exists, we have to find it."

"It was so kind of you to come with me, Peter." Eloise Bruckner's eyes filled with tears. Muller shook his head.

"My dear," he said. "It's the least I could do. It's been so sudden, such a terrible shock!"

The children were with her. They were white-faced and dumb.

"I couldn't have managed without you," she insisted. All

those dreadful arrangements to make and that inquest. Oh, I'll be so glad to get home!"

Muller knew that her grief was quite genuine. It had been a happy marriage, in spite of the difference in their ages. It had shocked him too, when he heard of Adolph Bruckner's sudden death. Irina had been brisk when she called with the news and told him to telephone Rakovsky at his hotel. She hadn't wanted to discuss what had happened. A heart attack, she said, and rang off before he could ask questions. It was unlike her to miss a heart condition in a special patient. And such patients weren't any use to Moscow dead.

Muller was sorry for Eloise, but a rich and attractive widow of forty wouldn't grieve alone for long. She wiped her eyes with a lace handkerchief and he caught the drift of her exotic scent. He had toyed with the fantasy of sleeping with her; the rich smell aroused him. He had never dared do more than imagine it while Bruckner was alive. Now—why not? A shoulder to cry on. He put his arm round her. She didn't resist.

"Some of Adolph's cousins are coming for the funeral," she said. "I don't know them; I think they're only coming in case there's any money for them."

Muller said gently, "Adolph left everything to you and the children. He told me. Don't worry about them. Susan and I will be there to support you."

"I know," she murmured. "I'm so grateful to you. We're not going to be late, are we? I couldn't bear it if we missed the flight."

She had begun to panic about things like tickets and time-tables. For twenty years all these details had been arranged for her. It was a symptom of widowhood.

"Plenty of time," he reassured her. "Just relax, my dear. Let me take care of you and the children."

Her luggage was packed. They waited in her suite at the Richmond for the hired car to take them to the airport. When reception rang through Muller answered it. It was not the car. There was a lady asking to see Madame Bruckner. He looked over to Eloise.

"Someone's downstairs. You're not expecting anyone?"

"No, no. I don't want to see anyone."

The receptionist sounded apologetic. The lady was very insistent. Could she speak to Madame Bruckner. Just for a few minutes. It was very important.

Muller said, "I'm afraid not, just get rid of her. Oh, it has. Very well. We'll come down." He hung up. "The car's here. They're coming up for the luggage."

They went down in the elevator and crossed the big reception hall. A woman moved quickly and caught up with Eloise. Eloise stopped.

The woman said, "Madame Bruckner? Please excuse me. I saw you at the clinic. I've got to talk to you. It's about your husband. I was the sister on his corridor."

They didn't catch the flight.

The sister was in her mid-forties, neatly dressed with a quiet air of authority. She spoke calmly enough. She had insisted on seeing Eloise Bruckner alone. Muller had smelled trouble the moment she said who she was. He'd tried to hurry Eloise away, to sidetrack the woman standing in their path. But he was overruled. Eloise Bruckner wasn't going without hearing what the sister who had nursed her husband had to say. They all turned back and went up to the suite.

"My name is Beatrice Duval. Your husband was admitted to my corridor. Let me say first, I've been nursing psychiatric patients for more than twenty years and I know what I'm talking about. I've never experienced a case like this."

"Why? What do you mean?" Eloise stared at her.

"The way Doctor Volkov treated him was nothing less than sadistic. I'm sorry, this isn't going to be easy for you, but

I've got to say it. It was deliberate cruelty. And it's been on my conscience ever since."

"Cruelty? How? I don't believe you!"

"I've nothing to gain," Beatrice Duval said. "I expect I'll lose my job for telling you. But it's preyed on my mind. The doctor wouldn't allow sedatives or painkillers when he had those dreadful headaches. She put him through the most intensive analysis with nothing to help him afterward. It's a wonder he didn't go mad. He suffered such terrible symptoms he tried to kill himself. He had to be tied down. In the end I got another doctor to sedate the poor man. Dr. Volkov was off duty and I didn't call her. She had me moved to another floor after that."

"My God," Eloise said. "My God, it's like a nightmare."

"It was a nightmare for *him*," the sister said. "I don't know why she did it, Madame Bruckner. If he hadn't died of that heart attack, he'd have been a mental wreck."

"You're sure? You're sure this is true?" Eloise was standing now. The scented handkerchief that had roused Muller's lust was tearing in her hands.

"As God's my witness. I asked the nurse on duty the day he died. She said the doctor and another man, a visitor, were in his room. She told me she heard him scream. A few minutes later *she* came rushing out saying he'd collapsed. I say she brought on that heart attack!"

Eloise said at last, "I'm going back home and I'll contact my lawyers. They'll want to see you and take a statement. All expenses will be paid, you won't be out of pocket. You will come, won't you? You won't change your mind?"

"I won't. I wouldn't have come if I wasn't prepared to tell the truth. What will you do?"

"If we prove mistreatment, they'll bring criminal charges. I've got the best lawyers in Germany. I'm very, very grateful to you. You're still working there?"

"Yes. I've been there since it opened. It's a very good place. It was just that one case. I hadn't worked with Dr. Volkova before."

"Give me your private address and telephone number," Eloise said. "Don't talk about it to anyone else. Wait till you hear from me. It'll be very soon." She went to the door of the suite. Her eyes filled up. "Thank God you told me," she said. "I won't let her get away with this, I promise you. My poor darling Adolph."

She turned away. When she closed the door she broke down in tears.

"I wouldn't believe a word of it!" Muller insisted. "The woman's got a grudge. She's probably trying to get money out of you."

"No," Eloise countered. "She said herself she could lose her job. I believe her, Peter. I don't want to, but I do. Something dreadful happened to Adolph and I'm going to find out what it was."

"It's nonsense," he said. "Doctor Volkova is a famous psychiatrist. That nurse didn't understand what she was doing. He was getting better. You were going to take him home very soon. For God's sake, Eloise, be careful. If you libel the clinic or the doctor you could be sued for a fortune!"

She looked up at him. "You needn't worry because you recommended her, Peter," she said. "I'm not blaming you. I know you were trying to help."

He hadn't expected that. He backtracked. "My dear! I'm not thinking of myself. I'm thinking of you."

"I'm thinking of my husband," she said slowly. "I'm going to follow it up. I can't forget what she said. He tried to kill himself. He was tied down. 'Sadistic,' that's the word she used. Deliberate cruelty. If that's medical treatment, it ought to be stopped. I'm not frightened of anything that doctor or her clinic can do to me. If she hurt Adolph she'll face criminal charges. And who was the visitor she took in there the day he died? She told me *no one* was allowed to see him. I want answers. I want to know why my husband was heard screaming."

My Christ, Muller said to himself. *If I go on defending Irina, I'm going to lose out.* He came up to Eloise Bruckner.

He said seriously, "You're right. I was only trying to spare you. Of course, this must be investigated. I'll come to the lawyers with you, if you like. Adolph was my friend, and I do feel responsible. I did recommend the clinic. I'm with you every step of the way."

"Thank you," she said. "Thank you, Peter. Now for God's sake let's go to the airport and get on the next flight home." She looked round her at the luxurious suite and shuddered. "I can't wait to get away from this awful place."

The flight to Munich took about two hours. They ran into bad weather and the turbulence upset the youngest Bruckner child. She was frightened and she was sick. Muller made soothing noises while Eloise moved seats to comfort her and settled back to plan what he must do. By the time they had risen above the storm, there was a slight smile on Muller's lips, as if he were thinking pleasant thoughts. And they *were* pleasant. Now it was his turn. Irina had put a black mark against him with Rakovsky. Fortunately Viktor valued him and they had a long association before he ever worked with Irina. Otherwise he might have been in serious trouble.

He wasn't going to warn Irina. He was going to report direct to Rakovsky in Moscow. She was about to be investigated and charged with malpractice toward a patient. Under Swiss law she would get a long prison sentence. She'd exceeded her brief with Adolph Bruckner and the operation through the clinic would have to be closed down. That, he decided, would put an end to Irina's career, if not to Irina.

He was very solicitous to the Bruckner family when they

landed, paying particular attention to the sickly daughter clinging to her mother's arm. He would end up in bed with Eloise;
he was hot with excitement at the thought of it. He watched
her lustfully, mentally fornicating. And he would somehow
persuade her to part with the Fabergé desk set.

Rakovsky wanted that. "Steal it if necessary. But get it. It
belongs in Russia." No Irina Volkova to goad him with her
arrogance and her interference. An affair with this lovely
woman who was so rich and inviting, and Viktor's brief to
him, track down the cross. "Use any means," Viktor had said.
"Spend whatever is necessary. Find it if it exists, or prove it if
it doesn't. I'll make sure your reward will be in proportion to
the value of your information." It was a glittering prospect and
gave him the courage to brush his hand against Eloise's breast
as he kissed her good-bye.

"We'll go to the lawyers," he said. "We'll see it through
together. Now sleep well, my dear. I'll call you in the morning."

Eloise's daughter frowned. When he'd gone she said,
"Mummy, I don't like that man."

"Now, darling, you mustn't say that. He's been so kind."

Viktor Rakovsky was in conference when the message came.
He couldn't leave, duty came first. His self-discipline had been
forged and tempered by years of training. He glanced briefly
at the written note, put it aside, and went on with the meeting.
His concentration was equal to his self-control. The last item
on the agenda was the renewed activities of anti-Soviet groups
in Europe and the North American Continent.

Their leaders covered a wide spectrum: free Ukrainians,
Catholics, Orthodox Christians, Liberal Socialists, even the
anomaly of a tiny White-Russian remnant hoping for the res-
toration of the monarchy. They were moving, these disparate
community leaders; visas and travel arrangements were re-

ported and the rendezvous was to be in Europe. The KGB had penetrated all these organizations over the years, but it could not determine the purpose and location of this summit.

In the days of Andropov, the solution would have been easy. Selected targets would have been eliminated. The rest would have understood the warning and the plot, whatever its form, would have fizzled out, as so many had done over the years. But not now. Now the KGB itself was subject to scrutiny, to accountability.

The murder of anti-Soviet activists abroad would stir up fierce controversy at home. The old powers and the impenetrable secrecy that protected them had been breached by the new liberties. It was ironic to Viktor and the colleagues sitting round the table that morning that Gorbachev had been the KGB choice as leader.

Other more subtle methods had to be employed. Rakovsky suggested that one of his protégés, an able and dedicated counterespionage officer, should take over the activist case files and plan the Soviet response. At thirty-five, Leon Gusev had reached colonel's rank on account of his excellent work with agitators in the Baltic Republics. He had scored notable successes in Estonia and Latvia. It was agreed that he should be the successor and at last the meeting ended. Viktor made the announcement.

Ivan Zobev, the Father of the partisans in the Great Patriotic War, was dying. His name and his exploits were part of every Russian child's curriculum. He was a hero who had become a legend. Every man there expressed his sympathy. They were genuinely moved by the news.

Viktor reached his dacha before noon. The nurse was waiting. Viktor raced up the stairs and the doctor opened the door to Ivan's bedroom.

"He's still conscious," he said. "He's been asking for you."

Viktor sat by the bedside. He held the frail hand.

"I waited for you, my son," the weak voice whispered. "I wouldn't go till you came."

"I'm with you, Little Father," Viktor said. "I won't leave you."

"You've been a good son to me," the old man said. "We fought together and we suffered together. I want to tell you something."

"Tell me," Viktor bent close to him.

"I loved your mother. There was no harm meant, but I loved her."

"I know you did," Viktor answered. "I found one of the men who killed her, Little Father. He was punished."

Ivan's eyes opened; he gazed up at Rakovsky.

"Too many dead," he said. "Too much pain. It's time to forgive, my son. I want to die in peace. I want you to live in peace. Remember that. I'd like a priest to bless me."

"I'll send for one," Viktor promised.

"Then I'll wait," the old man murmured and closed his eyes.

The priest was young and flustered; a number of churches in the district were open for services. Viktor stood while he blessed the dying man and anointed him. He intoned the prayers in a nervous voice, pulling at his beard. It was a privilege to send such a hero on his way to heaven. He summoned his courage and said so to the grim-faced man before he left the sickroom. He knew he was a very important Party official.

"Thank you, Father," Viktor said. "It's been a comfort to him."

He came to the bedside. The priest had gone, but he had left the smell of scented oils behind him. Viktor knelt beside the bed and bowed his head.

"Don't cry, my son. I'm happy now. I'm not afraid to go. Maybe I'll see your mother . . . and Stefan."

He died so quietly that Viktor didn't know he'd gone. The

silence told him. When he laid his hand against the old man's waxen cheek it was already cold. He got up and did what Ivan would have wished him to do. He opened all the windows to give the spirit easy exit.

Volkov looked round the apartment. There was no smell of Balkan tobacco. It was Irina's signature. Whenever she was at home, he smelled her cigarettes.

He went into their bedroom. The bed hadn't been slept in. He knew because his pajamas were exactly where he'd left them, dropped on the end of the coverlet. Untidy! She hated untidiness. Making a mess was one of his little rebellions against her. How trivial and demeaning it seemed to him now. How low he'd sunk through his own choosing. There were no messages on the machine. He'd forgotten to switch it on. She hadn't been home and she hadn't been able to call in. That would have infuriated her. When that happened it usually meant he was drunk, sprawled out on the sofa if he hadn't been able to reach the bed, sunk in self-induced oblivion.

He went to the window, made sure her car wasn't coming and turning into the communal garage. Then he started looking. He opened the drawers in her dressing table. They were full of make-up, boxes of this and pots of that; a case with her expensive costume jewelry, all the pieces meticulously fitted into their places. He opened everything, searched, put everything back. He'd learned to be very tidy when he was in prison. If the straw mattress was an inch out of true with the plank bed base, his food was reduced by one meal. A few drops of urine on the floor by his slop pail merited a scientifically aimed punch at his kidneys from the guard. He had thrown his clothes on the floor, spilled his food, gloried in deliberate untidiness in the first weeks and suffered terribly for his defiance.

Searching for his passport, he paused, remembering it all. The battles he won at such a cost to his health, that he couldn't help but lose the war in the end. The pain of coughing and the blood that frothed up in his sputum. The cold, that cruelest of all tortures. And the stink of those cigarettes in his tormentor's office, where he stood barefoot and shivering for hours on end.

He paused and suddenly tears welled up and he felt weak and overwhelmed. No passport in her private drawers. He forced himself to search the wardrobe, the chests full of her clothes. He went to the kitchen and found nothing but food and neatly arranged cooking knives and spoons, hanging like guardsmen from their hooks in perfect rows.

There was a desk in the sitting room. She never locked it. He'd gone through the drawers once, looking for something— he couldn't remember what, but there was nothing personal in that desk. Writing paper, envelopes, address book, a list of numbers where Irina could be contacted; paper clips, stamps, an India rubber and a packet of rubber bands; a stick of unused red sealing wax. He opened and shut the drawers and the flap and found what he expected. Nothing! She must keep her documentation at the clinic.

He sat down and wiped his brow. It was wet with sweat. The sweat of old memories, buried horrors, miserable lonely fears. No alcohol to dull the nerves; no soothing glow to warm the chill of despair into a muddled kind of peace.

Anger instead. Anger was making him sweat. Not anger for what he had suffered, but a deep and terrible rage for what had been inflicted upon others. Friends, colleagues in the movement who'd never left their bitter cells, or who'd spent their lives in labor camps till they died of exhaustion.

He had no passport, but that wasn't going to stop him. He'd been offered a second chance of salvation. The girl who found him that day by the lake was sent by destiny, by fate, the atheist's substitute for God. The holy relic passed down by who-knows-what route out of Russia, given to an orphan in an Austrian prison camp. Into Lucy's keeping. So she could give it to him and with it he could challenge the system that had tormented him and millions of the innocent. And win.

It was more than love he felt for Lucy Warren. More than appreciation of his cure and rejuvenation. It was his destiny, his fate that was moving him, and he knew that this time he wouldn't falter. He might die, but he wouldn't turn back.

ʼ The front door opened. He saw his wife come into the room. It was strange, but his hatred was purged. He looked at her and saw a stranger, who had never been anything else.

"You're up early? I tried to ring last night to say I wouldn't be home, but the machine wasn't on."

She looked very tired, he noticed—pinched and pale. He felt nothing. He wasn't glad.

"I do wish you'd remember," she said irritably. "It's not such a lot to ask! God, I'm exhausted. I think I'll go to bed and get some sleep."

"Did you have a crisis?" he asked her.

The passport must be in the clinic. But it wasn't going to stop him.

"Yes. Attempted suicide. God save me from Italians! They had the place in an uproar."

"It wasn't your special patient then?"

She stiffened, anticipating an attack. "No."

"Is he still there?" Volkov said it casually.

She was caught off guard. "No, he isn't. He had a heart attack. He died." She was on her way to the bedroom, slipping out of her jacket.

Volkov said quietly, "He was lucky. Are you off duty for the day now?"

She stopped at the door. "Why? What do you care? You're never at home these days anyway."

"I don't care," he answered. "I don't stay around here because I get bored. That might make me drink. I go out and about and keep busy. You ought to be pleased."

She sighed. She was tired and her spirits were low.

"I'm not pleased," she said. "I don't care either. I'm going to bed."

She went in and closed the door. He waited. She had left her handbag on the chair. He waited for a full half-an-hour by his watch before he opened it.

"What are we going to do? You can't go near that place!" Lucy leaned toward him. "Dimitri, you mustn't!"

He said, "It's the only way. My darling, you're not to worry; I'll be careful, I promise you. Now, drink your wine. This is our celebration, remember?" He smiled and reached out for her hand. "It's no good complaining now, you know. You were the one who made me brave." He turned her hand upward and kissed the inside of the soft palm. "When we're ready to leave I'll go to the clinic, get my passport out of the desk, and meet you at the airport. Simple!"

Irina's passion for neatness had caused her to label the key in her handbag: Office desk, left-hand drawer. Documents.

"What if she misses it from her bag?" Lucy protested.

Nothing could shake his calm or give him pause. He only laughed at her fears.

"She won't," he countered. "Because I've got this."

He put an envelope on the table and slid a rough white square out of it. "I'll have another key made with this," he said. "Candle wax, Lucy. You melt it and take an impression. It's an old prisoner's trick. My wife likes candlelight when her friends come to dinner. Very useful. So you don't have to worry about that!"

"Oh, darling, why don't we just try Mischa? Please? I can't bear it if you take any risks now!"

"Life is a risk," he said gently. "Every time you cross the road, get in a car, climb a ladder. The risks are all ahead and I don't care a damn! We're going to succeed, you and I, with the holy relic. How strange it all is. If I believed in anything I'd say it was part of a divine plan."

"My father was convinced of it," she said. They had chosen a table out of view in the café he called "their café." The waiter who'd tried to pick her up that first morning wasn't on duty. It was warm and there were flowers in a little silver vase with candles lit for them. He'd ordered champagne for her. He was flushed and happy and he hadn't let go of her hand since they'd sat down.

"You look so beautiful," he whispered. "When we're back home I want to marry you."

"Home?" she questioned.

"In Russia," he said. "It's such a beautiful country, so vast. The earth never meets the sky. It goes on and on forever. I want to show it to you. The little villages, the lovely cities— everything. I want to drink tea with you at the Samoyovska Hotel in Kiev and take you in the evening to a place where they used to play gypsy music when I was a student. If it's still there."

"It'll be there," Lucy said. "I love you so much. I'm sorry I've been frightened."

"But you're not frightened now, are you? You know it's going to be all right. Irina was meant to go to bed and leave that bag behind. I was meant to find that key. So I'm meant to get my passport and escape with you. Isn't that so?"

"She said, "It's so, darling."

He leaned close to her. "Nobody's looking. Kiss me. Ah, that's better. Again, sweetheart. I love the taste of you. Why don't we get under the table and make love?"

"Stop," Lucy begged him. "You're crazy."

"In that café where the gypsies were, we used to do that. When we were very drunk. I was wild in those days."

"You're wild now," she said.

By the end of their dinner she was imbued with his optimism. They were charmed because they were so much in love and so far everything had worked in their favor. They felt protected by the power of the holy relic in its hiding place so far away. They would leave Switzerland safely. Beyond that, she couldn't plan. He had taken command. He was in control.

He talked of the future; he made light of the present and its difficulties until Lucy lost sight of them too. They went home, walking the streets with their arms around each other. She rested her head on his shoulder and he whispered what they would do in bed that night. They walked slowly and clumsily, linked so closely together. The private detective following them cursed when they stopped and kissed in the middle of the street. By the next morning he had a full report on Dimitri Volkov and his lover ready for dispatch to Peter Muller in Munich.

3

LEON GUSEV was a Muscovite by birth. He had been born in one of the hideous concrete blocks of flats erected after the Great Patriotic War. His father was an engineer and his mother worked for a minor official in the Ministry of Post and Communications. He was an only son; his mother's old father and his aunt lived with them. The flat had three rooms. He shared his parents' bedroom and the old man and his widowed daughter slept in the other room with a blanket on a line dividing them.

Leon was clever as a boy; he was a dull-looking child, hampered by short sight. He had a squat body of surprising strength and quick fists that deterred bullies. Once the glasses came off, they ran away. He had a mind that delighted in problems. Mathematics fascinated him. He seemed destined for a career as an engineer like his father, but with much brighter prospects. But human puzzles intrigued him more. He graduated from Moscow University with a degree in psychology and political science and joined the Internal Security.

As compensation for his lack of height and pebble glasses, he was gifted with a charming smile and a friendly manner. He wooed and married one of the prettiest secretaries in the office on Djerjhinsky Square.

Promotion came rapidly once he caught Viktor Rakovsky's attention. He joined Rakovsky's select team of young Intelligence operatives. He saw service in the Baltic Republics and earned a special commendation for his analysis of the situation among the ethnic groups.

He had a pleasant apartment on the outskirts of Moscow with his young wife and baby daughter and hoped to achieve a small dacha. He was a dedicated follower of the new political initiative begun by Gorbachev. He believed in reform and modernization. He also shared Rakovsky's dread of the Soviet Union becoming fragmented by the Republics' achieving independence. A loose federation meant weakness. They couldn't contemplate such a situation with a united Germany and their allies in the Eastern Bloc in chaotic pursuit of democracy. His colonel's insignia was still bright and new; he was very proud of it. Now he had been given an assignment that demanded intuitive analysis to a sensitive degree. The anti-Soviet activists abroad were planning to strike a blow. Discovery and prevention were the methods available. The old strong-arm KGB response was not an option.

Gusev sensed that his dacha and further promotion were in the balance. He immersed himself in his work. Every file, every data sheet on the exiles and émigrés who'd caused trouble over the past thirty years was computerized and collated for him. He noted the dead as well as the living. The dead had children who might carry on their work.

In the very recent past, an English-based organization of so-called Free Ukrainians had led a worldwide campaign on behalf of the jailed dissident, Dimitri Volkov. The organizer and prime motivator was of Ukrainian birth though a naturalized British citizen, Yuri Warienski. He had died early that year. He had one child, a daughter: Lucy Warren had a Jersey-based interior decorating business and an independent income from her father's estate.

THE RELIC

The name Lucy Warren went into the computer at Moscow Center, along with hundreds of other names on the periphery of the various movements. Even a seventeen-year-old schoolboy in a French lycée was documented because his father and grandfather were involved in exposing the executions of the Cossacks after Yalta.

Gusev likened himself to an industrious spider, sitting at the heart of a complicated web—pulling a thread here, tightening one there—until finally he began to see a pattern. There was no pattern as yet. KGB agents among the various groups had no information beyond rumors of some kind of summit meeting between the leaders. That their destination was being kept so secret emphasized its importance. Activities in Canada and America were even more alarming. There were powerful and vociferous organizations of anti-Communist Russians in both countries, backed by considerable funds.

The venue of this gathering must be Europe. But its location and its purpose was Gusev's first priority. There must, he rationalized, there *must* be a unifying factor to bring so many divergents together. Something that bonded them closer than a shared hatred for Communism and the Soviet Union. If he could identify that.

There were many rumors. He didn't dismiss the wildest of them. Not even the fantasy that one of the czar's descendants was preparing to come out and offer himself as a leader within Russia itself, defying the authorities to arrest him and prove that they hadn't changed after all.

The theme of a leader kept recurring. It was necessary to check and triple-check the likely candidates. More lists appeared—long computer analyses of each individual's background, ethnic origins, age, record, and previous political activities. The web spread and became more entangled. Gusev recommended night and day surveillance by expert watchers on the heads of the organization and their families. Moscow

Center had facilities in all the countries concerned. Manpower was a problem, but he felt this deserved top priority.

An agent was dispatched from London to Jersey to check on the dead activist Warienski's daughter. His report that she had left the island and had not been seen or heard of since went into the computer bank with hundreds of similar reports and remained on file. Gusev knew from experience that sooner or later something would emerge and give the vital clue. It always did. Either by accident, or carelessness, or simply luck. And he believed that luck was the reward of diligence.

"It's late, honey," Susan Muller said. "Aren't you coming to bed?"

Peter Muller yawned and stretched. He smiled at his wife. "I'll just finish these accounts," he said. "I won't be long. Don't go to sleep!"

"I won't," she promised.

He kept the smile on his lips till she had closed the door. The accounts were his coded report for Rakovsky. With a new and important addition from the Swiss detective agency. Eloise had conferred with Bruckner's lawyers that morning. Muller had gone with her. The lawyers were cautious in their attitude toward the nursing sister's story. Muller could see they regarded Eloise as overreacting. "Naturally," they said. "She was shocked." The senior partner explained patiently that the nurse herself might have suspect motives in accusing the doctor of malpractice. Her reputation and experience would have to be investigated very carefully. Their case would stand or fall on her reliability.

Muller was surprised by Eloise's resistance. He'd always thought of her as pliable, sexy, more of an ornament than a partner for a man like Adolph Bruckner. Now he saw another side of her. She was determined. She possessed power and knew how to exercise it. She had silenced them all.

"I believe this woman. I believe my husband was ill-treated. I don't want arguments, gentlemen. I want this matter investigated. I want you to bring the nurse down here and let her tell you what she told me. Then, I want the best legal advice you can get for me. Good morning."

It made her more fascinating to Muller. If at first he had simply wanted the elegant clotheshorse, even more did he desire to strip and possess the woman of character. He had spent so much time with Eloise that he felt he must make love to his wife that night, however tired he was.

That fatigue disappeared when he got his detective's report on Volkov and his girlfriend. He rewrote his original report for Viktor Rakovsky, incorporating what the Swiss private detectives had outlined. Bruckner's widow was determined to pursue Irina through the courts. And Irina's husband, Dimitri Volkov, was involved in a passionate relationship with a woman of Russian descent, the daughter of a well-known anti-Soviet activist who'd recently died, Yuri Warren, alias Yuri Warienski.

His admirable Swiss detectives had checked up on her with the central police register of foreigners, and then elicited the information from the police in Jersey. Her reputation was confirmed as impeccable. In the course of establishing this, the agency had extracted the other information about her background.

He urgently advised the recall of both Volkovs to the safe confines of the Soviet Union.

Lucy took the call. Volkov had gone out. He liked to buy their food; he even enjoyed cooking it sometimes. He was always telling her how good it was to be alive these days. He seemed to take pleasure in the simplest things, like touring the delicatessens in search of a special cheese, or taking the water bus across the lake and mingling with the tourists.

He was putting on a little weight. They were so happy. She was waiting for him to come back when the telephone rang. It could only be Mischa. No one else knew where she was.

He spoke in Russian. "Are you alone?"

"Yes. Is anything wrong?"

"No. No, everything is very good. The meeting is in two weeks. The twenty-seventh. In London at the Makoff Galleries. There's an exhibition of Pre-Revolutionary photographs and memorabilia. It's a perfect cover for us. But is he ready? Is he strong enough?"

Lucy turned round as the door opened. Volkov was surprised by the brilliance of her smile and the heightened color in her cheeks.

"You can ask him yourself," she said. "Here he is." She gave the telephone to Volkov. "It's Mischa," she said. "They've set the date."

She watched him, listening to the one-sided conversation. There was no hesitation. He spoke calmly and with authority.

"I shall be there," he said. "I'll be happy to address them. No. That won't be necessary. I'll be with Lucy." He turned and looked at her. "As soon as possible," he went on. He hung up and he held out his arms. "I told you it would happen," he said. "Now we're ready to go. In two weeks I shall be speaking to the people who worked for me and campaigned and raised money when I thought I was as good as dead and buried. I'm going to make the speech of my life to them, my darling. I'm going to outline my plan for the new Russia! And it'll be born in the Ukraine!"

They held each other close. Then he said, "I must get that key cut today. If it goes well, we'll be on your island by the end of next week. And you can show me the cross. I dreamed of it last night."

Lucy didn't look at him. She was pale now instead of

flushed. The key. He had to get into his wife's office, open the desk and trust that his passport was inside. That was when the idea came to her.

"Darling," she said. "Why don't I take that wax and get it done for you? You've got so much to think about—your speech—let me do it. I know a little locksmith not too far from here. Please."

Lucy drove into the center of the city before she found a locksmith. The man looked at her suspiciously, the piece of hard white wax in his fingers.

"You want a key cut from this, *M'selle*?"

"Two keys," Lucy said. She forced herself to smile at him. "It's a bet," she said. "My friends said I couldn't get it done from a wax impression. I said I could. I do hope you can do it for me."

He shrugged. He examined the wax carefully. He hesitated.

"I'll get a big box of Bertier chocolates if I win," she added.

The locksmith chuckled. *Young people*, he thought. Bertier chocolates were the best.

"I'll make you two keys," he said. "It's a good impression, very clear. Come back tomorrow—the same time."

"Thank you," Lucy said.

Two keys. She drove home slowly. One key for Dimitri. And one for herself. She was not going to let him risk being recognized in the Amtel Clinic. She was going to get his passport for him.

Muller's decoded report was given a yellow sticker. It arrived via the diplomatic bag on Saturday morning. Viktor Rakovsky had left for his dacha. A courier was dispatched on the strength of that yellow signal. Blue was urgent, yellow was most urgent.

He was fond of fishing. When he wasn't sketching or painting for relaxation, Viktor took rod and line down to the banks of the Moskva and fished for the gray roach that lurked in the sluggish water. Often he threw them back. People couldn't eat them and the two cats at the dacha couldn't be allowed to eat too many of them. Viktor kept cats. The cat with the yellow eyes had disappeared into the forest the day the Germans came. He remembered pleading with his mother to take the little creature on the train to Moscow and safety. He loved cats.

He laid his tackle aside and opened Muller's report. He didn't fish that day. He went back to his office and summoned Gusev. Gusev's family didn't see him for the rest of the weekend. The banks of computers were busy and together Viktor and Gusev read the long printouts and the cross-references and the counterchecks on the information. At the end Rakovsky opened a bottle of his favorite Scotch whiskey and offered a drink to the young colonel. It was a great mark of favor.

Rakovsky listened to Gusev's summary.

"The daughter of Yuri Warienski disappeared after her father's death. She reappeared, according to this, in Geneva, where she made contact with Dimitri Volkov and became his mistress. For the last five years Volkov has been drinking himself to death. He had ceased to be a problem to us. This is the first woman he's been connected with in all that time. He's taken no part in politics since his release. Suddenly he becomes involved with someone whose father was an active anti-Soviet right up till his death. I think, Comrade, that we must conclude that she has seduced Volkov in order to use him politically. The surveillance team . . ." He glanced down checking something. "The Swiss surveillance team employed by our agent doesn't mention seeing him drunk at any time. His behavior is sober and normal. That is remarkable, given his alcoholic addiction."

"Very remarkable," Viktor said slowly. He was thinking while he listened to the logical thought processes of Leon Gusev. Irina had killed Bruckner on his orders. Only Irina knew that he was responsible for the collapse of Moscow Center's operation at the clinic. If Bruckner had lived, there wouldn't have been a complaint made to the widow. If he'd let his mother's rapist escape punishment... Muller said she and Volkov must be recalled. *Ironic*, he thought, *that Muller had plunged the knife into her back instead of the other way round. She must be brought home, before any further investigations are made by Eloise Bruckner's lawyers. She couldn't be charged with anything once she was out of reach.*

But Volkov's infidelity was more important than Irina's blunder. Volkov was not drinking. Volkov was in love with a woman who'd been sent to entrap him for political purposes, so Gusev deduced. He paid full attention again.

"Warienski was the originator of the London-based Free Ukrainians. We have an extensive file on him. The Free Ukrainians are in close contact with Catholic émigrés in Europe and the United States. They are a significant part of the dissident organizations we have been monitoring. As we know, they are suddenly very active. I have spent a lot of time on the question as to why. What are they planning and where are they meeting to organize it? It seemed to me—"

He cleared his throat. "Excuse me, Comrade," and took a sip of whiskey. He didn't like it. "It seemed to me that we were missing the key factor. The common denominator between them all. Is it possible that Volkov is this factor?"

He waited for Viktor's response. There wasn't one. He just nodded and said, "Go on. Take it further."

"Why should Dimitri Volkov, after five years of obscurity, become valuable to any anti-Soviet organization? That question had to be asked. The answer lies in his birthplace in the Ukraine and the reputation he enjoyed among dissidents and refuseniks before his arrest and during his imprisonment."

Viktor interrupted. "I know all that. I know how dangerous he was. Go on," he said again.

"He could be used as a figurehead. But a figurehead for what?" Gusev inquired and answered his own question. "For a full-scale political movement outside the Soviet Union. What purpose would that serve? I can't see the exiles and émigrés banding together and achieving anything of importance but limited media coverage." Gusev paused and frowned.

Viktor thought, *The keys are clicking into place in that computer brain of his. I can almost hear them.*

"His real use would be inside the Soviet Union. Here, he could be exploited by elements already working against the central government. Which brings us back to the Ukraine, where Volkov was born. If there is a link, and I believe there is, then that's where we must look. That's where we'll find the heart of this conspiracy. And he'd have huge popular support when he came home. I'm not suggesting he'd last long," Gusev continued. "Once the Ukraine demanded independence he could drop out of sight. There are plenty of others who'd come forward. I don't have to name them."

"No," Viktor muttered. "You don't. You may have found your missing factor. We can't take any chances. We bring Volkov home. Once here, we can make sure he gets inside the brandy bottle and stays there."

Leon Gusev said, "I'd like to investigate a little deeper. I'd like to run some cross-checking on Warienski. Before you take any action. Will you give me forty-eight hours?"

Viktor looked up at him. "I know you, Leon. There's a bee buzzing between your ears, isn't there? What is it?"

"From what we know about Volkov, he's not the whole of the missing factor."

"You've said he was. You agreed he has a limited damage potential, but he *could* be used to detonate a big political explosion. Isn't that enough?"

"It should be," Gusev said thoughtfully. "It should be, Comrade, but I still feel there's something we've missed. Let me research Yuri Warienski. Right down to the time he was born." He smiled at Rakovsky in his friendly way. "If there's nothing to find, I won't find it. If there is, we'll still have Volkov back in Russia."

Viktor stood up. "I'll make sure of that," he said.

Muller flew to London. He was popular in the trade. He was amusing and knowledgeable and he'd made no enemies. He started with the top dealer who specialized in Fabergé and Russian works of art. He called on Wartski in Conduit Street. Collectors from all over the world went to the firm for advice and to buy the exquisite objects fashioned for the imperial family and the old nobility. If a collector had acquired the ancient cross, Wartski might have heard of it through the dealers' grapevine.

An hour later, after admiring some of the rare and beautiful pieces in the shop, Muller left having learned nothing. He was advised to consult Eckstein, who also specialized in Russian and East European art. He had perfected a glib story. He had a client who thought he had missed a fabulous bargain when he refused to buy a paste cross from an impoverished Russian aristocrat.

This client was not only obsessional, but extremely rich. Muller had offered to help in the hope of persuading him to invest in something less fantastic. Heads were nodded in sympathy. Clients like that were not uncommon among the superrich. It irked them unbearably to let something slip through their fingers. But they had to be humored before they could be diverted from the unobtainable to the treasure that was actually for sale.

From the best in the business he worked his way down. He went from the reputable experts to the shadier middlemen who traded in dubious goods and from them to those who traded in anything without asking where it came from. Shops and dealers who specialized in old paste, in decorative objects, phony icons, and fake religious relics. He made two calls to contacts who sold to a private collector in New York. The collector was a woman. She hoarded like a magpie. The house in Long Island was referred to as Xanadu in the specialized trade that supplied her. It was crammed from the cellars to the roof space with furniture, pictures, sculptures, jewelry, and objets d'art.

They were never displayed. The criteria for her was that a piece be the only example of its kind. Then she bought whatever it was and paid their price without worrying too much about the provenance. She was the kind of acquisitive neurotic who would hoard a medieval paste cross or a Papuan shrunken head.

Nobody could help him. One even suggested he try a firm of theatrical costumers. They had a mass of worthless artifacts from crowns to papal tiaras that they hired out. Muller realized he was being ridiculed and hung up.

He decided to stop over in Paris and spend a couple of days following a similar route. He paid a call on the famous antique shop LaVieille Cité where he was politely entertained and actually bought a little Renaissance bronze relief, but no one had heard of a cross coming on the market in recent years. He knew the fakers and the fences in Paris as well as London and he skimmed through them, without any hope of success.

Muller was tired and frustrated by the end of his stay. The charming little bronze was a compensation. He decided to sell it to the Americans who had bought the triptych. He was packing in his room at the Georges V when his telephone rang. He supposed it was his wife, Susan. Or maybe Eloise; he'd kept in touch with her since he left home. She told him the nurse was coming to see her lawyers and make a statement at the end of that week. Things were moving, she said and the steely note in her voice excited him.

"I'll be with you," he assured her. "I'll hurry back."

THE RELIC

It wasn't his wife and it wasn't Eloise Bruckner. It was a woman with a vulgar Parisian accent. She had heard, she explained, that he was inquiring about an old Russian cross.

Muller kept his voice cool. Yes, he agreed. He was asking around. Did she have one? No, she answered. But she had some information. She could come to his hotel if he liked.

From the sound of her, Muller didn't like her. He suggested they meet at a bar he knew round the corner from the Place de Grève. Six o'clock, she suggested. He paused; he'd have to catch a later flight.

"My name's Levison," she told him. "I'm wearing a red dress."

"Six o'clock," he said and hung up.

He was five minutes early, but she was already there, conspicuous in the red dress, which was too tight for her. She wasn't what Muller expected. She was middle aged, overweight, and ill at ease in the chic little bar. He came up and introduced himself. She got up and they shook hands. Her bag and shoes were cheap. He had expected some kind of tart from Les Halles and found a respectable Jewish matron in an unbecoming color.

"Would you like something to drink?" he asked.

"No thank you. I don't drink." She brought out a man's handkerchief and blew her nose. People at nearby tables turned around.

Muller said, "I do have to catch my plane, Madame Levison, so if you don't mind, I'd like to get down to business. How did you hear about me?"

She had gentle brown eyes; they were her best feature.

"I've got friends in the business," she said. "My father was well known in the old days. He had a fine shop in the Avenue de l'Opera. Everybody respected him." She put the handkerchief away. "Excuse me," she said. "I've got a nasty cold. Summer colds are always the worst. My friend called me and said you'd been to see him and were asking about a Russian cross. He knew my father very well. He thought I might know something and he wanted to do me a good turn."

"That was kind," Muller said. "Who was this friend?"

To his surprise she named a reputable dealer in fine art that he had been to see that afternoon.

"Times have been hard since my father died," she explained.

"He took in a partner and we got married." She shrugged. "He was not like my father. He ruined the business. When he died I had to sell up. There wasn't much left. I do a little dealing from home. Small things. People offer me stuff they don't want."

Muller had wasted enough time. He interrupted. "You said you had information about a cross."

She nodded. "My father used to talk about it. He was nearly eighty when he died, but he had such a memory. Someone came to the shop and tried to sell him an old cross with paste stones in it. A long time ago—twenty years or more. He didn't offer for it. When he was telling the story, he used to bang his fist on his forehead like this. 'I wouldn't offer for it! I ask you!' "

Muller was on the edge of his seat. Bruckner's investigators had found a jeweler who'd refused to buy a cross that fitted the description of the holy relic. Twenty-five years after the war ended a man had come into the shop and been told that his treasure was studded with spinels instead of rubies. Paste wasn't accurate, but it served well enough. There the search had ended. Until now.

"My father never got over it," Madame Levison said. "He only found out what he'd missed a few years ago when some German came in asking questions. By chance, he said. The Germans were asking everywhere, advertising, making inquiries all over the trade.

"My father remembered the man with the cross; he remembered him because he was young and so nervous. He didn't want to sell the cross unless there was a lot of money. The German wanted to know about the man. My father got suspicious. He just said he was a foreigner, he couldn't remember anything else. He didn't want to help a German. Forgive me, but you can understand why. He'd lost a lot of relatives in the war."

"I understand," Muller said. "I'm sorry."

"It's not your fault," she said simply. "You weren't even born. I don't think you can hate forever."

"No," Muller agreed. For a moment he felt the old shame rise in him. "Tell me about the man. Tell me what your father said about him. You're being very helpful, Madame."

"He was a Russian," she said. "My father talked Russian. He'd learned it from his grandparents. They left Russia after a bad pogrom. He told the man it was very old, but the gold work was too fragile to be reworked and the stones weren't worth anything. He said the Russian said to him, 'Then it's God's will I keep it.' And he walked out. My father didn't think of it again till this German visited the shop and showed him an illustration. He recognized it. Then he looked it up and found it was some priceless czarist cross he'd turned down.

"He loved telling the story. My friend must have heard it from him and after you left he remembered and telephoned me. He said you were a gentleman who'd pay a fair price for anything I could tell you."

"What do you consider a fair price, Madame?" He could think of some people who'd say she'd told him nothing he didn't already know and offer a few hundred francs. But Muller had never done business that way. She was her father's daughter. She was a trader.

"Five thousand francs was what my friend suggested."

Muller smiled. "And how much are you giving him out of that?"

She blushed. "He made the introduction," she said. "Fair is fair."

"I don't have that much in cash. Do you mind a check?"

"No. A check is fine. Thank you." She opened the bag, took out the handkerchief and made a louder noise than before. "I hate colds," she said. "Especially summer colds. Good-bye, Monsieur Muller. If you're looking for this cross, I hope you find it. It must be worth a fortune!"

"Money couldn't buy it," Muller said. "Good-bye, Madame."

"A nervous young man who didn't want to sell the cross." Anyone old enough to serve in the German Army in 1942 would have been close to fifty. "It's God's will I keep it."

"Gold and fucking jewels. I'll be rich!" It wasn't the rapist and murderer called Boris. Bruckner was right. He'd been killed. It was another Russian who had got possession of the holy relic.

Muller got to the airport and caught the seven o'clock flight home. He had gone as far as he could go. He had no more resources to call upon. The cross had never surfaced since that one appearance in the shop owned by Madame Levison's father. Whoever had it then still had it, or had passed it on. A German would have thrown away worthless loot. A Russian who talked of God's will would have kept it. It was up to Moscow to start checking among the émigrés and escapees who'd gone to Paris after the war ended and had been there in the time scale.

He showed his wife the little bronze relief and when she was preparing dinner, he slipped into his study to telephone Eloise Bruckner.

"I'm home," he said in his warm voice. "I just wanted you to know I've been thinking of you."

He was thinking of her. And thinking that if he pleased her as much as he hoped, she might be persuaded to part with the Fabergé desk set.

THE RELIC

*　　　*　　　*

The letter reached Irina by special courier. She was at the clinic when it was delivered, working on some case notes. The Italian lady suffering postnatal depression was proving difficult to treat. Her husband and relatives were virtually camped in the clinic, driving Irina mad with their interference. She had been tempted to banish them and forbid all visits, but they wouldn't be intimidated. The director of the clinic was a reputable Swiss psychiatrist. He had no idea of the real identity of one of the major shareholders in the enterprise and regarded Irina as a dedicated and skillful doctor. He insisted that the Italians be humored. They were related to the Agnelli family and he was impressed by the connection with such wealth and power. Irina suspected that his own Italian origins made him sympathetic to the fuss they created.

She slit the sealed envelope open. It was written in Cyrillic. There was no heading on the paper, but she knew the signature. The military chargé d'affaires in Geneva was Moscow Center's top man.

The message was brief. "A civil action is pending against you brought by Adolph Bruckner's widow, alleging mistreatment of her husband. You are recalled to Russia as a matter of urgency. Your husband is to accompany you. You are responsible for his return."

She felt her pulse rate double; she flushed hot and then went cold. She was recalled to account for what had happened. Why had her methods been exposed? Why had Bruckner died, putting the clandestine operation at the Amtel Clinic at risk? Serious charges could be brought against her when she got home. Unless Viktor Rakovsky took responsibility. She snapped at her lighter; her hands trembled. At last the little flame flared and she set it to the paper, watching the end blacken, smolder, and curl as it burned. It lay in a charred heap in her ashtray among the cigarette butts.

Who had betrayed her? Who had given information to Bruckner's wife? A civil action alleging misconduct leading to her patient's death. It was Rakovsky's fault. She pushed her chair back and threw the debris in the ashtray into her wastepaper basket. Rakovsky had pursued his private vengeance. Then she paused, realizing that he had a faultless motive. The holy relic was his alibi. Bruckner couldn't be left alive with that knowledge. His defense would stand.

She'd aroused suspicion in some member of the staff and they'd reported her to Bruckner's widow. And she realized at once who it was—the sister who'd protested and overruled her by bringing in another doctor to relieve Bruckner's suffering. She'd seen the hostility in the woman's face and had her moved to another ward. That must be who had accused her.

Irina swore in fury. She should have taken precautions against such a mishap. She'd become careless, complaisant. Five years ago she'd have got the woman sacked on some pretext, rendering her harmless if she alleged anything against a reputable doctor in a famous clinic. The grieving widow was rich and powerful enough to hound anyone through the courts.

Irina forced herself to calm down. She lit a cigarette, composed herself. The pulse steadied, the cold sweats stopped. She would go home. She had given years of valuable service. Rakovsky would support her. She hadn't missed the sting in the tail in that curt directive. It was her responsibility to bring Dimitri back to Russia with her.

Easy for them to say, she thought bitterly. If it hadn't been for Muller's exposure, Dimitri might have been amenable. He might still love her and be capable of persuasion. But not now. Now he hated her. He hated her more in his sobriety than when he was drunk. And he was still sober, much to her surprise. The distance between them widened every day. They saw little or nothing of each other. He lived his separate life and she waited for him to falter and slip back into alcohol. But he didn't.

THE RELIC

Irina stubbed out her cigarette. She went to the window and opened it, gazing out at the magnificent view over the vast lake. It was coming to an end. Five years of exile among strangers would be over soon. Suddenly her heart ached for the sight of her native country, for the sounds and scents and voices of her own people. Once a Russian, always a Russian. She remembered reading a biography of a czarist émigré after the Revolution and the phrase came back to her. It was the only thing in the whole book that she related to: "We cherished our language and our culture. We never wanted to lose our Russianness, no matter what country we lived in."

She thought, *I'll come out of it unscathed. And when I'm home maybe I'll be happy again. No Russian is truly happy outside Russia. And I'll bring Dimitri with me, however I have to do it. Switzerland destroyed us. Russia may give him back to me.*

She took the key out of her bag and opened the locked drawer in her desk. Her passport was in order. His was out of date. She picked up the telephone and asked for a courier service. That afternoon the passport was delivered to the Soviet Embassy for renewal on an emergency application.

When Irina got home that evening Dimitri was not there. She realized suddenly how empty and unlived in the apartment had become. There were no signs of him about the place. No books left lying about, no newspapers scattered or folded untidily on a table, no dirty cups or glasses. He came home to sleep and as soon as he woke after she'd left, he went out. There were no weekends for them. No days spent together. He left the apartment in the morning. If she inquired, he merely said he was going walking and he didn't know when he'd be back. She wasn't to wait for him if she had anything else to do. It was so cold and self-contained, his eyes were empty when he looked at her. He hated her so much that he refused to see her as a person.

She had tried to follow him once. She wasn't skilled enough

and a tram ride lost him to her. She came home in despair and went back to the clinic to work rather than spend the Sunday alone or try to pass the time with friends. She went into their bedroom. He'd made his bed when he left; that was unlike him, but then the sober man was neat and organized.

Irina sat on the bed. He'll never come back of his own free choice, she admitted. There's only one way to get him home and I'll just have to take it. As soon as I have his passport.

Lucy dialed the number. A bright voice answered on the third ring. "Good morning, Amtel Clinic. Can I help you?"

Lucy's mouth was dry. She said. "Doctor Volkova's secretary, please," and swallowed hard.

"One moment," the switchboard said.

She waited; it seemed she waited for an eternity. It was less than a few seconds, but it seemed longer than time.

"Doctor Volkov's office."

The same honeyed tone, she thought. *They must be trained to speak like that, oozing reassurance.* She realized that she had betrayed her knowledge of Russian by using the feminine version of the doctor's surname.

"Good morning," Lucy forced herself to sound calm. "I would like to make an appointment with the doctor."

"And have you a letter from your doctor? Normally it's your doctor who makes the appointment." The voice was a little less friendly now.

"I'm visiting," Lucy said. "I came specially in the hope of seeing Doctor Volkov." She was careful not to make the same mistake. "I have no letter. My doctor's in England, but he promised to write to her before I arrived. Could you just check for me, please?"

"May I have the doctor's name, Madame?"

"Harrison," Lucy invented. "Doctor Philip Harrison, twenty-seven Sloane Square, London. I've been getting attacks of giddiness and I'm not sleeping well. He wanted me to see a specialist in Harley Street, but I'd heard so much about your clinic and Doctor Volkov, I said I wanted to consult her. Are you sure you haven't had a letter?"

"One moment. Doctor Volkov is off duty today, but I'll see if I can check through the files in case."

"Thank you," Lucy said. She hung up. Today. Her heart gave a frightened leap. She'd planned it differently. She'd rehearsed the lies till she was word perfect. "No, not that appointment. When was the next one available?" Finding out by elimination when Dimitri's wife wouldn't be at the clinic. Nerving herself to go there, to trick her way into Irina Volkova's office. To open the desk drawer with the key she'd kept back for herself. To find Dimitri's passport and get out without being discovered. Today. She had to do it today. The secretary would see she'd rung off and dismiss the call as the work of some crank hoping to bluff her way in without a doctor's recommendation.

She took a deep breath. They'd made their plans for escape. She argued in favor of a direct flight to London and then on to Jersey. Dimitri would be safe there. Nobody would think of looking for him in the Channel Islands. He would meet Mischa and the others in London at the exhibition in the art gallery.

And the next step would be to come out in public and call a press conference. That would guarantee his safety. So long as he was in the limelight, he couldn't be attacked or abducted. The media would be the best bodyguard of all. He was fired with enthusiasm. His spirits were so high he didn't detect the chill of fear in Lucy. She was so proud of him. It didn't seem possible for her love to deepen and grow, but it did. If she loved the sad victim of despair and betrayal, even more did she love the brave idealist. Loved him enough to steel herself to lie and excuse herself that afternoon, while she made her way to the Amtel Clinic.

"Don't be long, my darling," he said. "I'll miss you."

She forced herself to smile, to be lighthearted. "No, you won't; you'll be busy on your papers."

He was working on his speech and his press statements. He said, "I could come with you. Why don't I?"

She put him off with a kiss. "I can't see you sitting in dress shops all afternoon," she said. "I won't be too long. If I buy something nice, I'll wear it for you."

She waved at him from the door and went down to the street. She'd hired a car a few days before, with the trip to the clinic in view. No taxis, no chance of being delayed. In and out and drive like the wind.

She got in, checked that the newly cut key was in her purse, and switched on the engine. Clouds were gathering overhead and the windshield was spotted with rain. At midmorning the traffic was heavy, slowed down by the showery outbreak. Lucy kept looking at her watch. She had decided to reach the clinic by lunchtime. There was a good chance that the secretary would take time off for lunch while the doctor was absent. It was Lucy's only hope of getting into the outer office unchallenged. Once there, she had to gamble on the consulting room being unlocked. Her hands were sticking to the wheel. She sat behind a stream of cars stopped at the traffic intersections till they surged onward and then stopped again. The rain grew heavier and thunder rumbled over the mountains. *At this rate,* she thought desperately, *the lunch hour will be over before I even get there.* Then she remembered and calmed down.

The Swiss enjoyed their food. They started early and worked late, but they took two hours for lunch. If the woman she'd spoken to was having a break, she wouldn't come back to her desk before two o'clock.

It was just after one when Lucy finally turned down the Rue du Rhone and the traffic was lighter. She drove as fast as she dared down the handsome street with its expensive shops and at last she swung out onto the Quai Gustave-Ador. The sky was bright, the distant grumble of thunder died away and the sun shone, striking light off the puddles that had gathered from the downpour.

Driving along the quay, Lucy remembered that morning when she had gone to the little bistro on the Place de Truinant to find Volkov. She remembered the sinking despair when the smirking waiter shrugged and said, "He's always drunk." She'd needed courage then, to stand over him and introduce herself; to refuse to be sent away, to admit that she had come to Geneva in vain. *Perhaps I fell in love with him then,* she thought, *when I discovered he was a man and not a shining hero. The first time I looked into his eyes and saw how much he'd suffered; so hungry he'd tried to eat the straw from his mattress; frostbitten, isolated from the world. "You're only a number,"* they had taunted him. *"You don't exist. You're as good as dead."*

And I'm taut with fear, she reproached herself, *when all that can happen to me is to be thrown out of this damned clinic. If they call the police that would be different. I'd be arrested, Volkov wouldn't know what had happened to me.* Panic rose for a moment. She crushed it ruthlessly. *I can't afford fear. I've got to succeed. I've got to get his passport and take him away from here. Before our luck runs out. It's been too easy for us, we've led charmed lives till now.* There was a Russian saying her father liked to quote. "God doesn't always frown upon the wicked."

She put her foot down on the pedal and the car leaped forward. In her agitation she had taken the longer route onto the Quai de Cologny. She slowed and turned right-handed, crossing the Chemin de Belle-fontaine and down the Route de la Capite, upward off the main highway and into the Chemin Faguillon. There was a discreet sign pointing higher still to the Amtel Clinic.

She turned into the big car park. Expensive cars were parked in neat rows, the staff had reserved them. She saw the name Dr. Volkov on a smart little board above an empty space and her heart jumped. She found a parking space close to the main entrance. She put the key in her pocket and left her purse in the car.

She saw the building that Adolph Bruckner had looked at on his arrival that day, the pain in his head threatening like the thunder clouds coming back over the mountaintops. Clean architectural lines, gleaming glass, flower beds so neat and regimented that no weed would dare seed itself.

Two nurses in crisp white came down the main steps, laughing and talking, hurrying away. Lucy walked up the flight of steps; the plate glass doors slid open electronically as she crossed the beam.

More flowers inside. A small fountain pattered gently in the big reception hall. A desk with a RECEPTION sign in French, German, and Arabic loomed on her left. She saw every detail, her senses sharpened by a flood of adrenaline. She went to the reception and a smiling woman in a white blouse and neat gray skirt rose up and asked if she could help her. Lucy smiled back.

"I've come to see Doctor Volkov's secretary," she said.

The receptionist made a quick assessment. Nicely dressed, but not expensively enough to be a client.

"She may still be at lunch," she said. "I'll ring for you and see if she's there."

"Oh, don't bother," Lucy said quickly. "I'm a friend of hers. I've only popped by for five minutes. Second floor, isn't she?"

"Third," the receptionist corrected. "You can take the elevator over there."

"Thanks," Lucy said. Elevators could be on the wrong floor at the wrong moment. "I'll go up the stairs. Good for the figure."

"Round the corner, by the flower shop," she was directed. The woman watched her walk toward the stairway and gave a little shrug. If she wanted to climb all that way, that was her business. She had an English accent; the English weren't normally as health conscious as Americans, so they usually took the elevator.

Lucy skirted the kiosk overflowing with vases and baskets of flowers; the heady scents were sickening. A man came out with a big bouquet of regal lilies, festooned with white ribbons. He looked miserable and anxious, and almost bumped into Lucy.

He said, "Oh, *scusi Signorina*" and walked toward the elevator.

She hurried past him to the stairs. It was a longer climb than she expected. Nervousness made her breathless. She paused at the landing leading onto the third floor. Carefully she pushed the door open and looked left and right before stepping into the corridor. There were five consulting rooms, two waiting rooms, the elevator doors and another door marked FIRE EXIT ONLY. The floors were carpeted, the lighting soft; flower prints in gilded frames hung between the doors. It reminded Lucy of a luxury hotel.

Then she stopped dead. There was a nurse's cubby hole with a little desk behind a glass door. Someone was moving in there. She saw a glimpse of uniform and retreated behind the door onto the landing. She watched through a crack and at last a nurse came out of the tiny office and went to the elevator. Lucy could hear her humming as she waited. Then she was gone and the corridor was empty. The name was stenciled inside a brass frame on the fourth door along. DR. I. VOLKOV.

Lucy paused. She raised her hand to knock. If the secretary had come back early, if she answered, Lucy had decided to go in and bluff it out. "Doctor Volkov asked me to collect something from her office. Would you open the door please? She's in a hurry to get it." It had sounded convincing when she rehearsed it. She'd heard herself saying it and had been impressed by her confidence. Quiet authority was the key. She mustn't hesitate. Just walk in, say the few words, demand that the office be opened for her.

At that moment Lucy realized that no responsible employee in an ordinary office, let alone a hospital, would have admitted her without written instructions or a confirmation call. She knocked. She knocked again. Nothing happened. She couldn't hear any movement from inside. She tried the handle. It turned and the door opened. She slipped in and closed it very carefully. A quarter to two. She had lost precious time waiting for the nurse to leave.

She crossed the room in a few quick strides, grasped the handle of the door set in the wall and pulled. It was locked. She couldn't help it. She gave a stifled cry of disappointment. Then she swung round to the empty desk. Word processor, internal and external phones, a tiny switchboard with dead lights, linking the office to who-knew-what departments.

The key was in the top drawer, neatly labeled, I. Volkov. She couldn't turn it at first; she fumbled and wrenched, then made herself try again, without forcing. At last she was inside the consulting room and the door was closed behind her. The blinds were half-drawn against the sunlight. She ran to the desk, bumping against a large armchair, not feeling the impact. She had the key out of her pocket and in her hand. Her hand was trembling. She bent down and inserted it carefully into the left-hand drawer of the desk. She didn't hear the door open.

Irina slammed down the telephone. She had arranged to lunch with friends at the Lion d'Or at Cologny and call in to the clinic afterward to see one or two patients. The Italian lady was being particularly troublesome, demanding that the baby be left alone with her. Irina refused to allow it; the mother was a danger to her child as well as herself.

She gave the clinic the restaurant number. She always let

them know where she could be reached in an emergency. They telephoned in the middle of the dessert. She came back and excused herself. Both her friends were women. They were partners in an art gallery that specialized in avant garde paintings by young artists. Irina accepted their lesbian relationship without feeling threatened herself. They were intelligent and amusing companions and soon she would be leaving them forever. Without even saying good-bye, she had invited them to lunch as a silent farewell.

"I'm so sorry," she said. "It's an emergency. One of my patients has gone missing. Damned woman!"

She drove fast toward the clinic, her mood was angry. She had no sympathy for the rich, spoiled girl who'd walked out of the room and disappeared. Her frantic husband had gone to visit her and found the empty bed and her nightgown on the floor. Mercifully the new baby was in a special room with a maternity nurse. They were searching the clinic in case the mother was hiding somewhere. She hadn't been seen leaving the building.

Irina jerked her car to a stop in her reserved bay and hurried up the steps into the main hall. The receptionist called out to her as she went to the elevator.

"Excuse me, Doctor. There's a package for you. Vera's not back from lunch, so I kept it at the desk."

"Damn Vera," Irina said under her breath. "Taking extra time off because I wasn't in till late this afternoon. I'll have a word to say to her when she gets back." She took the envelope and stepped into the elevator.

It was special delivery. She tore it open. Dimitri's passport was inside. She pressed the third floor button to go to her office and put it away before she went down to her patient's room and the distraught Italian husband. No Vera, she noted furiously, striding across the empty office, ignoring the fact that it wasn't even two o'clock. She felt like punishing someone because her lunch was interrupted. She saw the key in her door and lost her temper. Now that was inexcusable. To forget to lock her private office and leave the key in the lock. "I'll sack her for that," she said out loud. "As soon as she comes back, I'll tell her she's sacked!"

She opened the door and then froze. A woman was going through her desk. Not her errant secretary, who was plump and dark. The intruder was blonde; her hair shone in a shaft of subdued sunlight from the slatted blind. She was bending down, absorbed in what she was doing.

Irina was startled, but she wasn't afraid. People didn't frighten her. She was used to controlling them. She stepped into the room on the soft carpet and said loudly in French, "What the hell do you think you're doing?"

Lucy jerked upright. She stood rooted, staring at the woman. She didn't answer. The drawer held various Russian documents and certificates, but no passport for Volkov. His wife's passport was there and the photograph inside was the same as the woman advancing toward her.

"Who are you?" Irina demanded. "What are you doing in my office?"

It must be a patient, she thought, *wandering about and creeping in to steal something. She might need assistance.* The emergency button to summon help was by the desk, under the ledge. She came close to Lucy. Then she saw the drawer she kept locked was open and knew this was no ordinary thief. She made a quick lunge across the desk surface to reach the call button. Instinctively Lucy grabbed at her wrist.

"You rotten little spy," Irina hissed at her in Russian. "You'll pay for this, whatever you're up to."

She wrenched herself free; she swung a fist and aimed a blow at Lucy with all her weight behind it. It sent Lucy reeling backward; the impact on her shoulder knocked her off balance.

She stumbled and fell to her knees. Irina reached the button and pressed hard.

Irina stood over her; she was triumphant, about to have the girl seized by trained staff and hustled away. She spoke in French so Lucy would understand her this time.

"We have male nurses here," she said. "They know how to deal with people like you."

Blind terror washed over Lucy like a wave. And from that terror she drew unexpected strength. She propelled herself forward and grappled with Irina. For a moment or two she was the stronger, but not for long. The other woman had one hand on her throat and she was squeezing brutally. At any second now, the door would open and she'd be seized.

"You bitch," Irina spat at her in Russian. "I'll have you in a straitjacket."

There was a box on the desk, just within reach. Lucy grabbed for it; she was choking with the grip on her throat. She slammed it down on her opponent's head as hard as she could.

Cigarettes scattered everywhere. In one blinding second she thought, *I've killed her*, as the fingers squeezing her windpipe slackened and fell away. Irina slumped backward against the desk and slid to the ground. Her mouth was open and her eyes had rolled back.

Lucy was sobbing, getting her breath. She stumbled across the floor to the door and kicked something. She saw it lying at her feet, half out of the opened envelope: dark green with the red hammer and sickle in the center. She stooped and picked it up. Volkov's wife had dropped it in their struggle.

It was Dimitri's passport. Her heart was pounding and her head felt light; she thrust the passport into her blouse and closed the door behind her. The key was still in it. She locked it. *She is dead*, Lucy said to herself. *I hit her so hard I killed her.* She put the key in her pocket and walked out into the corridor. She saw the bright red arrow of the elevator ascending. Help was coming for Irina. No time to use the stairs. She ran to the fire escape door and pushed the bar to open it.

Outside she found herself at the top of a fire escape. The ground dipped and swayed beneath her; she felt dizzy and clung to the rails, forcing herself to go down, to keep looking up, away from the void below.

At last her feet were on the ground. She was at the rear of the clinic. Thank God she'd locked the door. They couldn't get in and find the dead woman till they got another key or they broke it down. She had time to get to her car, to drive away.

She switched on the ignition; the engine coughed and didn't start. She tried again; it sulked, spluttering. She tried a third time. When she was about to abandon her car and get out and run, it fired. She put it in gear and eased out of the space, willing herself not to rush, not to panic.

Back down the way she had come, down the Route de la Capite, taking the direct route this time, going straight on to the Quai de Cologny and out onto the Quai Gustave-Ador. She overshot two traffic lights; cars hooted furiously at her. Her throat was still sore and painful where the other woman's fingers had dug into her. She banished the horrible image from her mind; the contorted face, the eyes rolling back as she fell under the blow to her head. The cigarettes scattered all around the floor.

Nausea welled up in her; she fought it down, forcing herself to concentrate on the road, to last until she saw the street sign Rue de la Tourelle. There was the apartment block. She was home. She was safe. She left the car and managed to get into the block and go up in the elevator.

Dimitri opened the door and she fell into his arms. She poured out the story. "She caught me in her office—we were struggling—I hit her on the head. Oh, Dimitri, I think I killed her!"

"You're crazy. Insane! How could you have taken such a risk? My darling, please stop shaking."

Volkov held her close, marveling at her selfless courage even as he reproached her. To go to the clinic alone, to chance getting in and out of Irina's office without being discovered. And to escape when his wife surprised her.

"I killed her," she repeated. "I hit her so hard because she was choking me. Oh, darling, what have I done?"

"I don't care what you've done to her," he insisted. "What terrified me is what she would have done to you. You'd have been drugged, confined in that place. God knows what lie she'd have made up to the staff and they'd have believed her. I am so angry with you, Lucy, and I love you so much for doing it."

Tears came into his eyes.

"What are we going to do?" she begged him. He soothed her gently. She was overwrought, exaggerating. Irina couldn't be dead. Lucy had only knocked her out and panicked.

He said gently, "The first thing is to find out what's happened."

"We've got to get away," Lucy insisted. "Just take a few things and get on a plane." She held on to him. "Where are you going?"

"To phone the clinic," he said.

Lucy watched him. *He's wrong*, she thought. He didn't see her face. The way she fell. She heard him say, "Doctor Volkova, please. It's her husband calling." There was a pause, a long pause while he waited. "What? But that's terrible! I'll come right over. How did it happen?" Lucy's heart gave a wild jump and started racing as she listened. "Yes, of course. Thank God it wasn't worse. Thank you, thank you, Doctor." He hung up and turned to Lucy.

"She's not dead, my silly darling. But you did give her quite a blow. She's concussed and they're keeping her in overnight. She doesn't remember anything about what happened. That was a doctor at the clinic. Her secretary said some crank had tried to get an appointment and a woman came to the clinic pretending she knew the secretary. They think they're one and the same and that she attacked Irina. He said they've issued a description and it's in the hands of the police."

Lucy said slowly, "I'm glad. I'm so glad I only knocked her out."

He came and put his arms around her. "So am I," he said. "For your sake. But you're right, we have to leave at once. By the morning she'll remember what happened. The doctor said so. She'll be able to describe you properly. The receptionist was vague. We have to leave today, Lucy. Before Irina realizes that I've gone and my passport is missing."

"We can fly to London," she said. "And then get a plane to Jersey."

Volkov picked up the passport and flipped through it. He looked at her and said, "No, we can't. It's my fault. I didn't think. I told you, I was moved around like a parcel. Everything was arranged. I can't get into England without a visa. No one from the Communist Bloc could go into the West without a visa. I'd be stopped and deported. My wife's friends in the KGB would be happy to escort me home to Russia."

"Oh, Dimitri! It was all for nothing! Why didn't I think of it?" She sank back in despair. "I thought all I had to do was get you a valid passport and we'd be safe."

He said gently, "You didn't think of it and I didn't either because we're like children playing grown-up games. We don't even know the rules. Me with my fine talk about liberating the Ukraine, and I can't even remember about a visa. It's my fault, not yours, sweetheart. You took the risks. You did the brave thing."

He reached out for her hand. "But we're not going to be beaten. I'm not wasting what you did for me. We can't fly, but we can go by car. We can travel from Switzerland to France. They don't bother about the frontier. It's all very casual now. Then we'll think of a way to get to your island. Come on, it's time to pack."

Lucy got up. "I love you," she said. "And you're wrong about us. We're not children and we're learning the rules pretty quickly. You've just proved it. I'm not shaking anymore."

They packed up her clothes and his few belongings, pajamas, shaving kit, a change of shirt. His experience was useful. If you're expected to be arrested, you cleared out everything that might give a clue or be used to incriminate you. Volkov scoured the flat clean of their presence, down to the last crumb in the kitchen cupboard and a twist of make-up-stained tissue in the wastebasket. No rent was due. Lucy had paid in advance. She left cash for the telephone, erring on overpayment, and put it in an envelope under the set.

At last they had her suitcases strapped up and they were ready to drive away from the little haven they shared together.

At the door, Lucy paused and looked back. "We were so happy here," she said. "I'll never forget this place."

"Maybe one day we'll be able to come back," Volkov said gently. He took her by the arm. "No more time, darling. We must hurry."

He threw the luggage into the trunk of the car and helped her into the front seat. He bent and kissed her quickly.

"We'll be into France in about twenty minutes," he said.

She looked up at him. "You're sure we won't be stopped?"

"My wife used to go across regularly. She said they only look at the car's registration number. If it's Swiss or French they don't bother. She was just waved straight through."

The car started easily for him. He put it in gear and they were on their way.

They crossed the French border. No cars were halted. Volkov put on a little speed, but not too much. The last thing they wanted was to be stopped for infringment of the speed limit. He smiled at her, squeezed her hand. It felt cold.

"We're through the first part," he said. "Our luck is holding, my darling. I told you we'd be all right."

He went on talking, reassuring Lucy. He'd mapped out a route for them, given it to her to follow. It would take two hours or more to reach the Autoroute du Soleil on the long way to Paris. He hadn't thought further than that and he didn't want to put more stress on Lucy than he had to.

He passed through the town of Isserre, and spots of rain spat onto the windshield. The sky had darkened and thunder rolled in the west. They were on a main road—wide, well-studded with signs. The rain came lashing down.

"Try and sleep," he suggested. "We've a very long way to go."

She looked pale and tense. "I'll try, but I don't think it'll work," she said. "Don't worry about me, darling. I'm fine."

Driving conditions were horrible and the visibility poor. But the traffic was light, which is why he noticed the Peugeot.

It didn't come close or overtake. It was a faster car than their small Renault. Volkov changed gear and increased his speed. He watched in the driving mirror. The Peugeot accelerated, its wipers flashing at double rate against the driving rain. He was being deliberately foolhardy. There was no reason for the driver of the Peugeot to copy him.

"We're learning the rules," Lucy had said, summoning her courage before they set out. But there were some rules he knew better than she ever would. And he hadn't forgotten them. He might forget about needing a visa because he'd developed the prisoner mentality so common among people who were never permitted to travel. You didn't know what you would never need to know. But he remembered very clearly what it felt like to be followed. Followed on foot, on public transport, in your car. They'd followed him for years when he was politically active.

He looked up at the mirror once more and saw the car behind him, keeping the same distance, the rain spurting fan-wise from its front wheels. They were following him again. For a moment the old fear ran through him, the fear associated with that word of infinite menace, "they." He kept going, watching them from time to time. He'd been allowed to cross the border. Was there another car ahead, waiting to pull out and sandwich them with the Peugeot coming up behind? He knew the technique. A half-empty road, a forced halt. A quick struggle and it was over.

First, he had to make absolutely sure—and to rationalize before he took the risks involved. He wasn't going to alarm Lucy. She'd been through a shattering experience already.

He said, "I'm going to pull in at the next rest area. I want to check the rear tire."

He pulled in and stopped the car, but left the temperamental engine idling. Lucy had relived the few desperate moments for him when it refused to start outside the clinic. There was noth-ing wrong with any of the tires. He walked round the back of the car and busied himself with the trunk. The Peugeot passed him. He waited, seeing it well out of sight down the straight road. A few cars sped by. He climbed back in.

Lucy said, "Everything all right? Oh, darling, you're soaked. Here, take your jacket off."

Ten minutes later they passed the Peugeot parked in a rest area. Within fifteen minutes he saw it again in his mirror, lurk-ing behind a large French container truck. He didn't look at Lucy. He laid a hand on her knee and said, "We're being fol-lowed."

He heard her gasp. "I stopped to make sure. They passed us, waited in a rest area for us to catch them up and they're behind us again. Are you a good passenger, darling?"

"Who is it? Oh, Volkov. Is it the police?"

"Not the police, no. We'd have been stopped long ago. There's a turnoff two miles farther on. Sit tight. I'm going to lose them."

He swung off the main road without signaling. The road ahead was narrow; a signpost flashed past them, too quickly for Lucy to read it. Behind them, the Peugeot came into view, veering unevenly.

"They weren't expecting that," he said. "It's thrown the driver off balance. Now!"

A right-hand fork came on them suddenly; he took it, the Renault's tires screeching; a rapid gear change gave them speed on the corner and he sat bent over the wheel, concentrating on the road through the sheets of rain.

"For God's sake," Lucy gasped. "We'll crash!"

"No, we won't. Shut your eyes if you're scared."

She was clinging to the seat with both hands. A hill loomed ahead of them. They went up and down as if they were on a roller coaster. An isolated house was on the right, guarded by dark gloomy barns. The country was deeply rural. He drove on the gears, cornering, accelerating into the twists and turns, and then without any warning, he braked so hard she was thrown forward against her seat belt.

"I'm sorry, darling," he said. "I only just saw it in time."

It was a farm track, little more than a rough pathway across the fields. He drove up, bumping over the potholes and the stones, and then reversed the car, facing the way they'd come.

"If they've managed to keep up," he said, "we'll see them from here. They won't see us, it's nearly dark."

She managed a shaky laugh. "You didn't tell me you were a racing driver."

He slipped his arm round her. "I used to enjoy playing the fool in a car when I was young," he said. "Country roads like this, no traffic. It was an old car, but I had a friend who worked in an engineering factory and he fiddled with it till it could go quite fast. We saved up for it together. He hit a tree and that was the end of the car. He wasn't hurt, but I was a full-fledged professor before I could afford another. We've lost them. Nothing's passed."

"Who were they?" Lucy asked. "Don't lie to me, Dimitri. Who do you think they were if it wasn't the police looking for me?"

"I thought it was a KGB trap," he admitted. "One following, one ahead. But they didn't know I was leaving. How could they? And they're expert drivers. I wouldn't have got away from them. I don't know, I don't know who it was, but I know we were being tailed. But now, we get back on the road. Let me look at our map and see where we go to rejoin the main road to the highway. Do you mind driving through the night?"

"I don't mind anything so long as we're safe," she said. "When you're tired, I can take over."

They reached the Autoroute du Soleil and settled into a steady eighty miles per hour. The little car had served them well, despite its temperamental starting mechanism, and he didn't want to stress the engine. Lucy slept after the first few hours and woke with a start after a nightmare where she was being chased and her feet were weighed down with heavy, heavy shoes.

Volkov stopped at an all-night motel. "We can stretch our legs and have some coffee and something to eat, but we'd better keep going," he said. "Of course, I haven't any money. I'm so hopeless you should have left me behind!"

"I needed a good driver," she said. "I can change some Swiss francs."

The coffee was strong and they were both hungry. It was self-service, presided over by a bored cashier. Three other late-night drivers were eating sandwiches and drinking beer. They glanced up without much interest at the couple who came in. Their trucks were parked outside.

Lucy paid for the coffee and the rolls full of ham and cheese. The cashier grumbled about changing Swiss money, but made a calculation that was to his advantage on the rate. She didn't comment.

"I can drive," she offered. She was still pale, with deep shadows under her eyes.

Volkov shook his head. "You sleep tonight and drive tomorrow. It's the highway all the way to Paris. Now settle down and go to sleep. But kiss me first."

She put her arms up and held him close to her. He kissed slowly, with great tenderness, gently exploring her mouth.

"You're a wonderful girl, Lucy Warren. You know that was a brand new passport? Issued from the Embassy. You *know* what you saved me from by that crazy thing you did today? They were going to bring me back to Russia."

She broke away and stared at him. "My God. They couldn't. You wouldn't have gone!"

"I wouldn't have had the choice," he said slowly. "They'd have left it to Irina to arrange that." He silenced her with another kiss, and gathered her to him. "I love you more than life, Lucy Warren."

"That's what you called me when we first met," she whispered.

"I know I did," he said. "You saved me then and you saved me today. Tomorrow night we're going to sleep in a bed, somewhere comfortable and small, not like that wretched motel place. Here, let me fasten that for you."

He clasped the seat belt across her. "Put your head back and shut your eyes. No more excitement for tonight. I'll wake you and we'll stop somewhere for breakfast. Now sleep, my darling."

*　　　　*　　　・*

Slowly Irina reached up and touched her head; the windows were shaded and the room was in semidarkness. The headache was thunderous. She felt nauseated. There was a dressing over a large lump; when her fingertips made contact she winced. Gradually her eyes became accustomed to the dim light and to her surroundings. She was in bed in a private room in the clinic. In spite of the pounding in her head she tried to concentrate. The day before was a blur; it had been a complete blank. *Concussion*, she diagnosed. *I've been concussed. I still am, that's why there's no light to hurt my eyes. I've had an accident. Hit my head. There should be a bell within reach to summon a nurse.* With her other hand she groped and found the switch. She pressed. *An accident. A fall. No, not a fall.* The sudden movement as she started to remember caused an agonizing throb of pain and she froze. The door opened and a nurse came into view.

"Doctor?"

Irina focused on her; her sight was clear now.

"I need painkillers," she said. "What happened to me?"

"Do you remember anything? Doctor Rodier said you weren't to try too hard, just let it come by itself."

"I know how to treat concussion," Irina croaked at her. She couldn't raise her voice. "Just tell me what happened to me."

The nurse hesitated. "You were attacked," she said at last. "Someone broke into your office. They struck you on the head and left you locked inside. You don't remember any of it? I'll call Doctor Rodier."

She hurried out. She didn't want the responsibility. X-rays showed there was no hairline skull fracture, but she had been unconscious even when the door was finally broken down.

Attacked. Yes, Irina whispered inwardly. *Yes, that's what happened. A woman. A woman stealing from my desk . . . I struggled with her.* Unconsciously one hand became a claw reaching for the other woman's throat.

The image came and went, but it was sharper, the fuzz was clearing round the edges. Blonde hair in the sunlit shaft coming through the blind. That's how she knew it wasn't Vera.

Vera who? Vera her secretary. She was struggling to reach the bell under her desktop. They were grappling, and she'd got her hand on the woman's windpipe, holding her off, squeezing.

Then nothing. Blackness, blankness.

"Good morning, Irina. How are you feeling?"

She opened her eyes and saw Rodier standing by the bed with the nurse hovering behind him.

"Terrible, thank you. I'm concussed; how bad is it?"

"Not too bad. How's the memory?"

"I can remember finding a woman in my office. We struggled, then nothing."

"She hit you with the cigarette box," he explained. "Very hard; I was worried about a hairline fracture, but luckily it was just a bad bump. We kept you sedated and put you to bed here. Can you describe the person who did it? We have a vague description, but if you saw her close up and could tell us, it would help the police. But only if it comes easily. You know you mustn't strain to remember."

"I know," she muttered. "She was blonde, quite young. Thin, not heavy. She didn't speak. The blinds were partly drawn. It all happened so quickly." And she had opened my locked drawer where I kept my Soviet documentation, but I'm not going to mention that. She was looking for something. She added, "Was anything stolen?"

"Nothing that we know of," the doctor answered. "Your secretary checked and everything was there. Your passport, personal papers. Some money, a diary."

Passport. The word danced behind her closed eyelids. Her passport. No, that wasn't taken. Why did passport mean something when it hadn't been stolen? Her headache seemed to split her skull.

"Your husband telephoned," she heard the doctor say. "He was very concerned. He said he was coming over."

"I don't remember," Irina said.

"He didn't come," the doctor said. "We telephoned your apartment, but there was no reply. We thought he'd call in again or come over. I tried myself this morning, in case you were fit enough to go home, but still no answer."

"He's drunk," Irina mumbled. "He's sleeping it off somewhere."

"I'm sorry," the young man said. "I didn't know."

"A shock would start him off," she said, more to herself than to him. "I knew it wouldn't be long before he went back to it. If I could get some relief from this headache."

"Nurse has got something for you. You sleep for a couple of hours and then see how you feel. You won't be going home, Irina, especially if your husband's not able to look after you. Just relax, take the tablets and don't worry. I'll come back and see you this afternoon."

She managed to swallow the pills with sips of water. The nurse smoothed the bedcovers. Irina could have screamed at her to go away and stop fiddling, but it hurt even to whisper. Passport. The word was running through her consciousness like a tune without a title. Her passport. No, not hers. And then the answer came to her. It came as the drug took control and she began to slide away.

Dimitri's passport. Ten minutes later the nurse checked on her. She was in a deep sleep. The hand reaching out for the bell had fallen slackly over the edge of the bed.

It was late afternoon and the nurse had gone off duty. When the bell rang again the new nursing sister hurried to answer it. She found Irina Volkova sitting up in bed, the bell switch gripped hard between her fingers.

*   *   *

"Have you seen the paper?"

"No," Peter Muller said. "I came straight from the shop. Why?"

Eloise Bruckner handed him the *Munich Zeitung*, opened to the second page. It was a small paragraph.

"That woman was attacked," she said. "Knocked out by someone who broke into her office."

"What woman," he asked. He wasn't really interested. He was aware only of Eloise sitting next to him, with her legs crossed at the knee, one delicate ankle encircled by a thin gold chain. He couldn't stop glancing at it and the foot in its black silk court shoe with the very high heel, swinging to and fro, making the erotic little chain glint.

"That doctor who treated Adolph," Eloise said. Muller stopped thinking about the foot, the ankle, the long leg, and what lay hidden out of sight under her skirt.

"Doctor Volkov?"

"Yes," she said. There was triumph in her voice. "Here, read it. She was hit over the head. Knocked out."

He took the evening newspaper and skimmed quickly through the story. A woman intruder. That was unlikely. The doctor was knocked unconscious during a struggle. Even more suspicious. People like Irina were trained to deal swiftly with a violent patient.

"Who could have done it?" he wondered.

"Probably one of her patients come back to give her a taste of her own vicious medicine," Eloise snapped.

She had conceived a real hatred for Adolph's doctor. *Irina was judged and found guilty before she was tried*, Muller thought. He was surprised by the depth of her vindictiveness. And excited by it too. He titillated himself with thoughts of her being cruel to him. He'd never tried that variation before. He had always dominated in bed, as he intended to dominate her. But a role reversal might be interesting to start off with.

He shrugged and passed the newspaper back. It sounded as if Irina was setting herself up for the planned return to Moscow, ahead of the Bruckner lawyers. For medical treatment after the assault. It was an old ruse, but useful.

"It says she suffered some concussion, but nothing serious," he remarked. "The police are looking for the woman. Never mind about that, my dear. I've been looking forward to seeing you so much. You're looking better, you know. I hope you're feeling stronger."

He leaned closer and lightly touched her hand. He let the contact lengthen, she didn't move away.

"I am," she said. "Thanks to you and all my friends. You know, Peter, all Adolph's friends have been so good to me. I knew they all thought so highly of him. He was so clever, so successful, but I never realized they cared about me too."

"Of course they did," he assured her. He slipped his fingers round her palm and held it comfortingly. "You underestimate yourself. You're beautiful, charming, and intelligent. And warm. Adolph was admired—he was quite awe-inspiring too. But you are loved by people."

"The children have been so good about it," she said. She let him hold her hand. *He was so kind, so steady*, she thought. *There is nothing sexual about this*, she insisted. *Just a warm hand holding mine.*

"You're sure you won't let me take you out to dinner? It would do you good," he suggested again.

"No, no." She shook her head and the rich scent flowed toward him. "It's too soon to go to restaurants after poor Adolph. . . . We can have a quiet dinner here if you don't mind. If you won't be bored?"

It was a little flirtatious; she admitted that. But pleasing men was second nature to Eloise. She smiled and lifted her eyelids at a man in a way that conveyed how attractive and interesting he was. It was a harmless habit and besides, she liked Peter Muller. He had beautiful strong white teeth.

His voice deepened. He squeezed her compliant hand for a moment and then let it go.

"You know I'm never bored when I'm with you. Now why don't I pour us a drink?"

"Friederich can do it," she protested.

"No need for that," he said, getting up. He didn't want the Bruckners' butler coming in and out. He wanted to mellow her with wine before dinner, and then advance a few steps after dinner. Good food, they kept a marvelous table, more wine, perhaps a little brandy.

An arm along the back of the sofa that could lightly rest on her shoulders, a casual pressure of his thigh against hers. Instant retreat if she signaled he was going too far. He wasn't going to rush this. Planning her seduction was an excitement in itself. He would be patient, stalk her carefully right up to the bedroom door.

He poured Moselle for her, brushed fingers as he handed her the glass and looked into her eyes. He drank Scotch whiskey. She said once she liked the smell. She was the kind of woman who convinced herself that she liked all the rich smells associated with men. Brandy, cigars. She told men this, with the lift and flutter of the eyelashes that was her trademark.

She used it now as she said, "It's so sweet of Susan to spare you tonight. I do hope she doesn't mind lending you for just one dinner. I've got so many problems at the moment."

"Of course not," Peter Muller said. "She's gone to see some Polish art film. You know the kind of thing, all black shadows and gloom. She's gone with a friend who likes that stuff. I couldn't sit through it. I like to be entertained, to be happy. And *you* must be happy, my dear. Adolph wouldn't want you shutting yourself away. All right, we dine here tonight and I'll help with any problems you want, but next time we go to the Hofburg!" He named the best restaurant in Munich.

Eloise smiled. "Just the three of us—that would be lovely."

"Just the three of us," he echoed. He didn't mind. He knew she didn't mean it.

Dinner was excellent, as he anticipated. Eloise was an accomplished hostess and Adolph expected and got perfection in his home. Looking round at the elegant dining room, waited on by the unobtrusive Friederich, Peter Muller wondered what it would be like to live on such a scale, with so much money to make life smooth as silk.

He and Susan lived well; their two sons in America wanted for nothing, but this lifestyle was majestic by comparison. He put the fleeting temptation aside, surprised that it had even occurred to him. He loved his sons and was fond of his wife. His plans were laid for retirement. Money and a house in the Caribbean sunshine. More than most spies, however successful, could dream of achieving at the end of their careers.

No, that was a foolish fantasy, impracticable. He was going to take Adolph's place in bed, but not at the head of his table by marrying the widow. He set out to be amusing; he had a fund of anecdotes, some about people Eloise knew well. They were funny without being malicious. She laughed and encouraged him. He thought she looked maddeningly attractive, and emboldened by the fine claret, pressed his knee against hers under the table. She let it rest for longer than she should have done and then moved slightly away.

"A wonderful dinner," he declared as they left to take their coffee in her sitting room. "As always, you spoil me, Eloise. Now I want to spoil you in return. I want you to unload all your problems on me and let me take care of them. If I can."

"That would be wonderful," she said.

He followed his plan, eased himself down beside her on the cushioned sofa and slid his arm along the back behind her.

Her hair was drawn back, skillfully arranged to fall in loose waves from a gold clasp. It brushed the back of his hand.

"My real difficulty is with dear Adolph's collection," she said.

He smiled at her. "Which collection? His pictures? The porcelain? There's so much, such priceless things."

"I know," she sighed. "It'll take months and months to settle the estate. He was even richer than I thought. No, I shall keep the house exactly as it was; he'd want me to do that. What worries me is his Russian collection. It worries the lawyers and the insurance company was always fussing about keeping it in a private house. The burglar alarm system is a nightmare, just because of them. All those boxes and objects, and the early jewelry. Apart from the desk set. As you know, Peter, that's absolutely unique. Not another like it in the world!"

"I do know," he said. "Clocks and calendars, but not a matching set with the Imperial provenance."

He had stopped thinking lewd thoughts; his mind was concentrated on what might be a perfect opportunity to obey Viktor Rakovsky's order. "Get the desk set back. Steal it if you have to, but it belongs in Russia."

"They say," Eloise went on, "that the value of the Russian works of art could make quite a difference to the total outcome, after taxes. And I must admit, I find the restrictions very boring. They're suggesting that I have a permanent security guard on duty day and night, apart from an alarm system that would be more suitable to the Bundesbank than a private house! They wouldn't have dared lay down conditions like that to Adolph."

"You mustn't let them take advantage of you," he said.

The steel flashed behind the velvety eyes. "Don't worry, I won't. They're not going to dictate to me just because Adolph's dead. In fact, the lawyers suggested something and I'm beginning to think it's a solution. It would put the insurers in their place as well. I want to ask you what you think of it."

She turned and looked at him. "Why don't I give the Russian collection to the Munich Museum of Fine Arts in Adolph's memory. The Adolph Bruckner Bequest. Don't you think it sounds rather nice? Wouldn't he have liked that?"

Muller's expression of concern was only too genuine.

"My dear Eloise—I don't know. Let me think a moment." It was worth trying, but he didn't have high hopes. "From the moral point of view," he said slowly, "there is an alternative. Everything Adolph bought was effectively stolen."

"Peter! You're not suggesting?" She flushed with indignation.

"No. No, my dear, of course I'm not linking Adolph with what I've just said. Let me explain what I mean. All those treasures were part of Russia's heritage. They were bartered for Western currency, sold by families desperate for money to buy food. Looted, smuggled out. It's one of the ugliest stories in the art world. I remember one very famous expert saying to me, it was the rape of Russia's heritage. I never forgot it."

"But you dealt in those things yourself," she protested. "Two of our gold boxes came from you. The one from Catherine the Great to Potemkin and the other one, the Orlov snuff box!"

He looked serious. "I know," he said. "I was no better than anyone else. But I have thought about it ever since my old friend said that. Eloise, why don't you do something remarkable in Adolph's memory?"

"What?" she said coldly.

"Give the whole collection back to the people of Russia. It would cause a sensation. And set a great precedent."

She didn't hesitate. She stared at him and he knew what the answer was going to be.

"I wouldn't dream of it," she said. "Adolph hated the Communists. Certainly not, Peter."

No easy solution to his problem, he thought. He forgot about sex; he was angry instead. Nothing showed on his face.

"If that's how Adolph felt, you're right, of course," he said. "But don't be rushed into giving such a priceless collection away till you've had plenty of time to think about it. The Museum will accept it, no doubt about that. They'll jump at such an offer. I'm just wondering whether there's any connection between your lawyers and the Museum itself? They don't act for the governing body, by any chance?"

"I don't know," Eloise frowned. It was a point Adolph would have made. He checked everything out. "Check first and trust afterward," he used to say to her.

Muller pressed the advantage. "It might be wise to find out," he said. "Would you like me to make inquiries? I can do it through friends of mine?"

"Yes," she said. "Yes, if you can, that would be helpful. If they are trying to use me to get something for the Museum, then I shall think of something else. It doesn't have to be Munich."

"You know, I haven't had a look at the things for a long time," Muller remarked. "I'd like to see everything again, refresh my memory. Then maybe I can advise you better. That's if we're not going to set off the alarm system!"

Eloise's mood had lifted. She laughed.

"We'd have half the police force here in a few minutes if we did," she said. "It's connected to all major stations throughout the city."

"Steal it if you have to." Muller wished Viktor Rakovsky in a special place in hell. Let Moscow Center try and organize a burglary and see what happened.

"All right," she said. "Let's look at it together. I haven't been into the room since Adolph died. I just went through the catalogs with those damned lawyers. He was so methodical, he kept everything documented and photographed. I wonder whether they weren't trying to get it for the Museum, they have a lot of government work."

Muller had sowed the dragon's teeth of doubt. Munich Museum of Fine Arts was unlikely to benefit now. Suspicion was inherent in the superrich. He followed Eloise out of the sitting room; she called it her boudoir, which he thought an affectation, and along the wide corridor toward the big first-floor room where the Bruckners held their parties and the guests were able to admire his Russian art collection.

In the corridor, Eloise paused by a console table; a superb bluejohn vase with Louis XVI ormolu mounts was in the center. An identical table and matching vase was a few yards farther on.

"This is the first switch," she said. "There are three on this floor, just for the ballroom."

She stopped by the table and pressed a carved and gilded flower head. It depressed a fraction.

"That turns the first part of the system off," she explained.

"How clever," Muller remarked. He had noted the flower head carefully. Third on the left of a larger floral carving. "Very ingenious."

"Adolph's idea," she smiled at him. "He was so inventive. Now, it's the same here, only on the other side."

She pressed another carved and gilded flower head on the second table. Third on the right of the larger flower group this time. He followed her as they approached the green-and-gold-painted double doors leading to the ballroom.

Eloise paused and said, "This is the last; it clears the system completely so we can open the door."

Muller stopped. He said, "My dear, I don't think you should let anyone know what it is. Even me. I'll turn my back."

"Oh, Peter, don't be so silly." She was herself again, fluttering the melting look at him. "It's so brilliant I want you to see it. You know that's one of the reasons I loved Adolph so much. He had the most amazing brain. Look!"

It was a bronze elephant clock, complete with gilded howdah and the clockface on its back. Eloise opened the glass case and adjusted the minute hand until both golden hands were on the numeral twelve. The clock chimed the hour.

"Isn't that genius?" she demanded. "There's no clock mechanism in there, just the final switch for the ballroom system."

"Supposing someone moved the bronze?" Muller asked.

"They couldn't," she said. "It's bolted to the table and the table is secured to the floor. Now we can open the doors and go in."

He remembered the first time he had come there, his first coveted invitation from one of the richest men in West Germany. A client of enormous potential if he managed to hook him.

Eloise switched on the lights. The room was flooded with a soft illumination, cleverly directed at the Gobelins tapestries that lined one wall. He glanced up.

"Ah," he said, and meant it. "How beautiful that is!"

Bruckner had brought the painted ceiling from Italy and had it fitted. Tiepolo no less, before the artist had commanded the fortune of the present day, but still a great deal of money, even twenty years ago when Bruckner renovated the old mansion and started filling it with treasures.

Together they walked across the carpet; a splendid Second Empire Aubusson that was always rolled up for the parties. At the far end, specially lit, Adolph Bruckner's collection of Russian works of art sparkled in a glass display case. It always excited Muller to see them.

"They are lovely," Eloise murmured beside him as they stood and admired. "Perhaps I should keep them. Adolph left it up to me what to do with everything."

There were the two gold and jeweled boxes Muller had sold him at a staggering profit, considering he had bought them from someone facing criminal charges and desperate for cash.

The early Byzantine pendants and a necklace that had graced some medieval noble's wife. Two fifteenth-century icons set in beaten silver studded with amethyst and quartz. Rarety was what Bruckner valued more than gems and gold. A pair of rock crystal goblets engraved with the cipher of Peter the Great. Boxes, portrait miniatures, and then in a section of its own in the center of the display, the works of Carl Fabergé in the high days of czarist glory.

"I think he's my favorite," Eloise said, one slim finger directed at a toad made of nephrite, its bulging eyes two big ruby cabochons surrounded by a ring of diamonds. Diamonds formed the wide mouth so that the little creature seemed to grin with light.

"He's got such a naughty look," she said.

Muller smiled. He thought if he'd had the choice, it wouldn't be the toad snuffbox, but the marvelous box in yellow-and-white opal enamel, with the unhappy Nicholas II's cipher and crown and the Imperial eagles in diamonds and black enamel.

By comparison the desk set was almost modest. It had the place of honor because, as he'd said earlier, it was unique. Designed and made as a present from the emperor for his niece. A Christmas gift, since the Easter feast was celebrated by the exchange of eggs and was the more important in the Orthodox calendar. They gleamed watery green, with the diamonds like frost, sparkling under the light.

He stood for a moment in silence. In his imagination he saw Bruckner stuffing them into his pockets, wrapped in the torn clothing of the woman he had raped, while his companion murdered her.

God knows, he thought, *how she got hold of them. Or how the greatest treasure of all, Saint Vladimir's holy cross, came to be hidden in a humble farmhouse in the Ukraine. For all those years* Adolph Bruckner had guarded his bloody loot and built his reputation as an art lover around it. The Grand Duchess Elizabeth, owner of the clock and the calendar, had been murdered by the Bolsheviks like her uncle the czar. Like the woman in the house by the woods. In the end they had driven Bruckner to near madness and death. It was no more than he deserved.

Muller caught Eloise by the elbow.

"It makes me think of Adolph," he said. "It makes me sad. Don't give anything to anyone, my dear. I was wrong to suggest what I did. Keep them; I'm sure that's what he would have wanted. Let's go back, shall we?"

Outside in the corridor she said, "I must reset the alarm. You see what I mean about it being a nightmare—and this is just this one room."

It worked in reverse. The elephant clock was set to twelve-thirty. Third gilded flower on the left of the first console table going the opposite way, third flower on the right of the second table. A light touch and not even a mouse could have scuttled through that ballroom without setting off the alarm all over the house.

"A brandy before you go?" Eloise offered.

Muller decided not. "It's late," he said. "Susan will be home by now."

He thought he saw a flicker of disappointment on her face. No harm in that. He came close and took her hand in both of his. He kissed it and then lightly touched her cheek with his lips.

"I've had a wonderful evening with you. And next week we are going to the Hofburg. I'll call you tomorrow. And you know, anything I can do for you—just ask. Give my love to the children."

She crossed and rang the bell.

"Friederich will show you out," she said. "Thank you for being such a dear friend. I look forward to our dinner."

He drove home slowly, thinking. The sight of the desk set had emptied him of all desire. He was reminded of his priorities. He had to get it. His reward, as Viktor promised, would be commensurate. The Volkovs would soon be back in Russia. That part of his operation was closing down.

As he drew up outside his own apartment, he shut off the engine and sat there, thinking through to the future. He'd boasted to Irina that politicians come and go, but spies go on forever. He was in his early fifties. He had a thriving business— a good life by any standard. But his secret life was contracting as the East-West tensions slackened. There would be less and less for him to do without the outlet at the Amtel Clinic. And therefore less reason to go on, to take the occasional risk, like an old servant being called out of retirement to help out. He didn't want that. He didn't want to play the game part-time. The risks were still there and the satisfaction wouldn't justify them. He would get Rakovsky the desk set and then retire himself before they retired him. It was a bonus that he could do it by way of Eloise Bruckner's bed.

He drove the car into the garage reserved for residents and went up to his apartment. Susan was waiting. She hadn't gone to any cinema and she hated art films with subtitles. He had explained that he was going to see Eloise in the hope she might be willing to sell him something. She came and kissed him in her brisk way.

"Any luck, darling?"

"I might get the two boxes back," he lied. "The Orlov one anyway. It's worth three times what he gave me for it."

"She won't give you any bargain," his wife said. "That lady knows about money."

Muller couldn't argue with that. "So do I," he said. "Leave it to me. I'll get it out of her."

They sat hand in hand and watched a late television movie. They were very companionable. The next morning the Swiss detective agency called to say that Dimitri Volkov and his companion had crossed over to France. Regrettably, their surveillance team had lost them.

4

THE SOVIET consul came to see her. He brought an assistant and it was the assistant who did all the talking. The consul itroduced him.

"This is Vladimir Turin from the Trade Department," he said.

Irina shook hands with him briefly.

"Please sit down," she said.

She didn't offer them a drink. It wasn't a social visit. She had discharged herself from the clinic as soon as she heard about the empty envelope lying on her office floor and that Dimitri's passport had not been found. That, she concluded, must have been what the intruder was looking for. And with a key, since the drawer had been unlocked. The implications were too serious to be concealed. She got back to her apartment and with a vicious headache, managed to search through the cupboards. Nothing belonging to him was missing.

But the emptiness had a special quality she recognized. Real emptiness, not absence. There was a difference. He wasn't out, he was gone. She had felt so weak and sick that she was tempted to delay. To go to bed and sleep on it before she called the Embassy. But that was failing in her duty. She had never failed. Except, she thought bitterly, when she fell in love with Dimitri Volkov.

The consular official was very understanding. This surprised her. He didn't express shock at what she told him. Later, with time to collect herself, Irina realized he knew already. She must rest, he insisted. Everything was in hand and he would come and see her tomorrow.

She wasn't surprised to see two of them when she opened the door.

"How are you feeling?" the young man called Turin asked her. She looked ghastly, with a dressing taped on top of her head.

"Better," she said to the consul. "Thank you for not coming last night. I'm much clearer this morning. Is there any news of my husband?"

Turin answered. "He was heading for the border into France two nights ago," he said. "Unfortunately the surveillance lost him."

"Surveillance?" Irina looked up sharply. "You were watching him? Why wasn't I told?"

"Not our surveillance," Turin corrected. "Swiss private detectives. If it was our operation, he wouldn't have got away."

She put a hand to her head; she felt dizzy for a moment.

"Swiss detectives? I don't understand."

"It was a routine precaution. Your husband was involved with a woman and Moscow wanted a low-key investigation. A private firm was chosen to do it."

"A woman? You say he was involved with a woman?" She stared at them in turn. Two bright patches of color blazed in her cheeks. The consul thought she looked very ill.

Turin proceeded without mercy. "He'd been having an affair with her for some time. Meeting in secret, sleeping overnight in her apartment. She was with him when he escaped. A blonde woman, in her twenties." He referred to a note he'd taken out of his pocket. He had flat brown eyes, deep set like stones in his face. "A similar description to the one you gave of your attacker," he said.

"Yes," Irina managed to speak.

"Obviously they planned to leave Switzerland and they had to get a passport for him. He couldn't travel through Europe without that. Did you mention returning to the Soviet Union to him at any time, Comrade Doctor?"

"No," Irina made an effort to control herself. "No, of course I didn't. He wouldn't have come. I'd planned another way of getting him there."

Turin smiled. "A sudden illness?"

"It's been done before," she retorted. "I had it all worked out. Excuse me for a moment."

She left them and made her way to the bathroom. A woman. Sleeping with her, staying together overnight. She retched into the basin. She drank some water, splashed her face, and dried it. Her reflection stared back at her, ashen, sunken eyed, the mouth caught in a rictus of pain. Years of lying beside him, hungry for the love he couldn't give her. Bearing the taunts, the drunken emptiness. He had betrayed her with someone else. Slept with her. Made love as they used to make love long ago when they first met. Stolen afternoons, long nights when the dawn came before they tired.

Five years of living in exile, the price she'd offered to pay to save his life and win his freedom from the gulag. She forced herself to stand up straight. She turned from that sorry sight in the glass and went back to the two men.

"Tell me about this woman," she said.

"I have no authority to go into details," Turin sounded apologetic. "Except to say that you are not being held responsible for what has happened. I can assure you of that. In fact . . ." he repeated the message received from his superiors that morning. "In fact, the official view is very sympathetic to you, Comrade. Also," he looked at his note again, "a reservation has been made for the Aeroflot flight out tomorrow morning at eleven o'clock. You'll go direct to Moscow."

A scheduled flight, not a special plane. She understood the significance of that. She was going home, but not in disgrace.

"Will you let my family know?"

"Your father will be at Sheremetyevo Airport to meet you and take you home," Turin answered. "Is there anything else we can do?" He turned, including the consul this time. "You seem to be still groggy. We can send someone round to pack up for you."

"That would be a help," she said. "I'm recovering every day. You know, I very nearly had her? I had my hand on her throat and a few seconds more and she'd have passed out. I'd got the carotid artery under my thumb." She stopped.

Neither of the men spoke. The consul looked at his fingernails. Turin nodded to him and they stood up. They each shook hands.

"I'll collect you in the morning," Turin said. "We'll issue a short statement to the press saying you are going home for a rest after your ordeal. It would be as well if you confirm this to the clinic director yourself."

"I'll speak to him," Irina promised. "Let yourselves out, please."

She lit a cigarette and put it out after a few puffs. She couldn't smoke. It tasted vile. The room was very quiet. Peaceful. She looked round it. Home for the last five years. It had never been home to her. She would leave it behind without a pang. She felt no attachment to the clinic or to the patients there anymore. To her they all seemed to assume the identity of that damned Italian whose antics had brought her away from her lunch that day. Into the office to find Volkov's lover rifling through her private papers.

Her mouth filled with a bitter taste; the bile of jealousy almost choked her. He'd stopped drinking for that other woman. She'd noticed the change and been too blind to guess the reason. How, where had he met her? On one of his endless, aimless walks, trying to kill time between the next drink?

She closed her eyes to shut out the torture of imagining them together. Younger than she by at least ten years; surely she'd glimpsed bright blue eyes in that surge of violence between them?

"If he were in front of me now," she said out loud, "I'd kill him. I know how to. I'd spring at him and smash my fist against his neck and he'd fall dead at my feet."

She started to cry and let the tears spill out and run down her face. So many tears she'd shed for him. When he was arrested, and she'd rushed from friend to friend, begging them to help, to use their influence. Her father, trying to comfort her and reproaching her at the same time, had said, "I told you not to marry him. I warned you he was no good for you."

The terrible anguish of seeing him in prison, hearing the rough consumptive cough and knowing that unless she did something, he would disappear into the Siberian wasteland and die. And the silent tears during the time they had lived together in that flat. Seeing him turn from her, degrading himself trying to escape in drink. Losing the man she had loved because Peter Muller had betrayed the deal she'd made to get him out of Russia.

Muller! Muller with his arrogance and his contempt for her husband. Opening his loud mouth as if the man sitting close by was no more sentient than a waxwork dummy. Dummy is what he'd called him to her once. Muller! She heaved herself up and sat by the telephone. She dialed the Munich number of his shop.

"Irina? How are you? I read about what happened."

"I'm all right," She kept her voice steady. "Can you talk to me?"

"Yes, the place is empty at the moment. Anything urgent?"

She paused, masking the mouthpiece for a few seconds with her hand. Does he know? Is he pretending? Was he part of this surveillance without telling me? Her instinct urged her to attack, to tear down his defenses.

"Volkov's disappeared," she said.

He'd been prepared since he got the apologetic call from his detectives saying they'd lost the trail. He'd sent the news posthaste to Moscow Center, just twenty-four hours after his dinner with Eloise Bruckner.

"My God," he said. "You mean he's vanished?"

The lie transmitted itself through his voice; she knew as soon as he spoke.

"He had a woman, Peter," she cut in on him. "You knew about it, didn't you? Don't lie to me. You knew!"

He thought very quickly. Why should she guess? Viktor must have broken confidence and told her.

"Yes, I did know. I saw them in the street together. Viktor didn't want you upset. He told me to say nothing, but to find out about her. Very low key, nothing to do with our people. I got a Swiss firm to keep a watch on them."

She cleared her constricted throat. "Tell me about her."

"Listen, Irina, I know you're blaming me. I'd have told you, but Viktor wouldn't allow it. He said, 'Irina's too valuable to be upset.' His own words."

"They were together for how long? Weeks, months? She's the one who broke into my office and knocked me out. She stole Volkov's passport. It had just been renewed. We were summoned back to Moscow. I was to bring him with me. Like it or not, Peter. You understand?"

"Christ, yes," he said.

He'd dismissed the story as a cover to get her out of Geneva before Eloise could bring a legal action. But it was true. The

woman called Lucy Warren had gone to Irina's office, bashed
her over the head, and made off with Volkov's passport. He'd
been right to alert Moscow when he discovered she was the
daughter of a Ukrainian émigré, founder of an anti-Soviet organization with wide affiliations. They'd set off by car the afternoon of the attack on Irina. And lost the experienced Swiss tail
after a hair-raising drive in the rain and darkness. He couldn't
believe it when he heard that it was Volkov at the wheel.

"We'll find them, don't worry," he said. "My people got
the number of the car. They'll be tracked down. He can't get
far without a visa."

"No," Irina said. "He can't. If you'd told me instead of
going to Viktor behind my back, I could have stopped it. I'm
going to point that out when I get home. They don't hold me
responsible. They've been very helpful, very sympathetic. You
let him cheat on me and kept it to yourself. You kept it as a
tidbit to feed Viktor, didn't you? Getting yourself in well. Just
wait till I get home! My father's got friends at the top."

Muller said what he'd been longing to say to her for years:
"Why don't you fuck yourself, Irina? No one else wants to."
He hung up on her.

She sat beside the telephone for some time. The headache
was less strident. She tried another cigarette; her hand trembled.
The taste was still disgusting. No alcohol, she knew that. Stay
quiet, rest. Apart from a mild concussion there's the element
of shock. She went into the kitchen and made herself a glass
of tea. She concentrated on being calm. She lay down on the
bed and forced herself to breathe deeply, keep her eyes closed.
She took her pulse at intervals. It steadied. At five o'clock the
buzzer sounded from the street entrance.

A girl came up and said shyly that she'd been sent from
the Embassy to help her pack. She could, if the Comrade Doctor
liked, make supper for her and stay the night. She was young
and pleasant; she said she worked as a secretary. She wasn't

KGB. Irina could scent them, however cleverly disguised.

Suddenly she was glad of the girl's company. She didn't want to be alone. Why not be looked after for a change? Have someone to talk to if she felt like it.

"You can stay, if it's no trouble," she said.

"I'd be glad to. You must be feeling awful. What would you like me to do first?"

Her name was Elena and she said it was her first overseas posting. Irina tried to smile. No, not left alone in the flat on that last night. Someone to take care of her. To deal with the packing up of her life for the last five years.

"You could make us both some tea," she said.

As they sipped it together, the girl said, "You must be looking forward to going home. There's nowhere like it, is there?"

"No, there isn't," Irina agreed. "Russians aren't happy outside Russia."

The girl looked away in embarrassment as the doctor's eyes filled with tears.

Colonel Leon Gusev was feeding the jigsaw pieces into his computer. Names, dates, locations, questions, suppositions, possible answers and conclusions.

Yuri Warienski had been traced to the early record kept in the Ukraine, when all births and deaths were registered and lodged in a central filing system in Kiev, with duplicates for the State Security in Moscow. Born in January 1930. Parents worked on a collective farm. The area was overrun by the German army in the attack on Smolensk. The civilians who had not escaped into the countryside were rounded up, the adults shot and the children sent back to Germany as slave labor. Warienski, Yuri, aged fifteen, was on the list of Ukrainian nationals rounded up at the camp at Spittal in 1945. No Ukrainians had been forcibly repatriated from that camp, except specific war criminals and members of the Ukrainian arm of the SS. A hundred and fifty out of ten thousand troops and thousands of civilians. The Allies, with the Pope's connivance and the pleas of their Polish brothers, had snatched the rest from Soviet vengeance.

He ran through the notes on the criminals. A lot of information had been extracted from those who'd been returned. Their interrogations, the sentences; death by shooting on arrival, or deportation to the labor camps in the Arctic.

The name Yuri Warienski came up in the brief report on one man, known to have served in the Einzad Commando, the SS death squads. One of his compatriots, hoping to save his own skin from the machine gunners, accused him of being a homosexual, and cited his friendship with a young boy in the camp. Fifty years later the man's bellow of contempt rang in Gusev's ears. "I buggered women, not boys! He was just a hungry kid!"

He had been condemned to death, along with his accuser. The name Warienski appeared on the Red Cross list of displaced persons in a camp in Rimini. Two years later, it appeared he had been issued with a set of papers and was allowed to settle in England under the guarantee of a Major Richard Hope. The same name as the officer in charge of selecting the war criminals at Spittal. Gusev found the pieces fitting, only to leave tantalizing gaps in the electronic puzzle he was putting together.

The murderous Boris Malik had befriended the boy. So had the English army officer, who got him to England and gave him a job. An interesting youth, this Warienski, to have attracted such diverse patrons. Perhaps the turncoat's charge of homosexuality was true.

The computer rejected this. No record of misdemeanor either at Spittal, in the DP Camp at Rimini, or thereafter in England. He had been thoroughly investigated as an active anti-Soviet in the hope of finding something that could be used to discredit him. There was nothing. He married, had a daughter, Lucy Eileen, remained on such good terms with his benefactor that Richard Hope left him his manufacturing business when he died. The computer flooded him with pieces for his puzzle after that.

Warienski, naturalized and known as Warren, had sold the business after a heart attack and moved to the Channel Islands to avoid punitive taxation in Socialist Britain. He had devoted the rest of his life to making trouble for his native country.

A founder of the Free Ukrainian Movement in the British Isles; in close communication with other anti-Soviet organizations throughout the world. A tireless worker in the exposure of the Yalta Agreement and the fate of the Cossacks. He had organized a worldwide protest at the arrest and imprisonment of the dissident Dimitri Volkov in 1983. A large piece of the picture slotted into place.

Within a few days of his death, his daughter had gone to Geneva and made contact with the exile. That contact had become a liaison. All his careful conclusions were being proved right. There was a political conspiracy, as he told Viktor Rakovsky. Times had made such a move possible. There was unrest, instability, opposing factions fighting a last battle for the way holy Russia should proceed. It was permissible to call it that, even applauded.

He rested, the computer screen was blank. He'd proved all the connections necessary, but he hadn't justified the extra time it had taken. By now they had pinpointed the venue for the anti-Soviet activists meeting. The Makoff Gallery was run by the grandson of a czarist émigré who specialized in pre-Revolutionary art. The coming exhibition had alerted the London Embassy, and a man well-known to them, Mischa Czernov, had visited the Makoff and asked for the use of the proprietor's flat above, during the reception. A rival gallery, specializing in Soviet art and on good terms with the Embassy, had obtained a copy of the guest list for the Makoff private view. The names of the activists in the United Kingdom were on it.

It wasn't enough. He hadn't answered his own niggling doubt. His conclusion lacked strength and depth to have real political significance. Volkov was Ukrainian, a dissident who'd suffered for his views. But he'd spent five years in idleness in Switzerland. He'd dropped out of the protest movement as effectively as if he were in the gulag. More so, since many of those imprisoned there had continued to smuggle out messages and make their commitment known to the outside world.

It fitted, but it didn't fit tight enough to satisfy him. He sighed. He couldn't go further. He decided to compile the information in a concise report and put it in front of his chief, omitting nothing—not a name, a date, or an observation. He knew Rakovsky liked to analyze for himself in depth. He didn't appreciate synopses. Gusev's report was on Viktor's desk by the next afternoon.

It was followed within the hour by Peter Muller's urgent message sent via the Russian Embassy in Berlin, that Dimitri Volkov had left Geneva and vanished. His wife, Irina, was on her way back to Moscow.

Leon Gusev was there to meet her when the Aeroflot jet landed at Sheremetyevo Airport.

Lucy saw the signpost, Auberge des Brumes, and slowed down. She had taken over the driving despite Volkov's protests and he had slept for the last four hours of their journey. It was monotonous driving, endless miles of auto route at a steady cruising speed of sixty miles per hour. It was very hot and dusty. She looked at him asleep in the seat beside her. The dark hair fell over his forehead and he had slipped down to lean against her.

She would never forget that feat of driving. He hadn't been

afraid, he'd been exhilarated, full of daring. They were going to spirit him back to Russia. Pumped full of drugs, suffering from some "illness" that his wife would certify, and flown home. Thinking of Irina Volkova made Lucy swallow, as if that steely grip was round her throat, the thumb seeking a pressure point while she choked for breath. If she'd faltered, not found the heavy box with her groping hand . . . she shivered.

A straitjacket, Irina had threatened in Russian, not realizing she would be understood. Lucy would have been restrained, locked away as a violent patient who'd attacked the doctor. She wouldn't have been listened to when she protested. She would have been helpless, at the other woman's mercy.

And Volkov wouldn't have known what had happened. He thought she was going out to buy a new dress. He'd have waited, worrying, wondering, and finally gone back to his apartment where his wife would have been waiting for him.

It was worse than the worst nightmare dredged up from the imagination. She felt cold with horror at what might have been. It was almost six o'clock. She'd been at the wheel for so long she felt stiff and numb. Auberge des Brumes. She slowed and followed the exit sign. It might be a motel. It might be shut, it might be anything, but she liked the name. Inn of the Mists. They were near the river.

They'd skirted Paris to the west and got onto the Autoroute l'Oceane. They were aiming for the Normandy coast because they dared not risk trying to get through customs and immigration at Jersey Airport. Their best hope was a sea crossing. It was vague enough and no details had been worked out. Fugitives don't plan, she realized. They run, as we are running, and trust their luck will hold.

Volkov stirred beside her, yawned, and woke up.

"Where are we? What time is it? I've been asleep for hours."

"You needed it," she said. "I've turned off the main road.

I saw a sign for a hotel. I think it must be by the river. We're going to have a bed to sleep in and something to eat. And a bath. Darling, that's the first thing I want—a hot bath!"

It was by the river. It was small and heavily beamed, with an overhanging medieval upper story and it sat in a garden full of flowers.

"The Inn of Mists," he translated. "It's a good place for us. We can hide here forever." He kissed her cheek. "We're husband and wife?"

"Mr. and Mrs. Warren," she said. "I'll fill out the registration cards. That's if they have a room."

They had two vacancies, the patron said. She was tall and thin, quite the wrong type to appear in the dark little hallway as they went in. But she smiled and said they were lucky, not the best rooms, but she had one with single beds and one with the *matrimoniale* . . . Both on the upper floor, one with a river view, the other looking down onto the garden.

Volkov spoke up. "We will take the *matrimoniale,* Madame. The view is not important. And we'll have dinner with you. Come on, darling. It's been a tiring day. We've driven from Paris and it's so hot," he explained.

The patron smiled at him. She thought he looked interesting, rather romantic. They got a lot of stodgy English and even stodgier Germans coming in off the highway.

"If you'll fill out the registration cards," she said.

"I'll do that, if you take the bags," Lucy volunteered quickly.

"Upstairs and the fourth door on the left. Number seven. It's a nice room; you'll be comfortable. How many nights? It's not booked."

Volkov paused with the suitcases, one foot on the stairs.

"Two nights, Madame. We're not in any hurry."

Lucy followed him upstairs. The room was low, dark-beamed, with leaded windows that looked out over the deep flowing river. He was stretched out on the bed. The *matrimoniale* was not very wide.

"French people must be very small or they like lying very close together," he remarked.

"Two nights?" She shook her head. "We can't."

"Why not?" He locked his hands behind his head. "Nobody knows we're here. Now go and have your bath; it's clean and the water's hot. Then come back and I'll make love to you before dinner!"

Afterward, lying side by side in the little room, listening to the cry of sea gulls swooping outside, he said to her, "I feel so free. I can't explain it. You wouldn't understand, Lucy Warren my sweetheart, because you've never lived in a country where nobody is really free. I was in prison in Geneva too; I'd made my own gulag and sentenced myself to life. Till you came along. Now I'm so happy that I could die tonight and not care, just because I've discovered what it feels like to be with you and to be a free man for the first time. So let me be a bit reckless? Don't scold me."

"Only so long as you don't talk about dying. I wouldn't scold you about anything, my love. I want you to be happy, as happy as you can possibly be, my beautiful racing driver!"

She held his face in both hands and bent down to kiss him. His arms locked around her.

He murmured, "I love your skin. Only witches have skin like yours."

"We'll be late for dinner," Lucy whispered in his ear.

"Yes," he whispered back. "We will."

Madame had given them a table that looked out over the river. She had taken a liking to them. They were obviously in love. She smiled on them benignly as they held hands and gazed at each other. Outside the ferry passed across their window, its lights sparkling, dancing on the dark surface of the river.

The food was delicious in the simple way of good French

provincial cooking. Lucy refused wine.

"Just mineral water," she said to the young waiter.

"Not because of me?" Volkov asked her.

"No, darling," she said gently. "I'd fall asleep at the table if I drank anything. I can't believe it's real. We got away just in time. I know you think it's nonsense, but I believe God was on our side."

"Somebody was," he admitted. "We're not going to talk about it tonight. We're going to pretend that we're on holiday and we can stay here as long as we like. Till your money runs out," he teased her. "Beware of a Russian when he's happy. He's capable of anything."

"I know," she said. "But tomorrow we've got to come down to earth."

They fell asleep in each other's arms and woke late the next morning to a glorious day. As they walked along the riverbank after their breakfast, Lucy turned to him and said, "I've been thinking, darling, and I know how we're going to do it."

"Do what?" he asked.

"Get you into Jersey without anyone even knowing you're there."

It was there, staring at him in the middle of Gusev's painstaking report. Viktor Rakovsky sprang up from his desk. He jammed a finger on the intercom and snapped at his secretary.

"Get Colonel Gusev up here. Immediately!"

The name had struck him like a punch to the heart. Boris Malik. His mother's murderer. Malik had befriended Yuri Warienski in the camp. Gusev had even repeated the dreadful retort to the accusation of homosexuality. The words mumbled by Adolph Bruckner to Irina's tape machine echoed in his head. She asked her question, in that cool voice, "How many times was she raped?"

The answer: "Boris did it twice. He turned her over. . . ."
Malik had stolen the holy relic. Malik had given it to the boy
at Spittal when he knew he was being repatriated. And it was
Yuri Warienski who had offered it for sale to the jeweler in
Paris. Yuri Warienski who'd sent his daughter to find Volkov
because she had the relic. And with the relic, Volkov could set
the whole of the Ukraine alight in bloody revolt against the
Soviet government.

When his secretary buzzed through to say Colonel Gusev
was in the outer office, he composed himself. He put his private
feelings aside. He came toward Gusev. He gripped him hard
by the shoulders.

"You've done it, Leon! Your instinct was right—there *was*
another factor in the Volkov scenario. And I've just found it.
I've been investigating something else and the two themes have
come together. I know why Volkov was singled out. Sit down.
Have you ever heard of Saint Vladimir's cross?"

They were shut up together for a long time; no one was
permitted to disturb them. At the end of the session Viktor
said, "Give the search for Volkov and the Warren woman top
priority. Put 'stringers' on the French ports and airports. Cir-
culate descriptions of Volkov and the woman."

Gusev said, "We have the car rental number—those Swiss
idiots managed to get that before they lost them! And, Comrade, one other thing." He hesitated.

"What?" Viktor encouraged him.

"It can't be a coincidence that the woman took such a risk
to get his passport. His wife must have let something slip and
that set them running. I'd like to talk to her again. Somebody
must be held accountable for his escape. I know you're on
friendly terms with her."

"She may even have warned him," Viktor said slowly.
"We'll both go and see her at home. Make it a friendly visit.
I'll arrange that now. If she did warn him in some way, she'll

be regretting it enough to admit it by now. She didn't know he had a mistress.''

He had asked Gusev to leave them alone. Irina was on her feet, walking up and down, her hands twisting in front of her. She had been crying at one stage.

"I didn't tell him," she said. "I didn't tell him anything! Why won't you believe me, Viktor?"

"It's not what I believe that matters," he said. "Leon is a good interrogator. He's reasonable and he's calm. He doesn't believe you. Our superiors won't either. If you can't convince him . . ." He let the sentence die away.

She swung round to face him. "How could you think I'd be such a fool? Why would I want to warn him?"

"Because you loved him," he suggested. "And you weren't sure what we had in mind for him when he came home. After all, you loved him enough to go into exile and work for us for all that time. You did very good work, but if we don't get the cross back, it won't help you."

"Love him!" She almost spat the words out. "I gave up everything for him. Do you know what my life was like for those five years? He hated me. He taunted and abused me for what I was doing. He never touched me in all that time. Not once. He hated me so much I made him impotent! You think I wanted him to run away? I wanted him back in Russia with me! I still hoped we might get back together. I told myself that if he was at home, among his own people, he'd change, he'd understand and we could try again."

She turned her back to him, fighting down the surge of bitter grief.

"And all the time he was with another woman. Making love to her. Lying to me about where he was while he was with *her*. Planning to leave me and go off with her." She turned back and faced him. "I had something prepared to give him.

It simulates a mild fit. I'd have been able to sedate him and fly him home."

After a little silence, Viktor said, "I believe you, Irina. But whatever happens you will be censured. I can't guarantee what form it'll take. You may be suspended from practice. You'll certainly lose your old job at the Lenin Institute."

She said in a harsh voice, "You mean I'll be sent to some provincial hospital to work? Dealing with common lunatics in some God-forsaken hole?"

He said truthfully, "That might be the outcome. I'll do my best for you, but I can't promise anything. It all depends on finding him and getting our hands on that relic."

"My life is ruined," she said slowly. "Now my career is finished. Viktor, what are you going to do when you find them?"

"Kill them both. Bring the cross back to Russia," he said.

"Let me do it."

He stared at her. "You're crazy. That's impossible."

"I've been thinking about it," she said slowly. "Ever since I got home, I've been thinking of finding Dimitri and that woman. You want them dead and you want the cross. Let me suggest something to you. Why not let your Colonel Gusev hear it. A witness is always a good thing."

Gusev and Rakovsky sat facing Irina. She was very calm now, her eyes hard and bright. Gusev thought her the most dangerous sight he'd seen in a very long association with trained killers. But she wasn't trained, that was the stumbling block. She was a doctor with a little basic training in handling unpredictable patients, but she had no other skills. Except her knowledge of drugs. He leaned a little forward, paying more attention as she talked.

"It's got to be an accident," Irina said. "A murder would be attributed to the KGB. That's not our image anymore. Isn't that so? Isn't that why a lot of people have got away with things when we'd have crushed them flat a few years ago?"

"Yes," Viktor admitted.

"So why not let someone handle it who isn't a professional? A woman. Who'd think a woman would be involved?"

"You weren't very successful in dealing with Warren," Gusev pointed out. "How would you cope with two of them?"

"I wouldn't," Irina said. She reached for the cigarettes on the table, lit one, and inhaled deeply. "I wouldn't do anything myself. I'd take someone with me for that. I told you, I've been thinking about it. I have a man who would do exactly what was needed. Exactly what I told him to do. And enjoy it."

"Tell us," Viktor said. "Who is this man?"

"The only survivor of 'Spartacus.'" She glanced at Viktor then at the impassive colonel who'd done nothing but put obstacles in her way. "Ten years ago," she said, "we ran a series of experiments at the Institute. We selected certain criminal types with a history of psychopathic violence and a talent for survival in the worst of the labor camps, and exposed them to reeducation and programming. My professor thought of the project and called it Spartacus. The Romans used to choose gladiators from the most rebellious of their slaves, like Spartacus. My professor was a great authority on ancient Rome. He wanted to see if we could harness their antisocial tendencies into the service of the State. I believe Andropov supported the idea."

"And it worked?" Gusev inquired. "I never heard of it."

"Only in some cases," Irina admitted. "Most of them went insane and had to be destroyed. About twenty responded satisfactorily. Some of these were sent back to the camps where they disposed of anyone who encouraged resistance. The rest were given special tasks. A few who survived were allowed a limited freedom afterward. One of them is still available."

"And you could trust yourself with him?" Viktor asked. He had never heard of Spartacus. But he'd never been involved with the most sinister branch of the Security Services.

"I helped to train him," Irina explained. "He was the most remarkable example. He did very good work till the scheme was abandoned. He would do anything I told him."

"It sounds like science fiction to me," Gusev said. "I couldn't support it."

Viktor ignored him. "Why do you want to do this, Irina? Personal reasons?"

"No," she said coldly. "Professional. If I solve the problem satisfactorily, my career won't suffer. I'll resume my post at the Institute. That would be the deal."

"If you solve it, and bring back that cross," Viktor said, "I'll recommend you for a professorship."

On the way back to Djerjhinsky Square, Gusev said, "You're going to authorize it?"

"Yes," Rakovsky answered. "I am. I believe she'll do it. She and her tame monster. She didn't warn Volkov; I'm sure of that. I'm going to give her the chance. I want you to help her any way she wants."

Gusev felt it his duty to make one more objection. He admired Rakovsky and he was anxious on his own behalf. He was sorry he'd been dragged into what seemed a high-risk solution to a problem requiring a team of skilled professionals.

He said, "Comrade, have you thought of the risk you are taking? The personal risk if this goes wrong? You could be charged with treason if Volkov escapes us. I have to point this out." He coughed awkwardly. "And I'm an accessory," he added.

Viktor shook his head. "You don't think I'd let Irina go without backup? We'll have our experts in place the moment we know where Volkov and Warren are hiding—ready to deal with them if Irina fails. And to deal with her if she succeeds."

Gusev drew a sharp breath. Viktor went on, gazing calmly

out the window as they drove fast down the reserved central lane into Red Square.

"A jealous wife who kills her unfaithful husband and his mistress. She'll be the perfect alibi for us. And then kills herself. Our team will dispose of her Frankenstein, whoever he is, and bring back the cross. A crime of passion with a Soviet dissident and his lover as the victims. The Western media will love it."

"It is a masterpiece of forward planning." Leon Gusev apologized. "I was being very stupid, but I thought she was a friend of yours . . ."

"I have known Irina for a long time, but I have no friends, Leon, when it comes to the safety of my country. Remember that in the future."

The car drew up outside the entrance to the Lubianka. They went up in the elevator together.

"I'll come to your office," Viktor said. "I want to ask your computer some questions."

"Well, Leon, there we have it. All the pieces fit the puzzle. There's the heart of the conspiracy. That's why the anti-Soviets are gathering from all over the world. Volkov appears and produces the holy relic. Think of it! The press conferences, the propaganda machine getting into gear in the Ukraine itself. And the hero, Volkov, returns to Russia with the whole Western media at his heels and Saint Vladimir's cross in his hand. Fifty million Ukrainians would take to the streets!" Gusev said. "It would be chaos, bloody revolution. The State would collapse. And you think that's where we'd find them?"

"I'm sure of it, even without your electronic toy," Rakovsky answered. "Warienski had kept the cross hidden. His daughter would never have risked bringing it to Geneva. She and Volkov are making for that Island to get the cross so he can declare himself in public. Concentrate your people there. As soon as they're sighted, we must be ready."

"He has no visa," Gusev pointed out. "He can't get into the U.K. without one."

Rakovsky smiled sourly. "He can if he goes by sea," he said. "That's how I'd do it. Let them get there, Leon. Watch the airports, but do nothing, even if they're identified. Have our team waiting for them in Jersey. Our first objective is to get that cross. In our hands, it could *unite* the Slavic ethnic republics under one leader."

A car met Irina at Sverdlovsk Airport and drove the short distance from the big Siberian city to the village on the western side of the Bashkir River. It was a poor place, a huddle of rough one-story buildings connected by tracks that were frozen solid in winter and choking with dust at that time of year. The inhabitants scratched a meager living from the land, growing a sparse crop of cereal, keeping the mangy hens that roamed scavenging for food in the yellow earth, cutting wood to keep warm against the savage winters. It was isolated, primitive, and an earthly paradise for anyone released from the gulag and allowed to live there.

She had christened him Remus, because he might well have been suckled by a wolf. He had no name, only the number that proved he existed. When she saw him first he had forgotten his name. He was wary as a wild animal, cunning, vicious in his determination to survive.

She hadn't seen him for ten years. She told the driver to wait and covered her nose with a handkerchief against the acrid smell of human waste. There was no drainage system. The people living there dug holes in the ground.

It was the nearest of the little wooden buildings; a woman in the long skirt and shawl of the region directed her with a wave. The foreigner lived over there.

He was eating when Irina came through the door. A woman, the one he'd chosen to live with him, was serving him from a bowl, standing beside him while he ate. The place was clean; the earth floor swept, the pine table scrubbed white.

"Remus?" she said, and he stopped with the spoon to his mouth, squinting at her. "How are you?" she said and came toward him.

He put the plate down, scrambled to his feet, knocking the stool over. The woman shrank back, receding into the background.

"*Matiushka! Matiushka,* is it you?"

Little Mother. By the time Irina had finished with him, that was what he called her. He peered closer and his mouth split wide open in a delighted grin. She noticed that he had lost several teeth.

"It *is* you!"

He stood towering over her, still so tall and built like a great tree in spite of his age. He bowed down from the waist. She held out her hand, smiling at him.

"You look well, Remus," she said. "Have you been well?"

"Well enough. She looks after me. I beat her if she doesn't!" He laughed like a bear grunting, deep in his throat. He turned and said to her in the dialect, "Get the lady some goat's milk to drink, you lazy bitch." To Irina he said, "Sit down, please. I have a nice chair. I made it myself. She'll bring something for you after your journey."

He hadn't changed, she decided. His response to her was the same mixture of respect and humble obedience. For such a brute he had become doglike in his dependence. She sat down in his chair. There was a big cushion on the floor, covered in the bright regional embroidery.

"Bring me the stool," he shouted over his shoulder, and the woman scurried forward, setting it for him to sit on.

"Does she understand?" Irina asked him.

He shook his grizzled head. "She speaks only dialect," he said. "This is an honor, *Matiushka.* A great honor." He beamed his broken smile at her. He watched her anxiously. She had always been a goddess figure who must be revered and obeyed and never made angry. She took the cup of goat's milk; the smell revolted her. She put the cup down and said, "Are you happy here, Remus?"

"Very happy," he said eagerly. "I have food, a warm stove, and the woman. She's a good woman. I don't have to beat her often."

His records said they'd had two children. She saw no sign of them.

She said, "How are your children, Remus?"

"They got sick and died," he said flatly. There wasn't a gleam of emotion in the deep-set eyes. "Last year. There was a lot of sickness here. She won't have any more. She's too old."

"I'm sorry," Irina said. "But you didn't catch the sickness?"

"No. I'm strong. I've always been strong," he said.

Irina nodded. "Yes. I remember how strong you were. Would you like a younger woman? If this one is too old?"

He looked over his shoulder at the swaddled figure, standing mute against the wall. Irina missed the expression on his face. It would have surprised her.

"No," he said after a moment. "I don't want a new one. She's a good woman."

"Well, then, would you like to move to a new place?"

His brow furrowed. He shrank into himself. He looked like an old man.

"What have I done wrong, *Matiushka*?"

"Nothing, nothing," she soothed. "I'm very pleased with you. You did good service, Remus. That's why I've come to see you. I'd like to put you to work again. Just once more. Then you can move away from here to somewhere not so isolated. Wouldn't you like that?"

"I'm content," he insisted. "But . . . yes. Yes, I'd be glad to live nearer my own people. They all speak dialect here. What do you want me to do?"

"Come on a long journey with me," she said quietly. "Forget about your life here. Speak Russian again. Dress like a Russian. And punish two people who are enemies of the State. You'll be rewarded. I'll send you to a nice village a thousand miles south. No more winters here, Remus. What do you say?"

He looked up at her. "I haven't forgotten my skills," he said. "Just show me the traitors, *Matiushka*."

"Good," Irina stood up. He was on his feet immediately, waiting respectfully. "Now you're coming back with me. You won't need anything. Say nothing to the woman."

He pointed to the cup of milk. "She can take this away and drink it herself. It's good when you get used to it."

He spoke briefly in dialect and the woman did as she was told. He followed Irina out into the dusty heat. His Siberian wife lurked by the window out of sight. He had told her he was going into the city and would bring her back a necklace. She watched impassively as the car started up, its wheels churning more dust, and disappeared out of sight.

They landed at Sheremetyevo Airport. Irina had bought him a suit of clothes in Sverdlovsk and had him shaved by a barber. He sat like a rock in the plane throughout the long flight down. No nerves, only a mild curiosity. He ate the in-flight food ravenously. She allowed him to drink vodka. Alcohol had never disturbed him.

He said, "I'm very happy, *Matiushka*. When I've done what's needed, can I have the woman in my new village?"

For a moment Irina hesitated. He had no emotional attachments. He hadn't blinked when he talked of the death of his children. He had never loved anything or anyone. That had made him so receptive to the programming.

"Why do you want her?" she asked. "There are other women."

"She suits me," he said. "She knows my ways."

Irina nodded. He was over seventy. At that age he wouldn't want to be bothered by a change of companion. He had his slave. Let him keep her.

He was lodged in a house on the outskirts of Moscow. Irina briefed him. She was in charge of him.

"You are a Pole, Remus. Your home is in Krakow and you have a Polish passport and an entry visa into England. Your name is Stanislaus Szpiganovitch. You are visiting friends. I will speak for you," she said. "But you must have the right answers ready if an official asks you. And you understand Polish, don't you?" The Ukrainian dialect was very similar to the Polish language. "And I am your daughter," she went on. "I am Polish too. My name is Marie Szpiganovitch and I am keeping you company on the journey. We are a simple Polish father and daughter from Krakow."

He laughed in his throat, growling at the joke of it all.

"*Matiushka*," he rumbled. "How can my Little Mother be my daughter?"

"Because I say so, Remus," she reminded him and he agreed at once.

"Yes, yes. As you say."

He didn't make any more jokes. He looked hunted and confused because she wasn't pleased with him. *It was a marvelous experiment*, Irina thought. *A pity it had only been effective with so few of the intake*. After ten years all it took was a look and a change of tone to bring him to instant obedience.

"This is Remus," Irina said.

He got up and bowed. Viktor nodded to him. He was standing at attention, like a soldier or a long-term prisoner. He was fit and tough for his age. He hadn't gone to seed in his sojourn in the Siberian village. The eyes were guarded, Viktor noticed. Whatever he thought or felt was carefully blanked out.

And he followed Irina's every movement.

"You're going on a journey," he said, speaking to the man.

"Yes, Comrade Excellency."

Viktor raised his eyebrows in surprise at the form of address.

"That's how we addressed all persons in authority," she explained. "Didn't we, Remus? It impressed them with the difference in their status and ours, you see. Remus has been one of our best pupils. Tell Comrade Excellency about what you did in Bashkir."

He actually grinned at them. "I got rid of a wasps' nest," he said.

"Muslims who were stirring up trouble," Irina explained. "It was the start of the fundamentalist movement; Iran had been taken over and we had copycat movements here."

"I remember," Viktor said. "I remember there was trouble in Bashkir and Azerbaijan."

"Tell him about the wasps' nest," Irina prompted.

"There was a mosque," Remus said. He rubbed his nose with a thick forefinger. "At Birsk, I think that was the name of the place. They were all meeting there, the men in one part and the women upstairs. They're made of wood, those mosques.

"It was quite easy. I jammed the main doors shut. Lucky I'm strong. It was a heavy wedge more like a tree trunk. Then I just threw a couple of Molotovs through the window. Like we did in the war with enemy tanks. It's the only way to get rid of wasps. Smoke them out."

Viktor heard him chuckle.

"Remus eliminated the leadership that night," she said. "We were very pleased with him."

"Killing doesn't trouble you?" Viktor asked.

"I kill enemies of the State," he said. "That's good."

"Yes," Viktor agreed after a pause. "Yes, it is good. Irina, could we speak for a moment? I wish you luck," he said. He couldn't bring himself to offer a hand to the man. He remembered that fire at Birsk. Over two hundred people had been burned to death. It was attributed to a rival Muslim faction and the fundamentalist movement in Bashkir collapsed.

Outside the room he said to her, "And that is the product of your experiment? He is a monster."

"He was born with all those tendencies," she said. "We merely made use of the material. As you are doing now." Her tone was sharp.

"As you are," he corrected her. "This is your suggestion. After this is over, I want him eliminated."

"I thought you might," Irina shrugged. "I didn't think you were so sensitive, Viktor. You knew what we were doing at the Lenin Institute. You didn't object to my work at the Amtel. You certainly won't object if Remus kills Volkov and Warren and I come back with your precious cross."

"I shall be the first to congratulate you," Viktor said and forced himself to smile. "I didn't mean to criticize, Irina. It was my first encounter with a mass murderer. Now, I've approved the cover story and the plan. Gusev's done an excellent job."

Stanislaus and Marie Szpiganovitch traveling from Krakow in Poland to pay their respects to the daughter of his old friend, Yuri Warren. With the strong religious and ethnic ties between Poland and the Ukraine, it was entirely credible. The papers were perfection: passports, visas, the best products of the forgery section.

Remus carried no weapons. Irina said that he knew how to use his hands better than most marksmen used a gun. He knew what was expected of him. Two enemies of the State. It might be necessary to persuade them to give up a piece of State property that they had stolen and he was very good at that too.

The wasps' nest at Bashkir was the climax of his service. He had committed half-a-dozen individual murders during the time he was on special duties. She didn't mention that to Rakovsky. His squeamishness irritated her.

"All we're waiting for now," she said, "is news."

"We expect it any moment," he answered. "Her house on the Island is being watched. You and Remus will leave for Warsaw tonight. As soon as we hear they've arrived on the island, you fly direct to Paris and by charter plane to Jersey. It's been organized down to the last detail."

And the trail has been laid both ways, Rakovsky thought, saying good-bye to her and setting out for his office. *If you succeed, our man will move in immediately. Gusev has sent a very good operator out for the job. If you fail or anything goes wrong, he'll be there and take over. Neither you nor that monstrous product of your perverted medical science will come back from this alive. The wheel would turn full circle.*

All those years ago his father had taken the same route through the Moscow streets with Ivan driving, carrying the holy relic as a bargaining counter for his family's life. He, as a little child, had seen it, glowing red and gold on the white comforter on his mother's bed. And sketched it secretly.

He had made a pilgrimage to the place where his mother and his brother, Stefan, were buried. A quiet spot under the trees near the old house, which was long destroyed. He had marked their grave with a simple stone obelisk, engraved with their names. From that house of death the cross had traveled with their murderer, all the way to the camp at Spittal and to an orphaned boy who'd been given it by a man going to execution.

Nearly full circle. He drove up to the steps of the formidable building just as his father Alexei had done, to plead with Lepkin.

The cross of Saint Vladimir would come back to Russia when Russia needed it most. To unify, not divide, as he had said. He dismissed his car and went inside. He had enough work to keep him in his office until late that evening. A lesser, personal matter came to mind.

Muller. What progress was he making with Bruckner's widow about the Fabergé desk set? He dictated a short memo reminding him.

"No," Volkov protested. "I can't let you do that. It's too dangerous. We'll think of another way."

"There isn't one," Lucy insisted. "If we fly you'll be stopped and you know what that means. Immigration is very strict with people coming from the Continent. We wouldn't get away with it on the ferry because all foot passengers have to produce their passports. If I had a Jersey registered car, I'd chance it, but not otherwise. And there's nothing to worry about—I've made the crossing dozens of times."

"With your father, not on your own," he said. "No, Lucy. What happens if something goes wrong? If there's a storm?"

"Darling," she said gently, "you don't know the first thing about sailing or the sea. I've been handling a boat since I was a child. I'll make the crossing back in a few hours. All you've got to do is wait for me in Saint Malo. Daddy and I sailed over once or twice a month. I could do it blindfolded!"

They'd been arguing for most of the morning. She couldn't convince him that she was an experienced sailor and that the trip from Saint Catherine's Bay to Saint Malo was a simple excursion, not a dangerous crossing where her life was in jeopardy.

"You'll see how easy it is when we sail back—I love the sea. There's nothing to be frightened of. Now let's go back to our hotel and have some lunch. You said it was a holiday, so don't let's spoil it arguing."

In the end he gave way, but he was unhappy and he kept referring to the trip, asking questions that made no sense. Supposing the engine failed on the boat? It wouldn't, and anyway it had a sail, she explained patiently. What if she hit a rock and started to sink? Then she'd drown, she agreed, except there weren't any rocks in the English Channel, so would he please stop being silly about it.

The next morning they set off again. The brief happy interlude was over; they said good-bye to the patron, and suddenly Lucy's mood clouded with the old fear so far kept at bay. She'd been too anxious and too busy making plans to feel afraid, but now the plans were made. As they drove the long miles past the lovely city of Chartres, toward Rennes, she felt increasingly uneasy. It was still very hot. Volkov was subdued; he couldn't come to terms with what she was going to do and it depressed him. They didn't talk much on the journey northward to Saint Malo.

The charming port was full of boats: sailing yachts, motor cruisers, ferry boats plying across to the Channel Islands. She made him walk along the quayside, pointing out the different types of craft, trying to reassure him.

"That's like our boat," she said, showing him a smart little single master. "She's lovely, so easy to handle. Now, let's find a pension where we can stay the night, and then I'll take you somewhere for a marvelous cheap dinner. The fish soup is wonderful."

"I'm not hungry," he said. "I can't eat when I'm worried."

"You and my father," she said. "You'd have got on so well. You're just as bad as he was. I said to him once, 'Why do Russians cry when they're happy,' and he said, 'Because we enjoy it more than laughing!' Please trust me, darling. I know what I'm doing."

He cheered up over dinner. He held her hand and admitted that he'd never even learned to swim, so naturally he thought the sea was dangerous. And she was right, the fish soup was delicious. He'd been ungrateful and ungracious, but then he loved her *so* much. He made love that night in the stuffy pension bedroom as if they were facing a long separation.

Lucy caught the early morning hydrofoil to Saint Helier. She had given Volkov money and told him to buy shorts and a sweatshirt in one of the tourist shops, and to wait for her on the quayside. He could amuse himself walking round the town till about four o'clock. She expected to reach the harbor at about that time, given a smooth crossing. And it would be smooth. There wasn't a ruffle of breeze on the water.

She paid the pension before she left and posted the keys of the rented car back to the Geneva hire firm. They had left it in a public car park. He insisted on coming to see her off. At the last moment when the sailing was announced, he tried again.

"Why don't I come with you. I'm sure I could slip through."

"No," Lucy said. "You promised last night, Dimitri. Go ashore."

Reluctantly he did. She saw him standing, watching as the hydrofoil began to move out of the harbor.

It was a simple plan. She went back home, picked up her boat at Saint Catherine, and sailed over to Saint Malo. Volkov sailed back with her. Anyone seeing them on board together would assume that she'd gone out for a sail with a friend. Fleets of private craft cruised round the Island and sailed across to Guernsey or Sark for a day out. Lucy was well known among the yachting enthusiasts. She could come and go without any-body suspecting anything. Least of all that she was smuggling a man over from France.

At Saint Helier she hurried to be among the first off and was waved through on a brief passport inspection and greeted by one Customs officer who was a friend.

"Hi, Lucy. Had a good holiday?"

"Yes thanks, Bob," she smiled at him.

"Sorry to hear about your father," he said. "I'll give you

a call—maybe we could have dinner."

"That'd be nice," she said and slipped away from him.

She took a taxi to her home. The Island looked so welcoming and green, with its abundance of lush flowers and the immense hydrangea bushes that grew everywhere, nodding their pink heads like friends welcoming her back. I've missed it so much, she thought. Dear God, it's so wonderful to feel safe, not to look over my shoulder anymore. Just let me get him here and we can shut the door on the outside world at Saint Catherine's tonight.

The watcher camped on the hill above the house saw movement and focused his binoculars. They honed in on the car arriving and the girl getting out, paying the fare, and unlocking the front door. The watcher carried a shortwave transmitter. He signaled across to his contact at Carteret on the French mainland. It was the closest shoreline to the Island.

"Target One has arrived. No sign of Target Two. Will report at 0300 hours."

Lucy opened the windows; there was a faint musty smell in the rooms. Dead flowers wilted in a stale vase. She threw them out. She went upstairs to her father's room and opened the shutters and the windows wide to let in the sunshine and fresh sea air. Volkov would sleep there with her tonight.

She changed into shorts, shirt, and a visored yachting cap, slipped rubber-soled plimsolls on her feet. She filled one thermos with coffee and another with water, and took some food from the deep freeze for their evening meal, leaving the dishes to defrost. The preparations were calming; it was real to prepare for supper, more real than taking a boat out to France and bringing back a fugitive Russian. *I'm not afraid*, she told herself. *The trip is nothing. It's Volkov fussing and fretting over me that's made me nervous for the first time in my life at going out alone.*

She packed the two thermoses in a canvas bag, looked round once more at the house where she had grown up and been so happy. And so sad that day her father left on his final journey across the lovely island. Then she locked the door behind her and began the descent down through the garden and across the grassy slope to the shingle beach, with its outcrops of massive rocks and the cluster of small boats swinging gently at anchor by the jetty.

The watcher saw her ease the single-mast motor yacht out of its berth. The boat was engine powered, its sail furled. It left a thin spread of white foam as it headed out to sea. He went inside his tent and sent another radio message.

It was a windless, sunny morning, without a ripple on the surface of the sea. A perfect day for motoring, giving her a good chance to reach her rendezvous at the time she had told Dimitri. Lucy had never sailed the sloop alone for any distance, but she knew the waters and before she set out, she had determined a navigation plan to take account of the wind or the lack of it, the tides, distances, and landfalls. She and her father had gone through the routine so many times over the years. She felt confident. She was well equipped with IMRAYs, folding charts, and instruments giving water depth, speed, and distance sailed.

At midmorning the west and then southeasterly tides would help carry them round the terrifying Minquier Plateau. At a steady speed and in favorable weather, she would reach Saint Malo by early evening, and mingling with the flotilla of French and foreign boats returning to Saint Malo and Saint Servan for the night, slip in unnoticed. No yellow Q flag would fly from the mast on this trip. Lucy checked her watch. It was time to set off.

She climbed down to the neat little cabin and readied for sea. She opened the sea cock under the port quarter berth to pass cooling water through the engine, turned the battery isolator switch, came back up to the cockpit, and pressed the starter button.

The engine was not really intended to make passage, but in the flat calm water there was no choice. It was a tough little engine, and it would cruise at a steady six knots until a breeze picked them up.

She had decided to take the Violet Channel to round the rock-strewn and hazardous southeast tip of Jersey. At last the Conchiere beacon was safely astern and she set her course, west, southwesterly.

It was a glorious day; she was safe and confident in her boat, no thought of danger occurred to her as the landmarks of the Island rapidly blurred. The engine thumped away, and at last she noticed some cat's-paws of wind starting to shimmer across the water. That meant an onshore breeze coming up, drawn to the warming mass of the French mainland.

Lucy drank some coffee. It was going so well. Fortune, like the sun overhead, was shining on her. The hours passed, and she set a new southerly course for the Saint Malo approaches. She thought of Dimitri waiting; sulking, anxious. The mental picture made her smile. In so many ways he was an innocent, despite his intellectual brilliance. It made her love him even more. One day, she promised herself, I'll teach him to sail. As she skirted the rocks there was a sudden change in the engine note. It began to cough and stutter.

"Oh, God," she exclaimed, "Don't you dare die on me . . ." But there were more coughs, then a final wheeze. Then nothing. Silence. Just the slip-slap of wavelets on the hull. Not a whiff of breeze.

"Get to know your engine," her father had insisted. "You can't rely on wind if anything goes wrong." She cranked the engine on the starter. Nothing. It wasn't overheating; she'd checked the fuel before setting off. There was plenty in hand for the trip. *Stay calm*, she told herself. *Go down and see if you can find the problem.*

In the engine compartment her worst fear proved to be

true. Pinkish froth and air bubbles swirled in the glass bowl of the fuel filter.

There was a loose joint in the fuel line. Even if she bled the line and restarted the engine, it would die on her in a few minutes.

She went back up to the cockpit, and she forgot about the engine. The east-flowing tide was setting her into the rocks. On the horizon a low bank of thick sea fog was looming, coming closer.

She was drifting toward shipwreck and drowning. Whatever she did, this was no place to linger. Better to keep starting the engine and pray that it lasted long enough to take her near a saving breeze.

She bled the fuel system, started up; the little sloop began to move. The rocks receded. The engine stopped again. She repeated the routine. A little progress, another half-mile or so; a westerly wind came up across her starboard quarter. "Thank God, thank God," Lucy prayed aloud. As the engine spluttered into silence, she managed to raise enough of the mainsail to swing the boat head to wind. She had to pull it to the top of the mast before the freshening wind laid her abeam. She had to find the strength. Dimitri was waiting helplessly at Saint Malo, watching for her. She would find it. She pulled with all her strength, her heart bursting with the effort. But the mainsheet had snagged and the boom couldn't run out freely. In desperation, Lucy tried to make fast the halyard round a cleat, but the rope slipped in her hands and ran free. The sharp cry of agony was caught by the wind and swept away. The speeding rope had seared and burned her palms; a trickle of blood ran down her wrists. Tears of pain blinded her. *She had to get the mainsail up.* At least high enough to make the halyard fast round a cleat.

Once more she exerted her strength and willed herself to

endure the pain in her hands. It was done. She swayed, sick with agony and shock.

Then she grabbed the tiller, held the boat head to wind and managed to unfurl the genoa, holding the boat motionless. She stumbled down below to find antiseptic ointment and bandages for her hands. They were raw and bleeding. She was shaking as she dressed them, awkwardly, wincing as the dressings went onto the ruptured skin. Her right hand was the worst. She could use the left with difficulty. She found painkillers and swallowed them. She would get there. Slowly and late, but she would get to Saint Malo and find Dimitri. She couldn't even think beyond that.

He had been walking the length of the quayside since half-past four. He didn't know what to look for; a single mast—a small boat. She'd promised to wave when she sailed in, as close to the rendezvous point as she could manage. A half-a-dozen times, Volkov had started up at the sight of some small craft, thinking it must be hers.

But there was no familiar figure among those who came into the harbor and soon there were no boats arriving. She was three hours late. He had left the café long ago; he sat on the damp jetty in his new shorts and the only sweatshirt he could find that didn't shriek Saint Malo across the chest in fluorescent colors, the smell of oil and seawater and refuse stung his nostrils. A rail-thin cat with hungry eyes stared hopefully at him from under a seat. He had nothing to feed it with. He felt sick.

Something had gone wrong. His instincts had been right. She hadn't made the crossing back. He sat there staring out across the forest of masts, listening to the transistor music blaring across the water and the noise of people on board enjoying themselves—calling out in the warm evening, drinking on deck, preparing to go ashore and eat.

A Brittany ferry loomed to his left, waiting to set sail. He could see lights along her sides. It was dusk now. Soon it would be dark. A group of small children scurried toward him, kicking a ball. They saw the cat and gathered round the seat. The animal crouched down, ears flattened. One boy found a pebble and threw it. Volkov leaped up and shouted at them in Russian to leave it alone. They stared at him, pulled faces, and ran away. He sat down and resumed his hopeless watch out to sea. In the end he couldn't bear it any longer. He went back to the café where he'd spent the afternoon drinking cups of coffee, looking at his watch as the time she was due came, passed, and lengthened into an eternity.

After five years in Geneva he spoke fluent French; he didn't even think about his accent.

"Don't talk to people, darling," Lucy had warned him. "You're such an obvious Russian, they'll look for the snow on your boots." They had to keep a low profile, blend in with all the other holiday makers and tourists. He forgot about being careful. He caught hold of one of the waiters.

"Can you tell me," he said. "I'm expecting a friend. She's so late—in a boat—has there been a storm out there?" He pointed wildly at the sea.

"Storm? Not that I've heard. I've been too busy to ask about storms." He pulled away impatiently. Some idiot ranting about a storm—as if he'd know. He was tired and fed up with serving the idlers on holiday while he ran around with their orders. He cursed Volkov under his breath.

Volkov went back to the jetty. He came close enough to one of the large cabin cruisers moored alongside it. A man and woman were sitting in deck chairs, drinking what looked like champagne. He shouted down to them.

"Excuse me. Can you help me, please?"

The man looked up with the wariness of the wealthy. The boat was flying a Dutch flag.

"What do you want?"

"My friend is missing. She was coming over in her boat

and she's hours late. Something must have happened to her. I don't know what to do!"

The man heaved up from his deck chair and came to the side.

"Have you notified the coast guard?"

"No. What is the coast guard? Where do I find it?"

The Dutchman decided that the poor fellow was not a member of the sailing fraternity. He looked desperately anxious.

His wife said quickly to him, "He's been walking up and down for ages. I noticed him. Dirk, hadn't you better go and help him?"

"Wait a minute," Volkov heard him say. "I'll come ashore. You'd better report it. I'll show you where to go."

He climbed up onto the port side and leaped onto the jetty.

"What sort of boat? How long is she overdue?"

"I don't know," Volkov said. "I know nothing about damned boats. She said four o'clock. It's after eight. I begged her not to do it."

He wiped his hand across his face.

"Where are you both from?" the Dutchman asked.

"Geneva," Volkov answered.

"She may have been delayed. You can't tell. Does she have a radio?"

"I don't know," Volkov said desperately. "It has an engine and a sail. She told me. That's all I know."

"Come on then, we'd better put in a report and see if anyone's picked her up. It's probably engine failure and she's just drifting with the tide. It's crazy not to have a radio."

He saw the look in Volkov's eyes. He clapped him on the shoulder.

"Don't worry; I'm sure she's all right. Just sitting out there cursing. The sea's like a millpond and the forecast is fine. Don't worry," he said again.

But the man wasn't listening. He had turned for one last look and there was a small boat, its sail bellied out in a light breeze and there was a woman at the helm. The Dutchman followed his point of vision.

"That's a single master," he said. "It's coming in. Is that your friend? It's a girl all right!"

Volkov was sprinting down the jetty. He followed. Now the figure guiding the craft slowly and skillfully among the anchored yachts was waving and the crazy fellow was waving back and shouting. He was jumping up and down, both arms in the air.

"It's her, it's her. Lucy! Lucy!"

"All's well, then," the Dutchman said. He smiled and shook his head. They might come from Geneva, but that lunatic certainly wasn't Swiss. "You'd better come and join us for a drink to celebrate," he said. "She's a good sailor, your friend. She's handling that little craft very well with all this traffic round her. I'm glad everything's okay. See you in a few minutes."

"Thank you, thank you," Volkov said.

When the Dutchman climbed back on board his yacht he told his wife the man had tears in his eyes.

"What a drama," he said. "God knows what the coast guard would have made of him. There they are. Hey, come and have a glass of champagne with us!"

They were walking back with their arms round each other. He reached up and helped the girl down onto the deck. Her companion was not at all sure footed.

His wife came forward. "I'm Beta, and this is Dirk. Come and sit down and tell us all about it. Your poor boyfriend was convinced you'd been drowned!"

She looked sunburned and exhausted, the kind-hearted Dutch lady decided. She gave her a glass of champagne.

"Here, this'll make you feel better. What happened?"

Volkov had his arm round her. She was trembling with fatigue.

"My engine conked out," she explained. "I couldn't get the bloody thing to go for more than a few minutes at a time. I tried everything. I just sat there drifting; there wasn't any wind. Then the wind did come up."

The older man shook his head. "Putting up sail is tough enough for a man," he said. "How the hell did you manage on your own?" He saw that her hands were bandaged. There was a blood stain on the right palm.

"Beta, I think we need the first-aid kit. You'd better let my wife look at your hands. What happened?"

"I let go the halyard," she explained. "I'm all right really."

"Where have you come from?" he asked her.

Lucy decided there was no point in lying. They were kind, friendly people. All sailors had danger in common, from the owner of the largest oceangoing yacht to the smallest dingy.

"From Jersey," she said. "It was my fault. I haven't been out for a while. I didn't check the engine. I'd plenty of petrol and that's all I looked at. We were sailing back today." She turned and laid her head on Volkov's shoulder. "I'm so sorry. So sorry. You had all those hours of worry for nothing!"

"Come below and let me see what you've done to your-self," exclaimed Beta. "Rope burns can be very nasty. And, Dirk, we can get our crewman to look at that engine first thing in the morning. We can't offer you a bunk, we only sleep three, but we can feed you. I hope you'll have some dinner with us." She spoke to Volkov. "Please, help yourself to a glass. The bottle's right there."

"I don't drink," he said. "But thank you. Thank you for asking us to eat, but I think we've been enough trouble already."

"No trouble," was the answer. "You're staying."

The Dutch couple walked back to the little boat with them.

They were a curious pair, impossible to place, but there was something touching about their relationship. It was nice, they agreed afterward, to see people so much in love, when so many treated each other with casual selfishness. They said good night, promising to send the crewman up to look at the engine. There was no way the girl could sail back, even with help, with her hands in that state. They bunked down in the bottom of the boat; there was a spare tarpaulin in the locker; Volkov pulled it out and they lay on that. He held her in his arms, her head resting on his shoulder.

"I thought I'd lost you," he said. "Your poor hands!"

"They're all right," Lucy said. "I've gone soft living in Geneva, that's the trouble. It's just blisters, they'll heal up very quickly." She closed her eyes; she was numb with exhaustion. "I kept thinking, what is he doing? He must be going crazy, thinking something's happened. I was terrified you'd start talking to people and give yourself away! That's what gave me the strength to sail here on my own. I held on to those bloody ropes because I had to get back to you. All our plans, the relic . . . Everything was at stake and I'd been careless and overused the engine. You had no money, no one to turn to. I knelt down in that bloody boat and prayed, my darling. I prayed for a wind. And thank God, it came."

He heard her sigh and knew she'd fallen asleep. He smoothed a strand of hair back from her face. At last, lulled by the gentle movement of the boat and the slap of little waves against the sides, he fell asleep beside her.

They took their seats on the flight from Warsaw to Paris. It was a long journey. Irina didn't talk to Remus. There was nothing to say. He was passive. He soon slept and even when they hit turbulence and the airplane lost height, he didn't wake.

She let her thoughts roam ahead. They'd hire a car when they landed in Jersey. They'd been booked into a modest bed and breakfast hotel in Saint Helier. She'd been shown the War-ren house on a map of the Island. It was secluded, on a hilltop overlooking the sea, in four acres of grounds. The woman had been seen by their watcher. The last report said she'd taken a boat out. That had been the signal for Irina and Remus to set off for Paris. Viktor had been right. The woman was going to smuggle Volkov in by sea from France.

She tried to imagine Dimitri's reaction when she surprised them. His face wouldn't come into focus. She tried to relish the scene when the man beside her put them out of action, and Volkov watched helplessly while he tortured the woman to make her give up the cross. She could see that in her mind's eye. But not the sequel. Not the moment when she gave the order, "Kill them, Remus."

Kill *him* . . . Would she be proof against him, even now? Was her love completely dead or merely paralyzed by hurt and jealousy? She couldn't answer that. She had staked everything on her promise to Viktor and the greater authority he repre-sented. "I'll bring back the cross and I'll get rid of them both."

I won't know if I can do it, she thought. *I won't be sure until I see him. Till the moment comes.*

They landed at Charles de Gaulle at two in the afternoon. By five-thirty the charter flight taxied to a halt on the runway at Saint Peter's, Jersey. Irina signed for and took possession of the Ford Fiesta.

"You get in the back," she directed and he smiled and muttered, "Yes, *Matiushka.*"

He smelled acridly of sweat and she didn't want him close to her. He looked out the window. She watched him in the driving mirror. He was showing interest in their surroundings.

"This is a nice place," he said. "Lots of trees and grass."

"It's just a little island where the rich come to escape paying taxes," she spoke sharply. "If they were Russians they'd be punished!"

He didn't speak for the rest of the drive. The bed and breakfast hotel was in a side street. There a sign outside said St. Margaret. It was a modern two-story house with a fine garden. Even Irina noticed the profusion of flowers and shrubs.

The air smelled salty from a breeze coming in off the sea. It reminded her of the Crimea, where she and Volkov used to take holidays when they first married. The same warm climate, the lush growth, the tang of the ocean. She registered and they were shown to their rooms.

"Where's the bathroom?" she asked.

The proprietress pointed down the corridor.

"Second door on the left. It's marked. Toilet is next to it."

"Thank you," Irina said.

She spoke to him in Russian.

"Go and bathe yourself, Remus. Then wait for me in your room."

She sent downstairs after the woman.

"Is it possible to get something to eat for my father? He's tired after the journey. Just bread and cheese would do."

The Jersey woman smiled. "Of course, dear. I'll find something for him. Come a long way, have you?"

"All the way from Poland," Irina said. "That's where we live."

"My goodness, that is a long way. On holiday, are you?" She was curious and Irina thought it best to satisfy her.

"We had friends who came here and they said how nice it was. My father wanted to come. He's never traveled before. I thought we'd do it properly and go on to England."

"Oh, yes, you weren't allowed to go anywhere, were you, while those Communists were in Poland. Don't worry, I'll bring a bite of supper up to him. Would he like some beer? I've got some in the fridge?

Irina managed a chilly smile. "I'm sure he would. That's

very kind of you. He doesn't speak a word of English, I'm afraid."

"That doesn't matter. We'll manage. You speak it very well."

"Languages were compulsory in our State schools," Irina said. "We all learned English and one other European language. Otherwise we weren't considered fit for higher education. I'll be back later."

She drove back into the center of Saint Helier. There was a small fish restaurant just beyond the port, called the Lobster Pot. *Not very original*, she thought.

The woman's remarks had needled her. Ignorant, prejudiced little bourgeois. It soothed Irina's irritation to imagine her fussing round Remus. Little did she know what kind of man he was! She parked the car and went into the restaurant. It was dim and cool, festooned with nets and plastic lobsters hanging from the roof. She couldn't bear the idea of eating with him, sharing a table. And it would upset the balance of her position. She was exalted, he was lowly. Mistress and slave didn't take food together. And there should be a message waiting for her.

She asked for a table and then said, looking round, "I was supposed to meet someone here. I don't see him."

The waitress said, "There was a gentleman, but he said he couldn't wait. Are you Mrs. Spigo? Sorry, I can't pronounce it."

"Yes, I am," Irina said quickly.

"Then he left a message for you. If you'd like to sit there and have a look at the menu I'll go and get it. The crayfish are very good tonight."

Irina slit the envelope. It was a scrap of paper written in French—from the watcher on the hill by the Warren house: "Nobody's come back. Do nothing till I contact you at the hotel. I'll leave a message from Rudi if they're in the house."

"Everything all right?" the waitress asked her.

Irina crumpled the paper and put it in her bag. "Yes, thank you. I'll have the crayfish. And a bottle of Moselle."

The girl smiled in apology.

"I don't know about wines," she said. "I'll get the list for you. Enjoy your meal."

"She goes sweet now," the Dutch boy said. He wiped the engine oil and grime from his hands with an even dirtier rag. He grinned at Lucy and shook his blonde head.

"Broken fuel line joint, must have come loose on the way," he said. "No surprise she won't go for you. Next time, don't ask too much of her, eh?"

"Next time," Lucy promised. "Thank you so much, Jan. I'm sorry it's taken you so long."

"Thank you," Volkov echoed. He wasn't sure what a fuel line was but he did know that the engine was working. It had taken the Dutch couple's crewman most of the morning to get it right.

"No trouble," he said. He spoke to Volkov. "You a good sailor?"

"No. I've never been in a boat."

"It's good. Not so good in a storm, but today—beautiful. Okay? Good trip!" He gripped Volkov's hand briefly and jumped ashore. "Mr. and Mrs. de Groot say good luck and good-bye," he called out. "They gone to buy provisions. If the boat don't start, they say come back to us. I tell them, she starts. I make sure of that!"

"Say thank you again from us, won't you?" Lucy called out.

He waved and hurried back down the jetty. She turned and hugged Volkov.

"We're all right, darling. We can cast off and start for

home. Now, you undo the tow rope and wind up the anchor. Here, you just do this."

He was clumsy and unsure, but he wouldn't let her use her bandaged hands. Everything had turned out well. They'd breakfasted with the hospitable Dutch couple and spent the morning watching the boy working on the engine.

She knew by the steady even throb that it was perfectly tuned. The sky was cloudless and a hot sun blazed down upon them. She went to the controls, leaving Volkov in the stern, and gradually backed away from the jetty and eased out among the other craft moored close by.

The boat began to rock and a swell built up behind them as they cleared the congestion and came out into the harbor mouth.

"Are you all right, darling?" she glanced over her shoulder at him.

He was sitting rigidly in the stern, holding the sides with both hands. Suddenly he smiled at her.

He laughed. "I'm very all right," he called back. "I like it! When are you going to show me how to sail?"

"When we're out at sea," she said. "Don't worry, it's not hurting me to turn the wheel. We'll keep to this speed. That boy knew what he was doing. She's going like a bird!"

He said, "They were so kind, those Dutch people."

"Very kind," Lucy agreed. "I got their address. I'll write and thank them properly."

"I was thinking last night while you were asleep," he said, "how brave you are. You have a brave heart, Lucy Warren."

She looked up at him. "Not as brave as yours," she said gently. "Now if you want to learn, come and sit here."

In the late afternoon after they left Saint Malo, Lucy pointed to a land mass on the horizon.

"Look, that's the west coast—you'll see Gorey Castle soon. We're home!"

5

THE WATCHER had set up a little tripod, with his binoculars fixed to it, trained on the bay below. He was eating out of a tin, hidden under a camouflaged sun shield. He had his equipment laid out ready. The automatic weapon was quite small, less deadly than the Armalite he preferred, but it had fitted easily into the struts of his backpack, the firing mechanism and ammunition sealed up in cans of food.

He was a big man, fit and well muscled. He'd trained with the French Paras and been dismissed after serving a four-year jail sentence for robbery. He hadn't hesitated when the offer of this kind of job came along. He had no political loyalties or prejudices. He had skills to offer which the French army had provided and he didn't care who paid him.

He had a bicycle hidden under more camouflaged sheeting outside. He had made one excursion into Saint Helier to leave the message for the woman at the restaurant. His instructions were to stay on watch and out of sight. He had spied out a little delicatessen in the village a mile down toward the bay. When he had to make the coded telephone call to the hotel, he could use the phone he'd seen at the back of the shop. He had his story ready.

It was sweltering under the canvas. He spooned up the last of his cold meal, tossed the empty can aside and swigged from a bottle of beer. It was tepid and the sweat ran down into his eyes. He swore; he was impatient to get the job over, slip back to France and collect his money.

His instructions were clear. He was to monitor what happened at the house when the Russian woman and her goon arrived. Their job was to kill the girl he'd seen take out the boat and her companion, after forcing them to hand something over . . . From this, he judged it better not to intervene if he heard screaming. When the Russians emerged, he was to eliminate them both, the man first and without worrying about how many bullet holes, the woman with a shot to the head that could be seen as self-inflicted. Her body was to be disposed among the other corpses, with a handgun left beside her. That had come in in pieces, in his saddlebag behind the bike. The body of the man she'd brought with her could be buried or thrown into the sea. That was his business. If the two Russians encountered any trouble, he was to go in immediately and take over. Either way, the result was to be the same. Four dead and the artifact, a cross, in his possession. A single radio call to Carteret would bring a contact to the same restaurant in Saint Helier, where he would hand over the artifact and get himself onto the next ferry to Saint Malo.

Payment would be waiting for him. He had already planned what he'd do with the money. Pick up his girl, take off for a holiday in the South. Bank the rest of the money. He didn't want to go on working forever.

He wiped his mouth and his sweating face and peered through the binoculars. He saw the small boat, its sail furled, cutting through the slight swell into the bay. He adjusted the focus. He could see the girl quite clearly. Blonde, blue shirt, shorts. A man with her. He watched as they came closer, as the boat slowed, inched into its berth at the jetty and dropped anchor. He was very still, concentrating like an animal stalking its prey.

The man helped the girl out. Then they began to walk up from the bay. He had his arm round her. They walked up from the sparkling sand to the pathway among the rocks. Up to the little road that ran along the coast, and out of sight until they came into view again, walking up the steep grassy incline to the lower reaches of the garden. Through the wooden gate, up a brick path among the flower borders.

He changed the focus, bringing them in clear close-up. She was a good-looking piece. The man looked like a Slav of some kind. She unlocked the front door and they went inside.

The watcher unscrewed his binoculars and folded down the tripod. He sent the radio signal to Carteret first. "Targets One and Two in place. Operation activated."

He crept out, keeping low, and hauled the bike from under its cover. A few minutes later he was pedaling toward the village. He stopped outside the delicatessen and went in. It was cool and he wiped his face with a forearm. The woman behind the counter said, "Good afternoon. Hot, isn't it?"

He smiled at her. He had strong white teeth and was not bad looking in a coarse way. She smiled back.

"It's hot," he agreed. "You have any Orangina on ice? And I need to make a telephone call, Mademoiselle. Can you help me? I'm meeting a friend in Saint Helier and I'm going to be very late."

"There's a phone through there," she said. "You're French? On holiday?"

"Only a week," he shrugged. "I like to do a bit of walking, biking round the Island, and swimming. I'm going home tomorrow. I'll take three Orangina, I'm that thirsty. Can I use the phone?"

"Just give me twenty-five pence for the call," she said. "I'll get the drinks. Bottles, not cans?"

"Bottles'll do fine," he said.

He grinned at her and made for the telephone. He dialed the number.

A voice said, "Saint Margaret's."

He lowered his voice.

"Can you give Miss Szpiganovitch a message? . . ."

He added a chocolate ice to his purchases and went outside. He ate the ice quickly before it melted. He went back the way he'd come and slipped under his shelter to watch the house. He guessed the Russian woman wouldn't waste time coming after them.

"I can't take it in," Lucy said. "I can't believe we're home and safe."

He had picked up a photograph in a silver frame.

He said, "This is your father and mother and you? She was very pretty."

"She had lovely coloring," Lucy said. "It doesn't show up there. It's very good of my father."

"I wish I had met them," he said.

He set the photograph down. He came to her and put both hands on her shoulders.

"It's time to show me the holy relic," he said.

"Yes," Lucy said. "Come with me."

The shutters were fastened in her father's study. Volkov had to open them for her. Her hands were still painful and very stiff. Sunshine poured in, lighting a million dust motes in its beam. Lucy looked round her. Everything was as he'd left it. The desk with his selection of pens, the shabby blotter he wouldn't replace because it was a Christmas present from his benefactor, Major Hope, the calendar with the date long past.

She said, "Move the desk out and pull up the rug."

Volkov pushed it aside and rolled up the bright Persian rug. The surface of the parquet glowed dark by comparison to the sun-bleached floor. Lucy stepped forward and pressed the fourth square on the left. The flap rose up. Volkov had moved quickly beside her.

"There's a box in there," she said.

He knelt and reached down. He brought out the plain wooden box and put it on the desk. He looked at it.

"This is what my father dreamed of," she said. "This very moment. Open it, Volkov."

The catch was simple, it slipped up and the lid rose. Slowly, reverently he lifted out the gold cross. Red lights danced and flashed as he examined it, and the frame was the honey color of pure gold.

"A thousand years of our history," his voice shook. "I don't know what to say."

"It belongs to you now," Lucy spoke quietly. "It will give you the power to free millions of our people. It's the proof that Communism didn't win."

He held the cross between both outstretched palms, and said in a low voice, "It makes me afraid." He looked up at her. "Am I strong enough, Lucy? Can I really go home and offer myself as a leader?"

"You must," she answered. "You have the holy relic. You've got no choice. You've been chosen."

"I could look at it forever," he said. "I could just sit here and look at it."

She came close and said softly, "I'll leave you alone for a while. I felt just the same when my father showed it to me for the first time. And don't ever doubt yourself, my love. You were born for this. I truly believe that."

She slipped out of the room and left him.

It weighed very little. The workmanship was delicate as lace. The big central stone was rounded and roughly polished so that the facets caught the light.

A blood-thirsty tyrant had commissioned it as a proof that

he was converted to the Christian faith and would bring peace to the land and mercy to its people. There had been little peace and no mercy from the moment it disappeared from its shrine. Millions starved to death, deported, murdered. Millions more were slain in Russia's most terrible war.

With the sun shining on him, Volkov's hands looked as if they were dipped in blood. He had never uttered even a mental prayer in his life. He didn't do so then. Lucy saw the hand of God. He felt the touch of history. Destiny had chosen him. She was right. He had no choice.

He laid the relic back in its box, replaced it in the cunning floor cavity and pressed the section of wood down. It fitted into the parquet, invisible in the design. The rug was laid on top, the desk maneuvered into its place. A dead man had guarded his treasure well.

He opened the door and came out. Lucy came to meet him. He looked very pale. She put her arms round him and they held each other. They didn't speak.

"Remus!"

She didn't knock. She opened the door and saw him lying on the bed, his shoes kicked off, his mouth ajar, dozing. His eyes opened and he jerked upright.

"*Matiushka!*"

"Get ready," Irina commanded. "You've got work to do. I'll be downstairs. Hurry."

She went down to the hallway. "Rudi" had telephoned and rung off without leaving any message. She'd turned her back on the woman's curiosity and gone upstairs to fetch him. They were on the Island together. They were in the house together. Celebrating their escape. Touching each other. She allowed herself a few seconds of mental torture before blotting out the image of Volkov with his hand on the woman, his mouth closing on hers. She was trembling.

He came downstairs. He moved very lightly for such a heavy man. He followed her outside.

"Get in the back," she ordered. It would take twenty minutes or more to negotiate the narrow country roads to Saint Catherine's Bay.

"You know what to do, Remus?"

"I know," he said. "We creep up on them, burst in, take them by surprise. I knock the man out and grab the woman."

"Not too hard," she reminded him. "I only want him stunned. Just long enough to tie him up."

"I won't hit him," he promised. "Just a tap on the neck."

"They must give me the treasure they stole," she said.

She saw his reflection in the driving mirror. His eyes were bright and he had wet his lips. He had always reacted like that; violence excited him.

"You'll torture the woman," Irina instructed. "To make him tell us. If that doesn't work, then we'll make her watch while you work on him. One of them will break. Probably him."

She bit her lip. She hoped so. She couldn't imagine sweeter music than the screams of Lucy Warren. But to see Dimitri suffer . . .

"I know how to make them squeal," he grunted. "He won't like it. The men always give in when their women squeal."

Irina concentrated on the road ahead. She drove as fast as she dared on the twisting roads. Twice they met an oncoming car, had to pull into the side to let the other pass. She didn't want to lose the light. It was better to rush the house in daylight. The backup was close by, she knew that. But he wouldn't be needed. Remus was at exactly the right pitch of controlled brutality. She could feel the energy coming from him in the confines of the car. He was like a coiled spring.

She slowed down and took a right, turning off the road.

It twisted and wound its way through green countryside and little wooded hills, and there, just ahead of them, was the driveway leading to the house. On her left she could see the blue sparkle of the sea in the bay below, with its little marina and the few boats bobbing up and down on the evening tide.

She stopped the car under some trees. She could see the white-painted facade up ahead. They wouldn't be visible.

He was so quiet she didn't hear him close the rear door. He came up beside her. She heard him breathing heavily. She remembered the formula. "You're serving the State, Remus. You're going to punish our enemies."

The watcher grunted. He'd seen the car and guessed where it was going. There wasn't another house in sight. He was right. They hadn't wasted any time. He bent low, watching the woman and the man begin to circle round the house to the back. He decided it was time for him to move closer in. He took his weapon and began to run bent double down the gentle rise to the level of the distant garden. He didn't waste time either. As soon as he was out of sight of any passing car on the road above, he straightened and broke into a fast loping stride that brought him to a shrubbery a hundred yards from the house. He waited. He heard a sharp scream that was cut short. He grinned. They were inside.

Irina saw them through the French windows. The windows were slightly open to admit a light breeze; the sun was sinking and it was suddenly much cooler.

She heard her husband say, "My darling, I want you to rest. I'll go and get us something to eat."

And, for the first time, Lucy Warren, speaking in Russian. A melodious voice, a little deep. It would find a new pitch very soon, Irina promised herself.

"I'll come with you. You don't know where I keep things."

"I'll find them. You sit down."

"Now!" she hissed at Remus.

He launched himself with the speed and lightness of a great predator. He was through the French doors and into the room before she could start to follow him. She saw Lucy Warren start up and heard the brief cry, choked at its source as Remus swept her to the ground. She lay dazed and without moving as Irina stepped into the room. Remus put a finger to his lips. They heard Volkov running from inside the house.

The door was flung open and he shouted, "Lucy! What—" when Remus snapped the ridge of his right hand up and across, striking him on the side of the neck. He collapsed, instantly unconscious as the blood supply from the carotid artery was halted by the blow. Remus left him there. He was silent, speedy. He hauled the girl up, threw her onto the sofa.

Irina came close. He had a luggage strap out of his pocket. He buckled her arms tight to her sides. He rolled his handkerchief into a ball and forced her mouth open, thrusting it inside.

"She'll give no trouble, *Matiushka,*" he grunted. "Now I'll fix him."

Irina stood looking down at them. He'd used two straps to secure Volkov by the hands and feet and pushed him into an armchair facing the girl. She was lying where he'd thrown her, her eyes wide open, her mouth distorted by the crude gag. Irina turned away from her; one hand instinctively touched her head.

"He's coming to," she said.

Volkov was moving, wrestling with the straps. He was conscious and Irina saw his expression and heard him gasp her name as he saw her.

"Yes," she said softly. "It's me. Look over there, Dimitri. My friend is going to amuse himself with your bitch whore. Let her scream, Remus. Nobody can hear her."

They were giving the girl a hard time. The watcher wondered what that old bastard was doing to her.

Volkov was begging, "Irina, stop him, stop him. Oh, Holy Christ!" The old Russian oath was dredged up from his subconscious.

He'd writhed and jerked in helpless agony when the man tore the bandages off Lucy's hands and dug his fingers into the raw skin. The sobs of pain drove him to a frenzy. He was shouting, pleading with his wife. She didn't answer. She stood and watched. She heard him curse her, beg her, cry out in horror as Lucy's shirt was torn from her and he saw his wife's lighter flicker into flame in the man's hand and hover in front of her breast.

"Wait!" Irina commanded. She turned to Volkov. "Where's the cross, Dimitri?"

There was a cry from behind her. "Don't . . . Don't tell them."

She swung round. She snapped, "Shut her up! Tell me where you've hidden the cross," she said. "Otherwise he'll burn off the nipple!"

Volkov didn't hesitate. He shouted, hoarse with anguish. "I'll get it! I'll give it to you. Tell him to leave her alone. Don't hurt her anymore."

"You tell me and I'll get it," Irina said.

He loved her. He loved her more than she imagined he could love anyone. His cries of agony and pleading were ringing in her ears. At one moment he'd said, "I'll give myself up. I'll do anything. Stop him."

He said, "You can't. You couldn't work the mechanism. Send him with me."

"Oh, no," Irina shook her head. "Oh, no. You'd try something. I know you would. He stays with her and I wait here. Remus, I'm going to untie him. If he makes any move, kill her."

He took his hand away from Lucy's mouth. He hooked his forearm under her chin.

"You do what you're told," he said to Volkov. "Or I'll break her neck."

Irina unbuckled the belts. For a second she thought Volkov was going to lose control and throw himself on her. She saw the temptation and saw him resist it. *How much he loved that girl. How much she meant to him.*

"If I give it to you, will you let Lucy go? I'll come back to Russia with you."

She said coldly, "Bring me the cross or I'll tell him to burn her."

She stepped away from him. He stumbled out. She took a cigarette from her bag. She snapped her fingers.

"I'll have my lighter, Remus." He handed it to her. "Don't choke her yet," she said. "I want him to see it."

Lucy closed her eyes. Her hands were on fire with pain. His arm was like a band of iron on her throat. She didn't want to see the woman's face. It was a mask, with the eyes glittering, exulting in her victims' agony. And her death was in those eyes. She shut them out and prayed for unconsciousness.

He threw open the door to Yuri Warienski's study. He heaved the desk out of the way and threw the rug aside. He was trembling, blinded by helpless rage and fear for Lucy. He might plead, he might bargain, but it wouldn't save her. As soon as he handed over the relic, he knew that they would both be killed. He stamped on the floor and the cavity opened.

"You do what you're told," that human beast had grunted at him. "Or I'll break her neck."

He closed his eyes, fighting nausea at the mental image of Lucy with that throttling arm across her throat.

He forced himself to kneel, to bring out the wooden box. He had no thought or fear for himself. He looked round the room. There must be something, something he could use. He wrenched open the desk drawers. Nothing. Then he saw it. It had fallen to the ground when he pushed the heavy desk aside.

A silver paper knife. A thin, sharp blade with a chased handle. He picked it up, felt the tip with his finger. With enough force it would penetrate a human body. He stuck it in the waistband of his trousers, out of sight. He carried the box in both hands and walked back down the passage to the sitting room. He couldn't hear anything. Silence. One chance in a million. He was going to take it.

Irina drew on her cigarette. Her hand was steady. She felt calm and drained. The catharsis was over. There was no dilemma about Volkov now. No doubt, no hope left. He belonged to the other woman. He would die with her.

Remus said, "He's gone a long time, *Matiushka*. You want me to look for him?"

"No," Irina said. "He hasn't run away. He wouldn't leave her."

As the door opened she turned slowly. She ground out her half-smoked cigarette on the carpet. She held out both hands when she saw the wooden box.

Volkov tried once more. The point of the silver knife pricked his back.

"Let her go, Irina. Don't punish her for what I've done."

She looked at him and there was a little smile on her lips. "The cross," she said. "Give it to me."

He lifted the lid and plunged his hand inside. He brought the cross out into the light. It flashed red fire. He stepped close and put it into her outstretched hand. She grasped it. He sprang at her. The cross fell to the ground. He had her arms pinned down and the knife point was aimed at her heart.

"Tell him to untie her," he said. He crushed her hard with his left arm. "Go on, tell him to let her go! Or by the Holy Christ I'll kill you."

He was gripping the handle of the knife so hard his knuckles were bone white under the skin; she felt the muscles holding her go taut. He raised the knife to strike. His strength was manic; she could hardly get her breath. She opened her mouth and found strength of her own.

"Kill her, Remus!"

But the arm had fallen away from Lucy's throat. He had come forward. He was staring at the cross. Volkov held the knife suspended. The man was bending, picking it up, holding it close to his face.

"My cross," he said. "That's my cross!"

"Remus," Irina screamed at him. "You heard me! Kill her!"

He didn't move. He was staring at the relic. "Gold and fucking jewels," he said and a grin spread over his face. "I'll be rich!"

"You'll be punished," Irina was shouting at him. "You'll go back to the gulag. Do as you're ordered!"

He glanced at her. The little eyes were bloodshot and they gleamed with cunning.

"You made a dog out of me. You made me lick your feet. Now you want to steal my cross. It's mine!" His voice rose to an infuriated roar. "You don't give me orders anymore, you bitch! You're not stealing my cross!"

He lunged at her and Volkov dropped the knife. The blow was so fast he hardly saw it happen. The man struck at her windpipe. It shattered and Irina fell.

"I'm Boris!" he shouted. "Boris! I'll be rich."

The watcher heard the shouting. It was time for him to move. He came up to the windows at a run, his weapon ready to fire.

Volkov had gone to Lucy. He was unfastening the straps, whispering to her.

"Run, my darling. Run!"

But it was useless. She was too shocked to move. He stood in the middle of the room like a great bear, Irina dead at his feet, holding the cross up to the light, exulting. He turned and

looked at them and smiled. It was a terrifying sight. He looked
like a happy child.

"I gave it to the kid. I gave it to Yuri. I thought they'd
shoot me. But there was a bastard of an officer—he said, 'Not
this one—he's strong! We'll work him till he drops dead in his
own shit—But I fooled them, I didn't die." He glared round
him; his voice rose in fury. "I did their dirty work, they scrambled my brains and I did what *she* told me—" he turned and
kicked Irina's body.

"They sent me to a stinking hole as a reward—no doctor,
no medicine, just a stinking dusty hole. I saw my kids die...
My woman cried...But now, I've got my cross back. My
cross!" The rage died in him; he gurgled with laughter. "It's
going to make me rich!"

The watcher took in the scene in a few seconds: the woman
dead, the targets still alive, the goon gloating over something
red and gold.

Boris heard him. He couldn't control his reflexes, they
reacted as they'd been trained to. He heard a sudden movement
and he sensed an attacker.

The burst of shots caught him in the chest. He spun and
staggered under the impact. The cross slipped out of his hand.
He gave a terrible roar of rage and anguish. With a burst of
superhuman strength he threw himself on the watcher before
he could fire again. His hands found the man's throat and locked
around it in his death throes.

He slumped suddenly and they crashed to the ground. He
lay, a dead weight on the watcher's body.

He had managed to strangle him before he died.

There was no report of any crime. The network in France had
no information for Moscow. Since the last radio message to
Carteret, Jersey, had gone silent. The house in Jersey was closed

up. Volkov and Lucy Warren had disappeared. So had Irina's team.

Leon Gusev was very nervous. He didn't sleep. His work suffered. He considered himself a ruined man for having agreed to Rakovsky's plan. It now seemed as insane as it appeared brilliant at the time. He fretted and wondered whether he might help his case by confessing his part in the failure before he was actually arrested. It meant denouncing Viktor, but even so— Viktor understood his feelings.

He sent for him three days before the Markoff Gallery private view. He offered him whiskey. Gusev refused it. He didn't have to pander to him now. Besides he hated the taste of the stuff. Viktor had been drinking a lot of it lately.

"Well, Leon, you'll be out of your misery soon."

"How?" Gusev asked him.

"The reception is on Thursday. If Volkov's going to make an entrance, that's where he'll do it. Our Embassy will have a man in place. Among the catering staff."

He actually laughed. Gusev felt his stomach heave.

"He'll come out of hiding," Viktor went on. "He'll appear among the faithful like Jesus walking through the walls into the upper room—with the holy relic to prove he's risen from the dead."

He finished his drink.

"With the connivance of the British, of course. They must have been waiting for us in Jersey. My guess is our three are dead. They wouldn't have been taken alive."

Gusev saw a faint hope.

He said, "The British may not want to foment trouble for us. They may be holding him so he can't come out into the open. They don't want to see bloody revolution here!"

"We've already sounded them out," Viktor retorted.

Gusev looked up, frowning.

"I didn't know."

"I reported the whole business as soon as it went wrong," Viktor said calmly. "Before you had a chance to make up your mind to do it. We're not living in the old days. We wouldn't be shot or sent to the Arctic Circle. Just retired and disgraced for failing in our duty. You can be honest with our president. I was honest with him. So whatever happens, we're prepared. No, the British didn't respond. If they wanted to avoid trouble for us, he could have been quietly deported. They said nothing. They knew nothing. Which means they have him. He's in England and by Thursday he'll be in London. Don't worry, Leon. I emphasized your resistance to the plan. You won't get promoted, but you won't be posted to Armenia either."

He stood up. "What worries me is how did the British know? Our security was absolute."

"Muller?" Leon Gusev suggested.

"No," Viktor dismissed it. "He only knew Volkov had left Switzerland. How could he know about Jersey?"

"He knew about Saint Vladimir's cross," Gusev pointed out. "If he tipped off the British, why wouldn't they draw the same conclusion as we did and expect Volkov and Warren to end up there?"

Rakovsky sat down again. He stared at the brightly polished toe cap of his shoe. He was a fastidious dresser. He looked up at Gusev.

"You think he's turned double?"

"You've run him for years. You know him. Do you think it's possible?"

"In the beginning he worked for a political ideal," Viktor said slowly. "But for a long time I've felt he was working for money. He's greedy for money. I think you could be right, Leon. We'll look into it. He has one little job left to do for me. After that . . ." He gave Gusev a cold smile. "I'll find a way to retire him."

*   *   *

He had introduced himself as Ian Freemantle. He was representing the Foreign Office. His companion, James Harper, was
from the Home Office. The head of the Jersey Police Force
brought them in his car.

Volkov saw them come up the steps of the old manor
house, two tall men in lightweight suits, with briefcases in their
hands, and he recognized officialdom at a high level.

The police had made him and Lucy very comfortable.
She'd been treated for shock and the injury to her hands and
she was recovering well. They weren't under arrest, but it was
accepted that they didn't leave the house.

"You realize, Mr. Volkov, that you've put Her Majesty's
government in a very awkward position?" Freemantle said.

"I know," Volkov agreed.

"You have asked for political asylum at a most sensitive
time in our relations with the Soviet government."

"I know that too," he answered. "I'm sorry. But they had
tried to murder us."

Freemantle had been shown the photographs of the dead
Soviet agents, and the equipment and weaponry found at the
watcher's hidden camp site. A serious KGB operation within
British territory. That was very awkward too. The Jersey police
had given him graphic details of the ordeal suffered by Lucy
Warren, a British subject. Their attitude had been aggressively
sympathetic to the Russian and the girl.

"You are also an illegal immigrant. Miss Warren has committed a serious offense in that respect."

He saw Volkov flush angrily.

"She was trying to save my life. Is that a crime in your
country?"

Freemantle looked at his companion.

Harper said soothingly, "No charges will be brought, Mr.
Volkov. My colleague was just making a point."

He looked at them with contempt. "Thank you."

"There have been inquiries from the Soviet authorities, unofficially, of course, and we have denied all knowledge of you up till now." Harper had taken it up. "We have been considering what line to take, if we do decide to grant your request and admit you to the United Kingdom as a political refugee. It poses a number of problems. You'll attract a lot of media attention."

Volkov said nothing.

"Worldwide, in view of your past political activities."

"I spent a year in prison," Volkov pointed out. "It wasn't just making speeches."

"And five years in exile in Geneva," Freemantle remarked.

There was instant antagonism between him and the Russian. He objected to the man's attitude. Britain owed him nothing. He had the government's decision in his briefcase, but he was going to drive a hard bargain.

"We would need assurances from you, Mr. Volkov, that you would not engage in anti-Soviet activities."

Harper played the emollient role again.

"That means refuse interviews and media coverage and avoid criticism of the present Soviet regime. In other words, Mr. Volkov, we would offer you a temporary entry visa, but play down any suggestion that you were seeking political asylum. If all went well that visa could be extended and a request for residency would have sympathetic consideration from the Home Office."

"So it's your Foreign Office who's objecting to me?" Volkov spoke to Freemantle.

"We could have legally deported you. That is still an option."

"Then you *would* get all the media attention," the Jerseyman spoke up. "I don't think it would look good for any of us. And I don't believe that the States here would sanction any action of that sort, sir." He made the last word sound an insult.

"We have kept the facts of the case sub judice as you asked, but I don't think I could guarantee that if any force was used against Mr. Volkov."

"There's no question of that," Harper interposed. His glance said that he was the senior of the two, and Freemantle had better retract. "Is there, Ian? I think you meant it hypothetically, didn't you?"

"It didn't sound like that to me," the Jerseyman said.

"Then I expressed it badly," Freemantle capitulated. "Mr. Volkov's attitude was rather provocative, I felt. There is no question of him being deported." He looked disdainful. "What my department is anxious to avoid is embarrassment to the Soviet president at the present time. There are a number of anti-Soviet activists making a nuisance of themselves already."

James Harper stood up. "Perhaps you'd like time to think about it?" he said to Volkov. "Your country has made remarkable progress in the last few years. People are enjoying a degree of freedom that was unthinkable before Mikhail Gorbachev. Surely the last thing to do is destabilize him and give the hardliners their chance to put the clock back. If you could see this attempt to silence you in that perspective, Mr. Volkov, you might take a different view. I understand that one of the participants was your wife. There must have been a personal element in the attack on you and Miss Warren. Why not consider the wider implications? We're at Government House until tomorrow morning. We can call back later."

Volkov didn't answer. Then he said, "You'll give me a visa if I promise to say and do nothing to call attention to myself. In other words to stay quiet in the background. Is that what you mean?"

"Yes. That is exactly what we mean. Do give it careful thought."

He didn't leave his chair to shake hands with them. He waited till the room was empty, then he got up. He watched them out of the window, the establishment personified, getting into the official car, driving away to their rendezvous with the governor of the Island.

He was a problem. An embarrassment. They didn't want him, but they couldn't deport him without the truth blowing up in their faces.

He turned away. Time to think about it. Time to agree to opt out, to stay silent, to relive the shame of Geneva all over again. He opened the door of Lucy's room.

"Have they gone?"

She came toward him. He'd wanted her to be present. That was not allowed.

"Yes, they've gone."

She looked so pale, he thought, and she'd lost so much weight from that terrible experience. He loved her in a new dimension now. She'd given all her strength and all her courage that night. He took her gently in his arms.

"What did they say?" she asked.

He was tempted to lie. But he had never lied to her.

"They'll give me a temporary visa—with conditions. One of them tried to threaten me with deportation." He silenced her anxious gasp. "No, no, my darling, it was only a threat. Our friend, the commissioner, soon stopped that. He's a real friend. They can't send me back, but they can keep me here. Beyond the meeting in London. It's the day after tomorrow."

Lucy looked up at him. He was overprotective. She insisted she was strong and recovered mentally as well as physically.

"What conditions?"

He said, "No publicity. No statements, nothing critical of the regime at home. I can stay in England as a private individual so long as I keep quiet."

"You can't do that, Volkov," she said. "You have the relic, you can't accept those terms! It would be Geneva all over again!"

"We could make a life together," he said slowly. "There'd be another opportunity—later, when you're recovered properly. My darling, I can't involve you in all this anymore. I can't stop thinking of what happened to you—and it was my fault. I brought you into danger. I'm not going to do it again."

"Volkov," Lucy said, "Listen to me. I went looking for you. I started this—I put *your* life on the line. And we're going to see it through together. You've got to attend that meeting. When they come back say you've decided on a quiet life. Agree to everything so long as they fly us out tomorrow and we get to London in time. If you don't, you'll have betrayed yourself and everything you believe in. And what that brute did to me will be for nothing." She held on to him.

"We're together," she reminded him. "That's what we promised after that dreadful day. Promise me. No going back."

He drew her close and kissed her gently.

"I promise. In my heart I hoped you'd say that. I'll lie in my teeth to the 'gentlemen' from London. I'll go to the meeting."

"And when you get there," Lucy asked him, "what are you going to do?"

He said slowly, "I'm going to talk to them. I've been thinking about it ever since. I've got a lot of things I want to say. It's not going to be the speech I wrote in Geneva.

"It's so easy to be brave when you're far away from the danger. I was always a hothead, Lucy. The Ukraine doesn't need a rabble-rouser. If all this is going to be worthwhile, I've got to grow to meet it. Our people don't want martyrs, they want statesmen, politicians who can get the better of Moscow. That's what I'm going to tell Mischa and the rest of them."

"They'll follow you," she said.

Freemantle and Harper caught the morning plane back to Heathrow.

"I never thought he'd give in so tamely," Harper said,

settling into his seat after take-off.

"I'm not so sure he has," Freemantle countered. "The girl's father was a bloody nuisance even before *perestroika*. All these émigrés are the same. They love to saber rattle, while we have to cope afterward. It's a pity they're going to London together. We'll keep a sharp eye when he gets there in case he tries to back out."

Harper opened his newspaper.

"There's not a lot we can do if he does," he said. "He got under your skin, Ian. Forget about it. We've got the undertaking signed, we've done our job."

They'd been booked into a hotel in South Kensington. Special Branch reported that they'd done a little shopping and spent their first evening quietly at the hotel. At six the following evening, they left in a taxi and were followed to the Markoff Gallery on Saint James Street. There was a private view of pre-Revolutionary photographs and memorabilia.

At ten minutes past eight, the press and the first television crews gathered outside the gallery. Ian Freemantle was on his way home to Sussex, listening to the car radio when he heard the news. He changed gears with such force that they screeched in protest.

"The bastard!" he said. "I knew we couldn't trust him!"

It happened after they'd been to the theater and to supper. Peter Muller had chosen a new play and booked a table at an intimate little night spot where a pianist played sentimental music and couples could inch their way round a tiny square of dance floor. The play was witty and frankly erotic. He noticed how often Eloise laughed, turning to smile at him.

At one moment he bent close and whispered, "I'm sorry. I didn't realize it was going to be so naughty."

Her answer was promising. "It's delicious," she murmured.

His wife was regrettably involved with a charity meeting and couldn't come with them. Their dinner at the Hofburg had been a great success, but instinctively Muller knew she wasn't ready. She was still conscious of her widowhood, still loyal to Adolph's memory. But she wanted to make love. He could feel the sexual restlessness in her and the constant moistening of her lips with the tip of her tongue made him sweat with desire.

She was a healthy, full-blooded woman and she needed a man. He was going to have her that night, he knew it. He thought she probably knew it too. The play set the mood for the slow piano music and the body contact as they circled, hardly moving, their cheeks close together, his pelvis pushed forward till their groins were touching. She must feel him through her thin dress.

At her door he asked softly, making his voice very low, "Can I come in?"

He discovered that she wanted him to be strong and insistent, to take command of her. Once only, as he abandoned her wet mouth for her throat and neck, did Eloise protest.

"Adolph," she murmured, "we shouldn't."

"He loved you," Muller said. "He'd want you to be happy."

It was better than he'd imagined. He lay in Adolph's bed and made love to Eloise until he was drained and slack. But he didn't sleep. When she dozed off he woke her with powerful caresses, demanding that she service him. She was imaginative. She surprised and delighted him. She filled him with fresh energy and at last he exhausted her.

There was no sham about her when she slept. She lay back with her mouth open and snored. Muller whispered to her. He stroked her. She didn't move. The rhythmic ugly breathing didn't check even for a second. She slept as if she was drugged.

Carefully he got out of bed. He drew on his trousers and slipped on surgical gloves. He paused by the bedroom door and waited, listening. She was not going to wake till the morning.

He had done this in his imagination many times. The long corridor leading to the ballroom. He had brought a pencil torch with him; the tiny spotlight was enough. He moved on his bare feet without a sound.

There was the first consul table, the bluejohn vase, its ormolu mounts gleaming in the beam of light. The third gilded flower head· on the left of the larger carving. He pressed it cautiously and it moved under his finger. The second consul table, its vase, its carved flowers. To the right this time. Again the slight depression as he touched the flower.

One more to go. And there it was. The bronze elephant clock, its trunk rising lewdly in the torch light, its clockface in the center of the gilded howdah. His hands were steady, though sticky with sweat in the tight gloves. With a tentative finger he moved the minute hand. The clock chimed. He jumped back. He'd forgotten the chime. It sounded so loud in the heavy silence. He shone his torch on the ballroom door and turned the handle. It opened. He closed it behind him. He didn't dare switch on the lighting system. There was a security guard on patrol outside the house. The insurance company had won that battle.

He followed the spot of light until he was in front of the cabinet and the treasures inside it sparkled as the beam played over them. It was never locked, because Bruckner liked to open it at will and handle his possessions. He loved the feel of the Fabergé animals. He was fond of saying so to Muller.

He lifted out the clock and the calendar. They fitted into each of his pockets. He took in a deep breath. Now, everything in reverse. The clock set to twelve-thirty. Another nerve-tingling chime, but this time he was prepared for it. Third gilded flower on the left of the consul table going back, third flower on the right of the next one.

The room was alarmed again. The theft wouldn't be discovered until someone went into the ballroom. That could be weeks. He crept back to the bedroom, peeled off the gloves, transferred the little objects to his jacket. She hadn't moved. He stepped out of his trousers and joined her in the bed.

He couldn't leave the house before she woke; he wanted it to be a memorable leave-taking.

"I'm going to fly to Kiev and meet him," Viktor Rakovsky said. "I'm to welcome him home. That's the official line."

No action had been taken against Viktor or Gusev. Not even a rebuke. Dimitri Volkov, followed by a planeload of media from all over the world, was on his way back to the capital of the Ukraine. Viktor was clever, but not as clever as the master tactician who was directing him. Volkov must be walking into a subtle trap, a political embrace that would eventually crush him.

Leon Gusev said, "Why didn't he produce the relic? What's he planning? So far we've had him saying the same thing to everyone. 'I'm going home to offer myself in the service of my fellow Ukrainians. If they'll accept me.' All good humble stuff and the West is loving it. He's the biggest hero since Solzhenitsyn. The Nationalists are planning a big demonstration. He's just what Rhykoh wanted."

"What Rhykoh doesn't want is for the government to upstage them, and that is what we're going to do. I'm leading a group of politburo members and we'll be there to shake his hand as he steps off the plane. We're not going to make a martyr of him, whatever he does. We had our chance and we bungled it. Thanks to Muller's treachery."

It was the accepted view that their agent, Peter Muller, had warned British Intelligence of the attack planned in Jersey.

It had mitigated the official anger at the failure of Viktor's department.

"And if he preaches sedition, with the relic as a rallying point? Are we going to kiss and hug him because of what the West thinks? I can't see it working. I can only see disaster."

"That's what I said to the president," Viktor admitted.

"Then I am relying on you, Viktor Alexzandrovich, to see it doesn't happen." That was the quiet response. He hadn't repeated it to Leon. Leon was still young and inclined to be nervous. He suffered from the legacy of the past.

"I'm leaving in half-an-hour," Viktor said. "You can watch it all on television."

He waited alone for the official car to take him to Sheremetyevo Airport. They were catching the internal flight to Kiev, scheduled to arrive an hour before the Illyushin jet came in from London. Volkov had made a point of refusing Western air transport. "I'm a Russian. I shall go home on a Russian aircraft."

He'd said that during a final interview. Bringing his wife. He had married Yuri Warienski's daughter in a Catholic ceremony in London. That closed the file on Irina. It was significant to Rakovsky that none of the activists who'd been present at the Markoff Gallery when he called the press and television were coming to the Ukraine with him. None had asked for entry visas. Whatever Volkov was planning, he was doing it alone.

The relic was the key. Only the cross could have given him this new authority, the steadfast sense of purpose that came across in every interview. Volkov was no longer the firebrand who'd talked himself into arrest and persecution. Viktor had monitored every appearance before the TV cameras and studied every word. This was a man with a mission and the maturity to accomplish it.

He'd noted his wife too; she had dignity and a quiet beauty.

They were a disturbing pair. She must be an unusual woman, Viktor judged, to have rescued the lost soul in Geneva and inspired him to escape and take up the challenge. She looked as if she'd suffered some baptism of fire. He recognized the marks it left; he'd borne them himself all his life.

Muller had sent the desk set back to Moscow via the Embassy. For a few hours it had stood on Viktor's desk in the same room in the Lubianka where Lepkin had wound the clock and changed the calendar every day, until he brought it home to the house in the woods and gave it to Viktor's mother. He remembered his mother putting it on the shelf above the stove. His brother, Stefan, had been forbidden to handle it; he was content to draw the exquisite trifles and admire them from a distance.

He found he couldn't bear to look at them. By the evening he had formally presented the Fabergé set to the State and it was put on display in the Hermitage Museum in Leningrad. It was out of the reach of human greed.

It was time to leave. He went down in the elevator and out onto the square, where his car was waiting. At the intersection he joined the cavalcade of officials on their way to the airport. The Illyushin had left London on time and would touch down on schedule.

Susan Muller picked up the telephone.

"Hello?"

"This is Eloise Bruckner."

She wasn't really concentrating.

"Hello, how are you? I'm just watching this Russian arrive at Kiev on television. Isn't it fascinating?"

"I want to speak to Peter. I've been robbed!"

"How terrible," Susan Muller exclaimed, still eyeing the screen. The jet had landed and was taxiing along the runway. A group of men were gathering on the tarmac.

"Look, Eloise, could I call you back?"

"No." The voice was shrill. "Just tell Peter I know he did it. I'm going to the police."

Susan Muller forgot about the scene at Borispol Airport.

"Peter? You've got a goddamned nerve. You must be crazy!"

"I showed him how the alarm worked," Eloise's voice was rising hysterically. "He's the only person who could have done it. He stole the desk set! The first night he slept with me! Just tell him he's not going to get away with it!"

The line went dead. Slowly Muller's wife put the phone down. "The first night he slept with me." Her husband had told her he'd bought back the gold boxes and told her he'd sold them immediately for a huge profit. He had assured her that when he stayed the night it was only to comfort a nervous woman. She believed him when he said that it was always innocent. She wanted to believe him. And he had stopped seeing Eloise Bruckner. She was becoming too demanding, he explained. It was time to phase out.

"Oh, Peter," she said. "You shit. Just for business!"

She switched the set off. After a few minutes she calmed down. She was a practical woman. Anyway, if he had screwed the bitch, he'd soon dropped her. That's why she was accusing him. He would never be involved in anything like theft.

She rang Muller at the shop and told him what had happened.

"I can explain," he said. "But you don't need to worry. I'll talk to her."

He sent the prints round to the Bruckner house by special courier. He put a note into the envelope: "My dear, I thought you might like to have these as a memento of our wonderful first night together. I treasure my set. Peter."

When they woke that morning he had persuaded her to pose for him. She had been excited by the idea. "We can look at them together," he suggested. She had adopted every erotic pose he suggested and then photographed him naked in turn. She had supplied the camera from one of Adolph's collection. They'd joked about it. A little different from his holiday snaps. She wouldn't put *them* in the album. Best of all, since Adolph was such an enthusiast, it was possible to take photographs by remote control. Muller had staged a series of unusual couplings, which the camera recorded. Eloise Bruckner wouldn't go to the police and risk these photographs being produced as evidence. He wasn't in the least alarmed by her threat.

In their apartment overlooking the Bremner Canal, the Dutch couple were also watching television.

"Isn't it amazing, Dirk," she turned to him. They were side by side watching the replay on Amsterdam television. "Just think, we helped that man get out of France!"

"I know," he said. "It makes you feel part of history. Nobody'd believe us if we told them."

His wife smiled broadly. "I've told everyone!" she announced. "Your sister says I should write about it for the newspapers."

"No, Beta, you mustn't do anything like that! We don't want a lot of journalists asking us questions. We were just doing a kindness. We leave it at that, eh?"

"All right, but it's amazing all the same. Look, they're coming out of the plane now. Look at all those people!"

"Sssh," he admonished. "Beta, listen to the commentary."

She had a bad habit of talking through a program if she got excited.

"I'm nervous," Lucy whispered to him as the plane door opened and the stewardess beckoned them forward.

"I'm nervous too," he admitted. "It's so long since I've been home. Last time I left in handcuffs."

The sunlight was blinding as they came down the steps and onto the tarmac at Borispol. They saw the flashing cameras and the TV crews behind a simple barrier. Volkov inhaled the earth smell of his country, the whiff of dust and pine trees borne on a hot breeze, and suddenly his heart lifted and he was happy. He caught Lucy's hand and walked toward the group of dignitaries: the president of the Ukrainian Parliament and his deputy, bureaucrats, one high-ranking army officer, and another smaller group ahead of them all. The representatives of Central Government in Moscow, making his welcome official. There were handshakes, warm smiles. The media captured every moment of it. Viktor Rakovsky was almost the last to greet him.

"Welcome back," he said. "I represent our Foreign Ministry. There's a reception and a press conference arranged for you. I hope you had a smooth flight."

"Very smooth," Volkov said. He brought Lucy forward. "My wife," he said.

Viktor shook her hand. He wondered how Irina had died.

"Welcome to the Soviet Union, Comrade Volkova."

She answered him in Russian. "Thank you."

It had all been arranged beforehand.

Viktor said, "Before we go in to meet the press, I'd like to speak to you in private. Just a few minutes."

"I thought you'd suggest something like that. What ministry are you representing?" Volkov looked at him coldly. "I think you were a friend of my late wife's father."

"I've known all the family for a long time," Viktor answered. There was a dark hatred in that steady gaze. His task was not going to be easy. "This way."

He ushered them ahead of him; his manner was friendly, even deferential. They were VIPs and they entered the exclusive lounge reserved for the highest Party members when they used the airport.

"A drink?" Viktor inquired. "What would you like? We

have excellent Russian champagne or vodka."

"I don't drink," Volkov said.

Lucy shook her head.

"Then I'll have to drink to your homecoming on my own," Viktor said.

He poured a measure of whiskey into a glass and raised it to them.

"What do you want?" Volkov cut the pantomime short.

"I want your assurance that you haven't come back to cause civil unrest in the Ukraine."

Viktor had dropped the pose. He stood taller than Dimitri Volkov. He was a man of years of hard authority facing an adversary.

"I'm bringing you a message from the president himself. We welcome you back. We apologize for the harsh way you were treated in the past. We hope you will forgive and forget and agree to work toward a Russia where such things can never happen again. If your intention is to stir up revolution and political chaos, then we are not going to stop you. That's the measure of the changes Mikhail Gorbachev has made. You speak a lot about democracy and justice, Comrade Volkov. You always did, when there was no hope of either under the old system. That is being swept away. But we need peace to do it. Peace and stability. Any other way means bloodshed and misery. Are you prepared for that?"

"No." To his surprise it was Lucy who answered. "Dimitri would never want that!"

Viktor said quietly, "Have you brought the relic with you?"

Volkov said, "I think it's time for the press conference."

"One more question, Comrade Volkov. What happened to your activist friends in London? They've left you to lead their crusade on your own."

Volkov took Lucy by the hand.

"They didn't like my speech. It wasn't what they were expecting."

Viktor opened the door for them and stood aside. He watched as Volkov took his place before the journalists and TV crews. He looked very slight standing there with the lights beating down on him. Viktor moved close to the woman who was responsible for it all. She was watching Volkov; she didn't seem to notice him standing beside her.

"I've heard his broadcasts in London," he remarked. "He's a fine speaker."

"Yes," Lucy answered. "He speaks as he thinks."

"And you know what he's going to say?"

"We wrote it out together," she said.

"With help from your friends in British Intelligence?"

"They're no friends of ours!"

The Ukrainian president was paying tribute to Volkov's stand against tyranny in the past. Her vehemence surprised Viktor.

"We understood they saved his life in Jersey."

She turned to stare at him. "They had nothing to do with what happened. It was the cross that saved us. They came when it was all over. We owe them nothing!"

He believed her. Perhaps Muller hadn't betrayed them after all. "We knew nothing about it," he had said. "You must believe that. His first wife . . ."

"I was there," she said. "I don't want to talk about it. My husband is going to speak now."

Volkov had a sheaf of notes. He glanced at them briefly and then put them in his pocket. He adjusted the microphone. The last speaker was much shorter than he was. He looked out over the faces turned upward, watching him, the TV cameras, the journalists—notebooks ready.

A slight flush appeared on his cheeks; he brushed his hair back from his forehead. In the audience Lucy tensed, knowing the gesture so well. He spoke and his voice was clear and resonant.

"My friends. Thank you for your kind words and your welcome. I would never have believed I'd live to see this day. The day I came home and could speak freely." He paused, took the notes out of his pocket. "I wrote all this when I knew I was coming home. With help from my wife, who's here with me. Now I don't need it. I can speak from my heart without forgetting anything. When you've been silent for five years, you can't believe you'll ever stand up and face people and talk openly again. I left this country in handcuffs five years ago.

"I remembered that when we came in to land. I was luckier than my friends who weren't sent into exile. Some are still in prison. Most of them are dead. Times have changed, they told me. Russia has changed.

"I have to believe that because I'm here. But so long as one man or woman is in prison because of their beliefs, then nothing has changed.

"The deputy spoke about what happened to me. He talked about injustice, suffering. But for seventy years, my friends, we have all been in chains. My country, the Ukraine, was the worst victim of oppression. Our culture, our religion, our lands were all taken from us. Millions died. Stalin built upon their bones. Still our people hoped and held on to their faith that one day, they would be free.

"Yes, I suffered, but I survived and I believe I've learned from it. I've seen cruelty and wickedness, but I've seen courage and nobility, and love." He paused and looked for Lucy in the crowd. He found her gazing at him. He raised his voice.

"In Europe the people have torn down the prison walls and cast off their chains. Just as we must do now."

Volkov felt the silence. No one moved; they had gambled and lost. He knew what would follow.

"I spoke of what I've learned, what experience has taught

me. The most important thing was the folly of violence. Violence achieves nothing in the end. It is self-defeating because the human spirit cannot be crushed forever. It degrades us, if we have any part in it. I renounce violence in all its forms. There's been enough death, enough tears in the last seventy years. If we want freedom and human rights, we have to build, not destroy. For myself I forgive the past. I want to serve my people, if they'll have me. I want to devote my life to the cause of liberty, of every man's right to speak his mind, to live without fear. I have no political ambitions, I belong to no organization. I have no supporters, only my wife, to help me. I am home and I look with hope to the future. But first, I have brought something with me that belongs to the Ukraine."

Viktor went rigid. Now. Now he was going to bring out the holy relic. For all his protestations of peace, he was about to declare civil war. *If I had a gun,* Viktor Rakovsky thought, *I'd kill him . . .*

He heard Volkov clear his throat. He gave a little cough.

"But what I have brought home doesn't just belong to the Ukraine. It belongs to Russia and to all the Russian people." He looked directly at Viktor. "If the president of our Parliament will escort us, we'd like to go now to the Cathedral of Saint Sophia."

Someone started to clap. Soon they were all applauding.

The Ukrainian delegation embraced him in turn. He looked very pale and the hair fell over his forehead, just as Lucy remembered it, the first time she saw him in the café by the lake in Geneva. He was moving through the crowd toward her. There were tears in her eyes. The journalists were pushing to get to their cars and follow them to the cathedral. The TV crews were already loading up to join in.

For a moment Viktor came face-to-face with him.

"You are a patriot, Dimitri Volkov," was all he said. Then he turned and walked away.

THE RELIC

*   *   *

It was all over. The media had gone. The demonstration organized by the Ukrainian nationalists party had dispersed with some feeling of anticlimax. Saint Sophia's Cathedral had emptied, the arc lights were dismantled, the commentators were gone; the patriarch had made a speech and announced plans for a mass of thanksgiving.

The Volkovs had retreated to a hotel suite provided for them. They refused all invitations for the evening.

The cross of Saint Vladimir glowed red inside its shrine above the high altar. People of all ages started coming in little groups to stare up at it. Many stayed to pray.

FIC   Anthony, Evelyn.
ANTHO
          The relic.

                                            501026